THE WARD BROTHERS

Vengeance
BOOK TWO

CAROL HELLIER

DEDICATION

A big thank you to my family for all the support they have shown over the time I have spent writing. Much love to my children and grandchildren.

I would also like to thank the girls in the NHS Histopathology office where I work, for their support and the giggles we have shared, so a shoutout to:

Kathryn Hadley
Karen (Sinman) Lee
Rachel Rolph
Sudha Durai

I would also like to thank Emmy Ellis for the fantastic editing and formatting and Francessca at Wingfield Designs for the fabulous book covers.

And my biggest thank you, as always, goes to those who have read what I have written. *The Ward Brothers, Meet the Travellers* had a fantastic reception, so I hope you like book two. Keep shining, you wonderful people.

Revenge is an act of passion; vengeance of justice.
Injuries are revenged; crimes are avenged.

Samuel Johnson

PROLOGUE

The last few years had been good to the Wards. Maeve was pleased that three of her sons were now married. Only Tommy Lee left to tie the knot, and that was arranged for September. She was grateful that he no longer disappeared for months on end working away. She had Millie and the twins to thank for that.

She now had six handsome grandsons with another grandchild on the way. Would Gypsy and John Jo give her a granddaughter? As much as she loved her family of boys, it would be nice to have a girl. Her eyes were always drawn to those pink frilly dresses on Romford Market. One day, she hoped.

Maeve kicked her shoes off and picked up her cup of tea. It was after midnight, but she doubted she would sleep. Everyone had gone back to Gypsy's while Tommy Lee had gone to the gardai station, waiting for the two fecking eejits to be released. There was still no news of John Jo or Sean Paul. Had they been charged or were they still being questioned?

With the boys now living on their own land, it was harder to keep them on the straight and narrow. Although they never listened to her or Paddy anyway, but hopefully this would teach them a lesson. Getting arrested at PJ's wedding was a step too far. Bringing shame on the Ward family name.

Well, at least things couldn't get any worse.

CHAPTER 1

April 1978

Tommy Lee sat slouched in the waiting area of the gardai station, elbows on his knees, eyes fixed on the scuffed floor tiles. The clock on the wall ticked past one-fifty a.m. He rubbed at his face, exhausted. All he wanted was to be home, in bed, Millie curled into him, the twins safe and sleeping.

He hoped she was all right. He'd left her at Gypsy's, restless and worried. She hadn't said much, but he'd seen it in her eyes, that unease, that fear. The kind that lingered even when you were told to stop worrying.

He stared over at the desk sergeant, whose head was down, scribbling into a logbook like time meant nothing. He frowned. That job had to be soul-destroying.

He stood, stretching out the tension in his back, and walked to the desk.

"Any update on my brothers?" he asked, trying to keep the edge from his voice.

The sergeant glanced up, expression flat, pen still in hand. "As I told you an hour ago, when there's news, I'll let you know."

Tommy Lee clenched his jaw. The man didn't even blink.

"Now," the sergeant added, nodding towards the chairs, "if you wouldn't mind taking a seat."

Tommy Lee stared at him for a beat longer than he should have, then turned without a word and sat back down. He'd wait. He had no choice. But he didn't have to like it.

Arrogant pig.

He sat back and closed his eyes. It was going to be a long night so he may as well get some sleep while he was waiting.

"Mr Ward?"

He opened his eyes to see a tall, suited gentleman standing over him.

"Who are you?"

"My name's Mr Barrett, I'm Mrs Kelly's solicitor. She instructed me to help get your brothers released."

The first thing that annoyed him was Millie being referred to as Mrs Kelly, the second was the fact she'd done this without his knowledge.

"Do you require my assistance?" Mr Barrett asked impatiently.

"Go ahead, get them out." Tommy Lee would deal with Millie later.

***

Gypsy sat biting her nails. Millie could see she was at her wits' end.

"Anyone want more tea?" she offered.

"I'll make it," Maeve replied. "I need to keep busy."

"Are you sure this solicitor can help?" Gypsy asked nervously.

"I'm sure he'll have them out within the hour." Millie stood. "I'll just check on the twins."

She headed to the end bedroom of the mobile. Both boys were wrapped up in the double pushchair, sleeping soundly. She wished she was, too.

The noise of a motor had her running to the door. Throwing it open, she came face to face with Tommy Lee.

He pecked her on the lips then headed to the front room, followed by John Jo and Sean Paul. She stood silently behind them.

"What have you done this time?" Paddy asked abruptly.

"We done nothing, Father, why do you think they released us," Sean Paul said while grabbing Shirley Ann around the waist. "Come on, let's get the boys to bed."

"We need to go, too." Tommy Lee eyed Millie. Was he annoyed? "Collect your stuff together and get in the motor while I sort the boys."

Yep, something was simmering just below the surface. She said her goodbyes and loaded up the Range Rover before getting in and clicking the seat belt into place. With the twins strapped securely into their car seats, Tommy Lee joined her.

"Are you going to tell me what's wrong?" She kept her gaze forward, tension hanging heavy in the air.

"Nothing's wrong." He tried to keep the irritation from his voice but failed miserably. He sighed; he didn't want to blame her. "That solicitor you arranged without telling me, called you Mrs Kelly."

"That is my name, and I only arranged the solicitor because Gypsy was so distraught. She's pregnant, remember, and this shit isn't good for the baby… I'm sorry."

He placed his hand on her leg. "It's not your fault, those two fecking eejits need their heads banging together." He peeked at her. "I knew they were up to no good. All this money they've been throwing about."

"They're choring motors," she said, spinning around to check on the twins. "That would explain why they had batteries and tools in that new shed."

"I've warned them, if they want to spend time inside that's their lookout… Anyway, enough about them, I want you to tell me what happened earlier, outside the reception."

"I told you, it's nothing to worry about, I just got spooked being outside in the dark."

"We promised we'd be honest with each other; Millie, I can tell when you're lying. Now what happened?" he pressed. He had a feeling he wasn't going to like what she said.

"Can we at least wait until we're home and the twins are settled?" she pleaded.

"No. Just tell me." He stared at her. "You've gone red."

"I just want you to know I've dealt with it. I told PJ—"

"I might have known it was to do with one of my brothers. I'll fecking kill the lot of them." He banged the steering wheel in temper, waking the twins.

Millie unclipped her seat belt and spun around, kneeling on the passenger seat to soothe them. "Shh." She rubbed each boy's head, lulling them back to sleep. "This is why I wanted to get home first."

He waited for her to sit. "You don't ever withhold the truth from me for anyone's benefit, and certainly not theirs."

"Please, Tommy Lee, stay calm, I don't want the twins woken again."

"Jaysus, it must be bad." Now he was certain he wasn't going to like it. "It's my job as the man to protect my family, that means you and our children. When you came back inside you were shaking. It was only because the gardai turned up that you didn't tell me, so spit it out, what happened?"

"Okay… When I went outside I heard a strange noise coming from the end of the building. I thought it sounded like someone injured, groaning in agony. Well, I was half right, they were groaning… It was PJ, he was doing stuff with one of the waiters."

"What stuff?" he quizzed.

"Do I really have to spell it out?" She looked at him. "He was having his cock sucked, by a man."

CHAPTER 2

P J ran the brush over Seraphina, the new mare his brothers had bought. She was a beauty with a healthy, shiny coat. He wasn't expected to work today, being as he only got married yesterday, but he had used John Jo and Sean Paul being detained as the excuse to escape Marina. He felt bad in a way, but after managing to perform like a real man, twice, in the night, he figured he needed time to recover. He had only managed it because he'd kept his eyes closed tight and thought of Pete, his ex-lover. That had gone pear-shaped when he was drugged and abducted by some rich pervert and the boys had found out.

He looked up when he heard a motor pulling in. It was Tommy Lee, with Millie next to him. Had she kept her word? Judging by the look on his brother's face, he thought not.

Feck.

Tommy Lee jumped out of the motor and headed towards him. PJ put his head down and continued grooming, knowing full well he would be unable to make a scene here in front of his new wife. His grip on the brush tightened. The steady rhythm of grooming Seraphina was the only thing keeping his hands from shaking. He kept his focus on the mare, on the warmth of her body beneath his touch, on the soft huffs of her breath. Anything but the heavy silence stretching between him and Tommy Lee who stepped closer, boots scuffing against the concrete floor of the stable.

"Well?" Tommy Lee said voice tight.

PJ exhaled slowly through his nose. "Well, what?"

Tommy Lee let out a sharp breath. "You know what." His tone dropped, dripping with disgust. "Millie told me everything."

PJ swallowed, but he didn't flinch. Couldn't. He just kept brushing, though his strokes were stiffer now, less fluid.

Tommy Lee took another step. "Feck, PJ. At your own wedding?" he said, almost growling. "What the hell were you thinking?"

PJ's jaw clenched. "I wasn't," he muttered.

"That much is clear." Tommy Lee huffed and shook his head. "You couldn't keep it together for one night? Not one fecking night?"

PJ finally turned, brush still in hand, his heartbeat thudding hard against his ribs. "I did what was expected of me," he said, quiet. "I married her, didn't I?"

Tommy Lee scoffed. "Yeah, and then you turned around and—" He stopped himself, eyes dark with frustration. He exhaled sharply, rubbing a hand over his face before saying, "If anyone hears about this, you know what'll happen."

PJ swallowed hard. Of course he knew. Their father had made it clear years ago, this wasn't something that would be tolerated in their family. PJ had done everything he was supposed to, had followed the path laid out for him, had even gone through with this fecking marriage. But that hadn't been enough, had it?

He could feel Tommy Lee watching him, waiting for an answer.

"I handled it," he said.

His brother laughed, but there was no humour in it. "You handled it? Yeah, sure. You handled it so well Millie caught you." He leaned in, voice dropping even lower. "You put her in a difficult position. Feck's sake, boy, I had to drag it out of her. My own woman, keeping your dirty secrets." He balled his fists. "I'm this close to battering you… Don't you ever ask her to cover for you again."

PJ's stomach twisted.

"If you don't get a grip, you're fecked." Tommy Lee took a step back. "And I can't save you if that happens, in fact, you won't deserve saving."

PJ didn't say anything. He just watched as he turned and walked away.

When he was alone again, he pressed a hand against Seraphina's side, grounding himself.

He had to be more careful.

***

"Tommy Lee's heading this way," Sean Paul warned. "And judging by the way he's walking, we may be in for a bollocking."

John Jo stood and peeked out of the window. "So what, we stole a few motors, that's not in the same league as killing for a living."

"I wouldn't mention that to him, he's likely to kill you if you do… I wonder what he wanted with PJ?"

"Dunno, but I reckon he's done something far worse than us, otherwise he would've come here first. Look out, he's here."

The door opened, and he stepped in, filling the room. "You pair of fecking eejits, what have you got to say for yourselves?"

John Jo smirked, leaning back against the table, arms crossed like he wasn't bothered. "We got motors to move, Tommy Lee, not bodies."

His eyes darkened, jaw tightening. "Oh, you think you're a fecking comedian now?" he snapped. "You two lifting cars like it's a game. Leaving tracks. Getting noticed."

He stepped forward, and Sean Paul instinctively took a half-step back.

"You think the gardai are thick? You think they don't clock a pattern when motors start disappearing in the same area?"

Sean Paul swallowed. "We're careful, Tommy —"

"Careful?" Tommy Lee barked a laugh. "The police don't turn up for no reason; you've fecked up somewhere."

He glanced between his two brothers. John Jo slumped back on the seat. Had the penny dropped, or did they still think they were invincible?

"You need to realise that now they have your names, they will be after you for any and everything that goes missing."

John Jo sat forward, exhaling through his nose. "What do you want us to do?"

"You lie low. No more stealing motors for now." He turned for the door, then stopped. "We're all building an empire to leave our children, so concentrate on the horses, let the gardai see that you have a good honest business keeping you busy."

With that, he left and trudged over to grab Millie so they could leave to see the priest about their upcoming wedding. Satisfied that he'd got business out of the way, he could now look forward to the pleasure.

Would any of them listen to him? No. Probably not, but he had warned them.

"Ready?" he called from the door of Shirley Ann's mobile.

Millie appeared carrying a twin under each arm. He grabbed baby Duke from her and headed to the Range Rover, strapping his son securely in.

"Do you think he'll marry us?" she asked, clipping her seat belt in.

"Yes, I do, don't you?" He glanced at her; she always worried about everything.

"We've had children out of wedlock, and I've never been baptised…"

"The priest is collecting money for repairs to the roof, I'll bribe him if he says no." He laughed at her expression.

"You can't bribe a man of the cloth," she said with a gasp. "Christ, we are both going to Hell."

"As long as I'm with you, I don't care where I go." He started the motor and reversed out of the driveway. Spotting PJ in the rear-view mirror, he shook his head slowly.

"What's the matter?" Millie spun around in the seat. "Did he listen to you?"

"I don't know, and to be honest I'm past caring. It's time he and the other two stood on their own two feet." He slammed the motor into gear and pulled away, knowing that if they didn't heed his warnings, things were going to get worse for them all.

***

It was two p.m. on the dot when Tommy Lee and Millie entered the dimly lit office at the back of the church. Father O'Reilly welcomed them in, his gaze resting on the double pushchair and the two noisy infants who filled it.

"Thank you for seeing us at such short notice," Millie said, her voice quiet.

Was she worried?

"So...you want to get married?" he answered, eyes still on the twins.

"Yes, Father, we're finally tying the knot." Tommy Lee grinned.

"We were waiting for the right time and, well, we've been busy," she added, pointing to the twins who were now fighting over a soggy, half-eaten biscuit.

Father O'Reilly cleared his throat. "Ah yes. Busy, indeed. You do realise marriage is a sacred institution, meant to precede—" He stopped when one of the twins burst out crying.

Tommy Lee grabbed the biscuit and broke it in half, giving each child a piece. That seemed to placate the little darlings. "You were saying?"

"Yes, umm, precede certain activities." He gripped his crucifix.

Millie sat forward. "Absolutely, Father, that's why we are here. To make things right. A holy union and all that."

"Hmm. It's rather unorthodox, you know. Two children already…wedlock is usually meant to come before the, uh, bundles of joy."

"Father, please, we just want a simple ceremony. Nothing fancy. Just a few vows, a blessing, and maybe some wine," she pleaded.

"Oh, I'm sure you'll have the wine covered." He scoffed.

Tommy Lee found his temper rising. He knew he had to keep calm, especially in a place of worship, but the last comment had obviously hit Millie hard. He wouldn't have that. "Look, Father, I know the church has been struggling lately…and that roof…it's a bit, what's the word…unstable?"

Father O'Reilly folded his arms. "The good Lord provides."

Tommy Lee grabbed an envelope from the inside of his jacket and slid it across the desk. "Of course, the good Lord often provides through generous, community-minded individuals."

The priest took the envelope and peeked inside, his eyes widening. "Well, the Lord does work in mysterious ways."

Tommy Lee nodded. He noticed Millie crossed her arms; was she disgusted?

"You just accepted a bribe, didn't you?" she gasped.

"No, no, no, dear child. This is merely a charitable donation. For the good of the church, and its, um, roof." The father tucked the envelope away.

"So, we're all set. Second of September," Tommy Lee confirmed.

Father O'Reilly nodded. "I suppose I can make an exception. The Lord is merciful, after all."

Millie sighed. "And easily bribed, it would seem."

CHAPTER 3

John Jo and Sean Paul had risen early and headed to their lockup. Whilst heeding Tommy Lee's words, they also had a couple of orders to complete. Having taken half payment up front, they didn't want to let the buyers down, and besides, the stolen motors were sitting right here.

"So once these are gone, we are going to stop for a while?" Sean Paul checked.

John Jo wiped his hands on his overalls and nodded. "Yeah. Got to keep things quiet, like Tommy Lee said. But let's get these done first."

The two men set to work, sparks flying as they sliced through the body of a black Vauxhall Viva with an angle grinder. Sean Paul moved efficiently, cutting along the frame while John Jo worked on stripping out the unnecessary parts. Once the back half was separated, they moved on to the second car, another wrecked Vauxhall Viva that had been written off but still had a solid front end.

Sean Paul examined the cut, measuring twice before making the final slice. "This will work," he muttered with a quick nod to himself.

John Jo helped drag the severed sections together, lining up the cuts as best they could. They used clamps to hold the pieces in place before breaking out the welding gear. The bright light of the torch illuminated their gritted faces as they worked with practiced efficiency, fusing the two stolen cars into one. It was a rough job, but once the car was painted and given new plates, no one would be the wiser.

"It's a shame." John Jo wiped the sweat from his brow. "We've become pros at this game. Could've made a lot of money."

"Money's not worth our freedom," Sean Paul warned. He exhaled heavily. "That's one done. Get the next one ready."

John Jo nodded, tossing his gloves onto the workbench. He knew the heat was on, but they had a business to run, and for now, that meant getting this job finished before disappearing into the shadows for a while.

***

Tommy Lee pulled the motor to a halt on Duke's land. They had set off to visit Millie's family straight after the church and tell them about the wedding. Millie was going to ask her father, Duke, to walk her down the aisle, a job she didn't want him to have, but after he had given her a talking-to, she had agreed. She still seemed upset at her parents moving from Stepney, but he knew Duke thought he was doing what was right. Her and Connie not speaking was tearing Millie apart, so him selling up and moving was, in fact, his way of protecting her.

"You all right, darling?" Tommy Lee asked softly. He placed a reassuring hand on hers.

Millie nodded but didn't speak. The lump in her throat was too thick. She'd spent weeks — no, months — avoiding this moment, but now the wedding was booked she had no other option but to come here and face her parents. With a deep breath, she opened the door and slid out onto the gravel path. Before she could reach the mobile door, it swung open, and her father emerged, his wide grin stretching across his weathered face.

"I wasn't sure I'd see you again," he said and drew her into a hug.

"I couldn't stay away forever, Dad," she murmured, her face smothered against his chest for a moment. She pulled back and smiled. "It's good to see you."

"And look at those chavie's," he said in surprise. "How they've grown."

Tommy Lee passed Tommy boy to her, grabbing his other son from the motor.

Duke gave him a firm handshake and, moving aside, he let them in. The warmth from the fireplace wrapped around Millie as she entered, but it wasn't enough to thaw the ice surrounding her and Connie. An awkward silence stretched between them. Millie shifted uncomfortably, waiting for her mother to say something.

"Hello, Connie," Tommy Lee greeted. "You're looking well."

Millie's attention dropped to her mother's bump; she must only have about four months to go. "I'm going to see Aron?" She turned then heard Connie's voice.

"Millie."

She took a shaky breath. "I didn't come here to fight, Connie. We only came to tell you we're getting married."

Connie's lips parted slightly, surprise flashing across her face, then she masked it with indifference. "Congratulations."

Millie's heart sank at the coldness in her mother's voice.

"Tommy Lee, let's take the twins out to see their cousin." Duke grabbed the boy from Millie and left.

"I'll put the kettle on." Connie busied herself making the tea. "Take a seat."

"It's nice here." Mille stared out of the window. "Proper countryside."

15

"We like it. Do you still take sugar?"

"No thanks." Millie felt stifled by the tension, almost struggling to breathe. It was as though they were strangers.

Connie placed the cup in front of her then sat opposite. "Your father has missed you."

Millie didn't know whether to laugh or cry at the statement. Didn't Connie miss her or the twins? No. That was crystal clear. They sipped their tea, both avoiding eye contact.

"You're all invited to the wedding, but it's up to you if you come." Millie stood, ready to leave. "I hope the birth goes well." She headed towards the door, her heart heavy. How had it come to this?

"Wait," Connie called. "Are you happy?"

"I'm the happiest I've ever been. I have a man who loves me, twin boys who are adorable, mainly when they're sleeping, and I'm getting married… This is what I dreamed of in the children's home. I thought it was parents I longed for, but it was a family of my own. Being loved unconditionally and wanted." Millie smiled with sad eyes. "I'm sorry it didn't work out with us, and I'm sorry for whatever part I played in it. If I could go back and change things, I would. But life isn't like that, is it? We must live with our actions. Anyway. All the best, Connie."

She felt Connie's hand resting on her arm, stopping her from leaving. "I'm glad you're happy, that's all I ever wanted for you… I will be at the wedding. Now, I think it's time I see my grandsons."

***

PJ sat at the table, his fingers nervously tracing the rim of his teacup. The hum of the radio filled the trailer, a soft croon of some love song he barely listened to. Across from him, Marina stood at the sink, scrubbing the dinner plates with that same determined force she seemed to apply to everything in life. She was a good woman, loyal, kind, eager to please, and guilt ripped through him. He hadn't realised how hard this would be, but the need for male company was calling, and he didn't want to fight it.

He cleared his throat, already rehearsing the lie in his head. "Marina, love," he began and tried to keep his tone light, casual. "It's been a hard day with the horses, you know? Thought I might go for a couple of pints and see Jasper about a horse he's got for sale. I won't be late."

She turned slightly, a soap-covered plate in her hand. Her brow furrowed, just a bit. "But we only married yesterday. I thought we could have a cosy night together."

He hated himself, the hopefulness in her voice got him right in the gut, but still he knew he had to go. "I won't be long, darling, just a couple. I need to see him about this horse so we can make a future for ourselves. I don't want to work for John Jo and Sean Paul for the rest of my life… You can warm the bed up."

She sighed and rinsed the plate, setting it on the rack. She wiped her hands on a dishcloth and turned to face him fully. "All right. But don't be stumbling in at all hours. It don't look good, you leaving me so soon."

He grinned and stood. "Course not, darling." He pecked her on the cheek and lingered just long enough to feel the warmth of her skin before grabbing his coat and heading for the door.

***

The place was tucked away, hidden behind an unmarked door in an alley. He knocked twice, then again, in the rhythm he'd been taught. The door cracked open, and a pair of sharp eyes met his before it swung wide, revealing the pulsing warmth inside.

The club was alive, filled with bodies swaying to a beat that felt like freedom. The scent of cologne, cigarettes, and sweat filled his nostrils. Men in shirts and flared trousers laughed in corners, whispering secrets into each other's ears, fingers brushing in ways that weren't allowed outside these walls. PJ exhaled, a weight lifting from his chest. Here, he wasn't PJ the husband, the brother, the son, a man with expectations draped over him like a suffocating blanket. Here, he was just himself.

He moved through the room, catching the eye of a tall man at the bar, a familiar face, one he'd only seen in places like this. The man smirked, lifting his glass in a silent invitation. PJ hesitated for just a second before stepping forward, already knowing that afterwards he would hate himself again.

***

Tommy Lee sat on the sofa waiting for Millie to join him. She entered the room, two cups in hand, and passed him one.

"I think today went well." He glanced at her over the rim of the cup.

"It could have gone worse, I suppose," she said.

"Duke's excited about walking you down the aisle." He laughed. "And Connie seemed to be making an effort."

"I guess."

"What's wrong?" He placed his cup on the coffee table then grabbed hers and set it down. Tugging her closer, he wrapped his arm around her.

"How can anything be wrong when I'm sat here with you?" She smiled. "Monday I'm going to see about selling the club and put feelers out for the scrapyard. Once they are sold, we can look at houses."

"You're changing the subject." He stroked her cheek then turned her face, so he was looking in her eyes. What was she thinking? "Tell me what's on your mind."

"The visit went better than I expected," she agreed.

"But?"

"But I had to go to her. She's made no effort to see the twins, never mind me. I apologised for whatever part I played in the situation. She didn't. It's like she's brushed over it, until the next time it happens." She paused briefly. "It's like I'm disposable."

"You ain't disposable to me, or our boys. We are your family and we'd be lost without you. I love you."

"And I you." She smiled.

"We've got a lot to look forward to, Mil." He leaned in and nibbled her ear. He hardened immediately. "I think an early night is in order."

He stood and helped her up, pushing away the bad thoughts of his brothers.

CHAPTER 4

June 1978

Life was good, Millie had decided. Things were finally falling into place for her and Tommy Lee. Her best friend, Rosie, had now married Tony, days after he was released from prison, and the newlyweds had moved closer to the docks, where Tony ran the business for Millie and himself as he had a twenty percent share. Did she trust him? Not fully, that's why Tommy Lee or Scott, Rosie's brother, kept an eye on her interests when she couldn't get there.

The club was up for sale with a few interested parties, and the scrapyard was in negotiations with a man called Larry Smith. Slimy chap, always making innuendos. She had made the decision that Tommy Lee could deal with him while she focused on the impending wedding. Everything had come together nicely, especially as there were no more hiccups from his brothers.

She drove up on the driveway leading to Maeve and Paddy's ground. He was in the paddock doing something with the horses. She waved as she mooched towards the mobile. Shirley Ann, Gypsy, and Marina were already there.

She took a deep breath as she stepped up to Maeve's door and smoothed down the front of her skirt. Wedding preparations had been going well so far, and she was looking forward to discussing the next steps with Maeve. She knocked, and the familiar sounds of laughter came from inside.

The door swung open, revealing Gypsy's grinning face. "You finally made it," she teased, "Come on in."

Inside, Shirley Ann was perched on the armrest of a chair, a cup of tea in hand, while Maeve stood over a table covered in magazines. Everything seemed light-hearted, yet Millie immediately caught the tension in Marina's face. Unlike the others, she wasn't smiling. She sat with her arms folded, eyes distant, her lower lip caught between her teeth in thought.

Millie didn't like it. She knew her well enough now to recognise when something was wrong. As the others fell into chatter about floral arrangements and seating plans, she moved closer to her and gently touched her arm.

"Can I have a word?" Millie murmured.

Marina hesitated but eventually nodded. She led her to the kitchen, away from the cheerful chaos.

"What's up?" Millie asked softly. "You look like something's weighing on you."

Marina's eyes flickered away before she took a deep breath. "It's PJ," she admitted, voice low. "I… I don't know what's going on with him."

Millie's brow furrowed. "What do you mean?"

Marina swallowed hard and glanced around, as if afraid someone else might overhear. "He goes out at night. A lot. Never says where he's going. And when he's home…" She hesitated, clearly struggling with her words. "He barely touches me. Barely seems interested in me. And when he does…" She stopped. Bit her lip before finally forcing the words out. "It's either my arse or my mouth. That's all he wants."

Millie blinked, cursing as she absorbed the confession. A pit formed in her stomach. "Have you asked him what's going on?"

Marina gave a short, bitter laugh. "He just shrugs it off. Says I'm imagining things. But I'm not, Mil. I can feel it. Something's wrong."

Millie reached for her hand, squeezing it gently. "You need to talk to him. Really talk to him. Find out what's going on."

Marina sighed, shoulders slumping. "I don't know if I even want to hear the answer."

Millie's heart ached for her. This wasn't just about sex; it was about trust, about love, about something deeper breaking between them. And Marina was terrified to face it. Millie didn't blame her. If Tommy Lee treated her like that she'd be devastated. But as it was, she'd no need to worry, the horny sod had her knickers off at every chance he got. Morning, noon, or night. She decided all she could do to help was tell him. Let him handle PJ; after all, he was his brother.

"I'm here," she said firmly. "Whatever happens, you don't have to deal with this alone."

Marina nodded, her eyes glistening. "Thanks, Mil."

They rejoined the others, but the laughter and wedding talk felt distant now. And as Millie sat back down, she couldn't shake the feeling that whatever was going on with PJ, it wasn't going to end well.

***

Tommy Lee had survived some tough situations in his life, but nothing, and he meant nothing, compared to being left alone with eight-month-old twins for an entire morning. At first, he'd thought, *How hard could it be?* Feed them, change them, let them crawl around. Easy.

Wrong.

By mid-morning, he was already on the brink of collapse. One twin's nappy had fallen off, and before he could react, there was a tiny streaker zooming across the living room, leaving a trail of piddle on the carpet. Millie was going to have a fit. The other twin, perhaps inspired by the chaos, somehow got hold of a banana and decided to mash it directly onto the carpet, clapping delightedly at his masterpiece. Tommy Lee had never rushed around so much in his life.

By nap time, both babies were finally asleep, one draped over his chest, the other snoring softly on his thigh. He was trapped. Was he scared? Yes. Any movement, any slight disturbance, and the whole cycle would start again. He lay there, staring at the ceiling, wondering how the hell Millie did this every day.

When she finally walked through the door at lunchtime, he could've wept with relief. He gently extracted himself from under the babies and all but crawled to her.

"Thank God you're home. I need a long, cold shower and a nap," he told her.

She laughed. "Not so easy after all then?"

"When did they start moving so quick? It's like chasing two little madmen hell-bent on causing destruction and chaos." He sighed. "It was easier in the army, and less scary."

"I'll put the kettle on, looks like you could do with a cuppa."

He followed her out, taking a seat at the kitchen table. "How's the wedding preparations going?"

She turned to him; her face darkened. He knew something was wrong.

"I hate to bring this up after the rough morning you've had." She hesitated and took a seat next to him. "I need to tell you about PJ."

He stiffened. "What about him?"

She sighed, rubbing her temples. "Marina wasn't herself; she was distant…like she had the weight of the world on her shoulders. So, I pulled her aside and asked what was wrong… She told me PJ doesn't show any interest in her in the bedroom, but when he does he wants to do it up her bum or, failing that, he wants her to suck his thingy."

Tommy Lee's stomach plummeted. His exhaustion vanished in an instant, replaced by something colder, something tighter. He swallowed hard, but the bitterness remained lodged in his throat.

That fecking eejit was on the road to ruin, and it seemed he'd take no heed nor help from anyone.

"She also said he goes out at night regularly... He's still chasing sex with men..." Her words hung heavy in the air, the silence suffocating.

A moan came from the lounge. Millie went to check on the twins. He followed. He peeked at them, still sleeping soundly.

He glanced at her and shrugged. "Well, isn't that just fecking fantastic."

"Is that it, is that all you've got to say?" she said, rolling her eyes.

"What do you want me to say, Mil? I've spoken to him more than once, reasoned with him and pleaded with him. He's on his own."

She grabbed his arm. "I'm not interested in PJ; he's chosen his own path. I'm worried about Marina; she deserves better than being used to make him appear normal."

"Fine, I'll talk to John Jo and Sean Paul later. They'll have to keep an eye on him. I have my family to look after, a wedding fast approaching, and the scrapyard to sell. Now, can we not discuss him anymore?"

"You do realise we are both complicit in this farce of a marriage. We both knew he was into men and yet said nothing." She stormed to the kitchen; Tommy Lee followed. "I don't know about you." She reached for a glass then a bottle of wine. "But I feel guilty."

She poured a hefty measure, and he watched her take a large gulp.

"Okay. You're right. We'll go over later and have it out with him, but I'm still telling the others. They deserve to know so they can help." He snatched the glass from her hand.

"Hey," she whined.

"Drinking won't help, and I'll tell you this for nothing, I'm probably going to batter PJ, the fecking selfish eejit."

***

The sun was setting behind the trees, casting giant shadows over the paddock. Tommy Lee coasted in and stopped the motor close to PJ's. He and Millie walked with purpose, their footsteps heavy on the pavement as they made their way to his trailer. They had dropped the twins off with Maeve, telling her they wouldn't be long. The woman was in her element, having small ones to care for again. Millie didn't want them here, not for this.

They hadn't said very much to each other on the way over, instead both choosing to focus on the conversation ahead. They reached PJ's trailer; Tommy Lee rapped on the door with sharp, deliberate knocks. A few moments later, the door cracked open, and there stood PJ, bleary-eyed and annoyed.

"What the hell is this?" he grumbled and rubbed his face.

Tommy Lee shoved past him and stepped inside. "We're done letting you treat Marina like dirt. Get your arse in here, we need to talk."

Millie followed and closed the door behind her. "Where's Marina?"

PJ frowned, his jaw tightening, but he moved back and crossed his arms. "At her sister's. Talk about what?"

"Don't play dumb," she said. "We know you've been sneaking out, seeing men behind her back. She told me everything, how you have no interest in her other than her arse." She stabbed a finger at him. "Make you feel good, does it, fucking men and then slipping back into bed with her?"

PJ's face paled for a moment before he forced a laugh. "Oh, come off it. You don't know what you're talking about."

Tommy Lee took a step forward, his voice low and firm. "Don't insult us, PJ. You think Marina doesn't notice how distant you've been? She's not stupid, and neither are we."

Millie crossed her arms. "You chose to marry the girl; you said your vows in front of God and a whole fucking congregation. But the way you're treating her now, like she's nothing? You had a choice, she didn't. That's what makes me sick."

PJ's bravado faltered. He glanced away, sighing. "It's not like that."

"No?" Tommy Lee challenged. "Then what's it like? because from where we're standing, it's exactly like that… Jaysus, PJ, only wanting your wife's arse… How the feck do you think she feels?"

"I think I'm more disgusted at him wanting her to suck it." Millie glared at PJ. "Is this after you've stuck it up some bloke?"

Silence stretched between them before PJ finally muttered, "I don't know what I'm doing."

"Well, you better figure it out," Millie shot back. "And fast. If you think we're gonna let you keep hurting her, you're wrong. You need to get a grip. Treat her like a proper wife, love her, care for her, and make her happy, and that includes in bed."

Tommy Lee nodded. "And just so you know, we're telling John Jo and Sean Paul about this. They'll be keeping an eye on you, too. You're not going to get away with this anymore."

PJ's head snapped up. "You're serious?"

"Dead serious," he said. "You either sort yourself out or you'll have more than just us to answer to."

Millie glanced at PJ one last time before heading for the door. "You've been warned."

Without another word, they left, leaving PJ standing there, more rattled than either of them had ever seen him.

They headed towards John Jo's, hand in hand.

"Do you think he'll change?" Millie asked Tommy Lee.

"No. It's gone on too long. I thought after what had happened to him, he would have learnt his lesson, but I guess the urge is too strong." He stopped and turned to her. "We've done all we can, Mil, it's up to him now."

She nodded but said nothing. The thing that pissed him off the most was the fact she felt guilty and was now worrying. He hoped that once John Jo and Sean Paul were told, then he had done his part. Only PJ could resolve this mess.

He tugged on the door and stuck his head in. He really wasn't looking forward to this.

CHAPTER 5

2nd September

The wedding day soon arrived, a grand Gypsy and Traveller affair bursting with music, laughter, and a touch of organised chaos. The air buzzed with excitement as family and friends gathered, dressed in their finest, the women in dazzling dresses and the men sharp in their suits. But none could outshine the bride.

Millie stood at the entrance of the church, breathtaking in her gown, an elegant, fitted masterpiece that shimmered under the golden midday sun. Her hair was adorned with delicate flowers, woven into a style so perfect it was as if the wind itself had designed it. She was both glamorous and ethereal, a picture of sophistication.

Tommy Lee, waiting at the altar, swallowed hard when he saw her. He had never been one for grand speeches or poetry, but even he could admit she was like something out of a dream. He tugged at his collar, the heat suddenly overwhelming, or was that her, the vision he thought he wasn't good enough for?

The organ roared to life. Duke walked down the aisle with Millie on his arm, his chest puffed out. He appeared every inch the doting father. Rosie walked behind them, taking her role as maid of honour seriously. With his gaze glued to Millie, Tommy Lee could hear the whispers from the guests, about her beauty and how lucky he was. He didn't need telling, he already knew.

He turned when a thud caught his ear. In the front row, Maeve was having a battle of her own. His eleven-month-old twins were now walking, or rather, running, everywhere, and had chosen this moment to showcase their newfound independence. One had somehow wriggled free from her grip and was making a beeline for Millie, while the other was bawling his eyes out for absolutely no reason.

"Tommy boy, you come back here this instant!" Maeve hissed and grabbed at his tiny hand.

"You all right there, Maeve?" someone asked, their laughter muffled as she balanced one child on her hip and used the other hand to corral the other like an unruly sheep.

"Yes," she huffed. "Wouldn't be a wedding without a bit of mayhem, would it?"

Tommy Lee laughed before turning his attention back to Millie.

She glided down the aisle, taking in as much as she could. Connie had turned up along with Millie's brothers and their wives. She glanced at the baby Connie was holding. Baby Nelson, her new brother. She felt a pang of guilt, having not made any attempt to go see the infant. Of course she had congratulated her father when he had phoned to inform her of the good news, but she hadn't visited. Was this tit for tat? Her mother hadn't bothered for months to see the twins. Millie made a mental note to congratulate her at the reception.

Finn was sitting in the second row, with his new lady friend, Brenda Webster, a petite type with a fiery temper. Millie had no doubt she would keep the six-foot Irishman in check, it was just what he needed. He had met her on a night out at the dogs, a trip he had laid on for the pub locals. She was with a group of friends, they'd got chatting, and a new romance had blossomed. Scott sat the other side of the couple. Millie didn't recognise the woman he was with. He seemed to have a new one each week.

Back at the altar, Father O'Reilly cleared his throat, trying to bring order back to the moment. Duke handed Millie over to Tommy Lee, clapping the younger man on the back with enough force to make him stumble slightly.

"Look after her, or you'll answer to me," he said, only half-joking.

Tommy Lee nodded solemnly, though his lips twitched into a smile. "Wouldn't dare do otherwise or she'd kill me."

Millie smiled and turned to face Father O'Reilly. She was about to become Mrs Ward.

***

The reception was held on Paddy and Maeve's land. A giant marquee had been put up with round tables holding ten to twelve people at a time. They had a makeshift bar, well stocked with every drink they could think of.

The accordion player at the wedding stood gracefully at the corner of the elegantly decorated marquee, effortlessly drawing the attention of guests with his warm smile and infectious energy. Dressed in a crisp white shirt and a dark vest, he exuded a charming blend of sophistication and approachability. As he began to play, the familiar, joyful notes of traditional Irish Traveller songs filled the air, weaving through the laughter and chatter of the attendees. His fingers danced across the keys and buttons, skilfully pulling the bellows to create a rich tapestry of sound that resonated with both nostalgia and celebration. Guests couldn't help but sway to the rhythm, some even joining in, singing along, as he infused the atmosphere with a sense of joy and togetherness, making the special day even more memorable.

***

Nighttime had settled in, and Sean Paul and John Jo stood outside the marquee, away from prying ears and eyes, with their cousin, Billy. He was telling the brothers about his new business, stealing posh motors to order.

"I'm telling you, boys, it's a game changer. These high-end motors are worth a fecking fortune," Billy boasted.

"How do you know what ones to nab?" Sean Paul asked eagerly.

"I work for a well-known face; he tells me what's needed. It's like having a shopping list. Then I pinch them. I meet him at a destination, which always changes to reduce the risk of getting caught. He loads them into the back of a lorry and transports them somewhere, not sure where, then he changes the plates and ships them out of the country. It's money for old rope."

"Why are you telling us this?" John Jo said while sipping his beer.

"Because I can't handle the number of motors he needs, thought yous might want to dip your hands in the honey pot?"

John Jo slowly nodded. They had kept their heads down long enough, and this sounded an easier way to make money. Without the hard work and greasy hands that accompanied the cut-and-shuts. Not wanting to sound too keen, he rubbed his chin.

"Can we have a think about it?"

"I'll need an answer by Monday, because if yous are not interested, I'll need to find someone who is. Right, I best go find the wife." With that, he returned inside.

"What do you reckon?" John Jo asked Sean Paul.

"I think we'd be mad not to give it a go, even if we only chore one to see how easy it is," he said.

John Jo nodded in agreement. "I'll go give Billy the nod."

***

Tommy Lee finally managed to get away from his aunts and uncles and made a beeline for Millie. She was leaving the dance floor with Duke after having a father-daughter dance.

He grabbed her around the waist and guided her towards a quiet corner. "At last, I feel like I haven't seen you all evening... Mrs Ward."

"Mrs Ward, I like the sound of that." She grinned. "Did you —?"

He planted his lips on hers before she could utter another word. Drawing back slowly, he smiled. "I've been wanting to do that since we cut the cake."

"And was it worth the wait?"

"You're always worth the wait. Come on." He pulled her towards the exit.

"Where are we going?"

"It's a surprise." He beamed.

***

PJ stood in the entrance, watching Tommy Lee drag a giggling Millie into their father's spare trailer. It didn't take a genius to work out what they would be doing. He glanced at Marina. She looked happy for a change, sitting with Maeve, both fussing over the twins. His stomach twisted in shame. She would make a fine mother. He only prayed that she would fall pregnant soon, so he didn't have to perform every night. He had been contemplating ways to escape without her or his brothers' prying eyes watching every move he made. The only thing he had come up with was travelling to a horse fair, but then he would have to return home with an actual horse. His life was spiralling out of control, and he didn't know how much longer he could keep up the lie.

CHAPTER 6

October 1978

It was the twins' first birthday. Everyone had gathered at Maeve and Paddy's for the special occasion. After they had opened their presents, not that were very interested, the infants and their cousins had more fun playing with the empty boxes, the adults sat drinking tea and eating cake. PJ winced at the racket, and mess, the children were making. It was like a free-for-all at the local jumble sale.

"I've got some good news," Marina said loudly over the din. She glanced at PJ, a smile covering her face.

Strangely enough, it unnerved him. She appeared too happy.

"What is it?" he asked.

"PJ and I are going to have a baby." She grinned.

It took a few seconds for the news to sink in, his brain trying to process the information. He was going to be a father. Would that get the others off his back? He vaguely heard the cries of congratulations. When he looked up he was greeted with smiling faces. He glanced at Tommy Lee. He wasn't smiling, he was studying him. Was he waiting for a reaction?

Grabbing Marina, PJ pulled her into a hug. "That's fantastic news."

And it was, he wanted children. It was also a bonus that she would now be kept busy, leaving him free to do what he wanted.

"When did you find out?" Gypsy asked while collecting the empty cups.

"This morning, I phoned the doctor for my results. I was going to tell PJ later, but I couldn't wait," Marina said.

"Maeve's gonna have an army of grandchildren." Shirley Ann grinned.

Sean Paul poked Tommy Lee. "'Bout time yous had another one."

"You have met the twin destroyers?" Millie laughed. "They're enough to put anyone off."

"We will when the time's right," Tommy Lee chipped in. "Right now we need to sort business and find a house."

PJ stood, he'd had enough baby talk. The air was so thick with it, he could hardly breathe. "I need to check on the horses."

He left the mobile and stepped out into the cooler October air. Marching to the paddock, he relaxed until he heard the gravel crunching behind him. He checked over his shoulder.

"Thought I'd join you," Tommy Lee said, falling into step beside him. "Marina's happy," he added.

"That's what you wanted, wasn't it?" PJ said.

"Surely as her husband that's what you want, too?"

PJ stopped at the fence, keeping his eyes forward. "Of course I do." He sighed. "I also want everyone off my back."

"I've got to admit, I thought you'd be happier." Tommy Lee placed his hand on PJ's shoulder. "Or are you still having those thoughts?"

"Thoughts?" PJ blew out slowly. "I'm doing what's expected, the other stuff is all in the past." He wasn't sure he believed him, but that was the best he could offer. "I'm going to see about a horse on Saturday. It's time I start building a future, especially now I'm going to be a father."

"Good. Is John Jo or Sean Paul going with you?"

"Jaysus, Tommy Lee, I am capable of buying a horse. I know more about them than the rest of yous put together. Or is this in case I sneak off?"

The question hung in the air. Tommy Lee showed no emotion, just a stony glare.

"We're going now," he eventually said. "Duke and Connie are coming over." He turned to leave. "Just remember, you've a lot to lose if you stray," he threw over his shoulder as he walked away.

***

Tommy Lee sat in the lounge with Duke and the children. Millie was in the kitchen making tea with Connie.

"Do you remember that gym we went to last Christmas?" he asked.

Duke nodded. "That was a profitable night, until we spent half the winnings in the pub." He grinned. "Why, is there another fight coming up?"

"No, it's up for sale. I'm thinking of buying it. The scrapyard is as good as sold, and I want to put the money into a business, so we have a steady income."

"Millie agree to that?"

"Yes, she thinks it's a good idea." He glanced up when the women walked into the room, Millie holding two cups.

"Here." She handed one to him and the other to Duke.

"I was just telling your dad about the boxing gym," Tommy Lee said, placing the cup onto the coffee table.

She took a seat next to him and smiled. "Yeah, we've been to see it and had a look over the books. The place seems to be doing well."

"Bit far from Stepney, though, isn't it?" Connie asked.

"We're moving to Romford, it's closer to Maeve, Paddy, and his brothers," Millie said as the twins ran towards her. She scooped them up and planted a kiss on each boy's forehead, then set them down, watching as they ran around the room giggling.

Tommy Lee noticed Duke's face twitch. Was he jealous that they would be nearer to his family than them?

"You not thought of moving to Kent?" Duke asked.

"No, Dad, I still need to be close to the docks. That business is thriving, and Tony can't manage it on his own," Millie explained. "Tommy Lee has been overseeing it."

Did she now feel guilty? Tommy Lee sighed. "Mother and Father bought the boys a pony for their birthday, so it will be good to be close so they can learn to ride and care for it."

"They're one," Connie gasped. "Surely you're not teaching them to ride already?"

"They sat on her today and loved it." Millie laughed. "She's called Trixie. You'll have to come over and see her."

The mood in the room had changed since mentioning the move, and after mentioning the pony it had become worse, awkward.

"You'll have to come and see the gym, Duke, when your next up."

"Hmm, right, we better make tracks." Duke stood and turned to Connie. "Ready?" He took baby Nelson from her.

"It was nice seeing you all, and thanks for the twins' presents," Millie said, standing. "We'll come down and see you in the next few weeks."

They collected their belongings and headed out.

Tommy Lee waved them off then turned to Millie. "Are you okay?"

"Yeah, I'm used to being a disappointment," she replied quietly. "Why would my dad think I'd move to Kent after he left me in Stepney, and why's Connie got to moan about the pony?"

He grasped her around the waist and brought her tight to his body. "You are not a disappointment to me or the children... Whatever their thoughts are, they are theirs and theirs alone. We do what's right for us. Now give us a kiss."

***

PJ ordered a whiskey and leaned against the polished edge of the bar, drumming his fingers lightly on the wood. The low hum of music and murmur of conversation filled the dimly lit room, familiar and oddly comforting. He hadn't been here in a while, not since he'd promised himself he'd stay away for good. But promises didn't hold up well under pressure, and tonight, the pull had been too strong.

The drive over had wound him tight with anticipation, a knot of desire and danger coiled in his gut. It was stupid, reckless, but it was real. By the time he'd parked, the rush had taken over, quickening his breath, clouding his better judgment. Just the thought of what might happen had his skin prickling, heart thudding. He needed it. Fast. Quiet. No names.

His gaze swept the bar. Faces turned away, deep in drinks or laughter, until one man caught his eye, older, alone, dressed sharp, like he didn't belong here but knew exactly why he was. The man held PJ's stare for a beat, then offered a nod. Subtle. Deliberate. PJ didn't hesitate. He took his drink and made his way down the bar, his pace calm but his blood surging beneath the surface.

"Mind if I join you?" he asked, voice low.

The man gestured to the empty stool beside him. "Be my guest."

PJ slid onto the seat, their shoulders nearly touching. The tension between them wasn't loud, but it was there, thick in the space they shared, pulsing with unspoken understanding.

This was what he came for. Not conversation. Not connection. Just release. Something clean and quiet to take the edge off the mess of everything else.

***

It was the early hours of the morning, pitch-black and silent on the streets of Dagenham. John Jo sat in the passenger seat with an air of confidence, while Sean Paul drove. They drew up across the road from their target. A brand-new Range Rover, with its sleek black paintwork.

John Jo checked his watch.

"All right, let's make this quick," he whispered to his brother, who seemed increasingly nervous.

He slipped out, jimmied the lock, and within minutes the Range Rover roared to life. He peeled away, Sean Paul close behind him, keeping an eye out for any unwanted witnesses. John Jo headed out of town and onto the quieter country roads. With his heart racing, he picked up speed and kept it steady for a further two miles towards a pre-arranged destination. The lorry, already waiting, came into view. Slowing down, John Jo parked up behind it. The doors opened immediately, and two men tugged out the ramps.

"Come on," the boss, in his immaculate suit, called, with a wave of his hand.

John Jo nudged forward a little. He glimpsed the man, his eyes greedily viewing the new motor.

Once loaded, he jumped out of the back, landing with a thud on the road. "All done."

The man handed John Jo an envelope with money and a list of cars he wanted.

"When you find one on the list, give me a bell and we'll arrange pickup." He turned and walked to the cab, opening the door, and climbed in. The lorry started and moved away.

John Jo joined Sean Paul in the motor. He opened the envelope, scanning the cash.

"Well, Billy boy was right, money for old rope," John Jo said.

"So, what do you think?" Sean Paul asked.

"I think we would be a right pair of eejits if we don't… We are going to make a lot of money." John Jo grinned.

"As long as we don't get caught," Sean Paul added.

CHAPTER 7

December

The weeks passed quickly, and everything seemed to be falling into place for Tommy Lee and Millie. She had sold Kelly's nightclub, and on his advice, invested the money in land. The scrapyard they had sold to Larry Smith, and the purchase of the boxing gym had gone through. Things were on the up. The only thing left to do was find a house they both liked. Funnily enough, he was the fussy one; everything they had viewed so far was not to his liking. Was it because he wanted to impress her, give her better than she had? He knew she wasn't the type to compare, and many times she had told him she'd live in a shed as long as they were together. Maybe it was for him. He was building an empire for not only them but also his sons.

"So what do you think?" the estate agent asked as they stood outside the latest viewing.

Millie shook her head. "The garden's not very big." She turned to Tommy Lee. "What do you think?"

"No, it's not what we're looking for. I've already given you an in-depth description of what we want. Four bedrooms, large garden," Tommy Lee said, trying to keep the annoyance from his voice. "Let us know if anything else becomes available with that criteria."

The estate agent nodded, then turned and left.

"I'm starving, let's go to Mother's for lunch," Tommy Lee said while he strapped Tommy boy into the motor. "I need to check up on PJ after, so we'll nip over there later."

"What's going on with PJ?" Millie climbed into the passenger seat. "I thought he was behaving?"

"I don't know, I've got a bad feeling that he's up to his old tricks. You speak to Marina, find out if he's going out in the evenings, while I keep him busy."

***

John Jo and Sean Paul sat in the shed counting their money. They had stolen another two cars, to order, and were stashing the money beneath the ground in a tin box. To make it more secure, they had a stack of tyres neatly piled on top. It was a pain to keep moving them, but it was a necessary safety measure.

"We're going to need another box after this, no more will fit," Sean Paul said while shoving the money in.

"We need to invest it…could buy land in the girls' names, then there's no comeback on us."

"What about asking the farmer if we can buy the field next to us? Then we can expand the horse business," Sean Paul said thoughtfully.

John Jo nodded in agreement. "Is that a motor?" He poked his head out of the door. "Shit, it's Tommy Lee. Put the wood over it and replace the tyres, quick."

He grabbed the first tyre and rolled it over the wood covering the hole. Sean Paul grabbed the next, and they piled the tyres before heading out to see their older brother.

***

Millie knocked on Marina's door, opened it and then stepped in. "Hello," she called.

"I'm in the bedroom, come through," Marina called back.

Millie entered to find Marina packing a case.

"Going anywhere nice?"

"Only to stay with my mum for a few days. I've been getting bad morning sickness, so she suggested I stay with her for a bit. I'll be back for Christmas."

"PJ going with you?" Millie said, throwing the question out casual like.

"He's taking me, but then he needs to get back as he's seeing about a horse." She placed a jumper in the case then closed it. "He's been after it for the last couple of weeks, reckons the man is close to selling."

Millie said nothing, only offering a smile and a nod in return.

Marina pulled the case off the bed and placed it on the floor. "He should be back soon."

"How are things between you now?" Millie grabbed the luggage and hauled it out. "Christ, that's heavy." She stood it by the door then leaned against the worktop.

"Good...everything's good. PJ's so excited about the baby." Marina grinned. "We've started buying baby bits already."

"It's an exciting time... Anyway, I best check on the twins. Tommy Lee can only handle them for short periods." Millie rolled her eyes. "I'll see you Christmas." She turned and left.

***

John Jo strolled to the shed, his hands tucked into his pockets, trying to keep them warm. Sean Paul was already waiting. It was now dark, and the already cold air of day had become colder, damper, with the darkness.

"They've gone," John Jo muttered.

"I didn't think he was ever going to leave, and why's he still questioning us about PJ?" Sean Paul asked. "The boy's having a baby."

"I don't know, maybe he thinks he's up to something. Anyway, enough of him. I've had another look at the motors on the list. Have you seen how much he's willing to pay for the Jag?" He grinned.

Sean Paul shook his head slowly. "No. We can't thieve a motor like that. It'll be more than likely kept in a garage. Locked. We would not only have to break into the motor but also wherever it's stored." He sighed. "There'll be more chance of getting caught."

"I know what you're saying, but if we find one, follow it, see the routine…"

"No," Sean Paul said firmly. "It's in a different league, and I'll have no part of it."

John Jo stood there in the dimly lit shed while Sean Paul walked away. He hadn't told him he had already found the perfect motor. Or that he knew where it was parked, the routine the owner had. It seemed he was on his own with this one, unless he could talk him around.

***

Tommy Lee climbed the creaking metal staircase that led up to the office of the gym. It overlooked the boxing ring and training area. The perfect vantage point for matches or to keep an eye on things. Through the door to the right of the ring there was also a changing area, with toilets and showers.

The office itself had a large desk with an old, ripped leather chair behind it. The sofa opposite wasn't in much better condition. Millie had already decided they should get new furniture when she had sat on it and scratched her leg on the jagged, stiff material. He smiled; the fun he'd had kissing that better. His mind wandered to the two hours of passion that had led to.

Concentrate, man.

He struggled to shake the images from his mind but eventually sat behind the desk and focused on the paperwork. Millie had already checked the books to make sure everything was in order. That was her domain, his was decision-making and keeping everyone in check. He placed the accounts on the edge of the desk, ready to take home. A loud thud caught his attention. Standing, he walked to the window. Four men were making their way up the stairs. He opened the office door and blocked their way at the top.

"Can I help you, gentlemen?"

"We've come for payment," a burly man said.

He had a slight accent Tommy Lee couldn't place.

"I haven't bought anything," he said, annoyance edging his voice.

"It's for protection. We look after your premises, make sure nothing untoward happens." The man took another step up.

"I'm not interested," Tommy Lee said.

"I don't think I made myself clear, it's compulsory."

"Compulsory?" Tommy Lee laughed. "Fellas, I am an Irish Traveller, I have four hundred cousins, now if I need protection, I'll be asking them, who, by the way, will do it just for the craic."

With that, he brought his foot up and kicked the man in the chest, sending him tumbling down the stairs, knocking into the others as he fell. The four men lay in a crumpled heap on top of one another at the bottom, groaning.

Tommy Lee jumped down the stairs and grabbed the first man, dragging him up to face him. "Whoever sent you, tell him to come see me himself."

He kicked out at the man's leg. The snap of his bones echoed around the empty gym, accompanied by the man's cries. He hauled him to the door and shoved him out. The man landed on the pavement. He then turned his attention to the other three who were now running towards him. The first received a punch to his face, splitting his nose. Tommy Lee pushed him outside to join his mate on the ground. The last two put their hands up in surrender.

"Take them." Tommy Lee pointed. "And feck off."

He locked the door behind them and headed back to the office. First he phoned Millie, then his brothers.

***

Tommy Lee perched on the edge of the desk. John Jo and Sean Paul sat on the sofa, elbows balanced on their knees.

"So you don't know who this bloke is?" Sean Paul asked.

Tommy Lee shook his head. "I'm hoping Millie can find out. She was going to check with Tony, the man who runs the docks for her. He's been in the game all his life, he may have some idea."

A loud knock suddenly rattled the door. All three men jumped up, guns in hand, and stormed down the stairs. When Tommy Lee opened the door, his mouth curled in anger.

"What the feck are you doing here?" He grunted.

"Last time I looked I owned half the place," Millie said dryly, brushing past him.

"I don't want you involved, this could get dangerous if it escalates." He sighed. "Please, go home."

"If?" She laughed. "You've attacked his men, there's no ifs about it." She climbed the stairs and took a seat behind the desk.

Tommy Lee stared at her, cursing himself for phoning. "I can't concentrate on sorting this out if I'm worried about you," he reasoned.

"Okay, you want me to go, fine, but hear me out first… Whoever this is, there's two ways they can play this. The first, they will strike fast, all these gangster types are big on revenge." She placed a bag on the desk and rummaged inside, taking out sandwiches, scotch eggs, sausage rolls, and pasties. There was enough to feed an army. "You've made them look weak; they will want to rectify that in case anyone else has similar ideas."

Tommy Lee blew out slowly. "This is exactly why I don't want you here."

Ignoring him, Millie carried on. "You need to set up vantage points outside, eyes on every corner. When they come, and they will at some point, you can then grab them, before they get near."

"What's the second?" John Jo asked.

"They will bide their time, lull you into a false sense of security, and just when you think you're safe, *boom*." She threw her hands into the air.

Was that for dramatic effect?

She stood and adjusted her coat. "You've started a war, Tommy Lee, and now you need to win it… Anyway, I'll leave yous boys to it. I'll go and do some digging, find out who and where these people are based. Oh, and enjoy the food, you'll all need to keep your strength up."

She stood, kissed Tommy Lee on the mouth, then stood back. "Please be careful." She sidestepped him, continued out of the office, and descended the stairs.

Tommy Lee followed to the door. "I'll see you to the motor."

"It's okay, I'm parked right outside." She stood on tiptoe and kissed him again. "I love you," she mumbled against his mouth.

"I love you, too," he muttered, easing back reluctantly. "I'll be home as soon as I can. Now you stay away until it's safe."

"I will, and I'll phone you as soon as I have something."

He stood and watched her drive away, wishing he could have gone with her. It was all that prick's fault, thinking he could demand money. Tommy Lee grinned. That fecker would be the one to pay.

CHAPTER 8

Millie had spent the entire night curled up on the sofa, her eyes fixed on the silent phone as if willing it to ring. Sleep had come in brief, shallow snatches, never enough to quiet the churning in her chest. She glanced at the clock on the mantel, six-thirty a.m. The dull grey light of early morning was creeping through the curtains. The twins would be stirring soon.

Her body ached with tiredness, but her mind was wired. She'd already called Scott, Tony, and Rosie the night before, asking them to meet her here first thing. Tommy Lee wanted answers, names, faces, details, everything they could dig up on the coward threatening their businesses with demands and violence.

Millie and Tommy Lee were done waiting. Whoever was behind it had made it personal. Now it was their turn.

Scott was the first to show up, followed by Tony and Rosie. She was going to babysit, freeing Millie up to work.

"Right, what have you found out so far?" Millie asked Tony while placing a cup of tea in front of him.

"Romford has been run for years by a man named Cole. Rumour has it, his son has taken over the running of the business. He's younger and is eager to prove himself to his old man."

"Do we have a first name?" Millie stood. The twins were awake. "Rose, do you mind?" She motioned to the door.

"Not at all. Bet they miss their Aunt Rose." She grinned and jumped up; she almost skipped to the door.

Millie waited for her to leave the room then refocussed on Tony.

"Mickey Cole," he replied with a nod. "And I have his address."

"Perfect. Jot it down, then I'll phone Tommy Lee." She handed him a pen and notepad. "I've been thinking, can we spare a couple of men to watch the gym at night?"

"I'm not being funny, Mil, but does Tommy Lee want our help? He is, after all, a proud Travelling man." Scott glanced at her.

"No. Probably not, but him and his brothers stand out like a sore thumb. We need men who can blend into the background... I'll speak with him first, I just need to know if it's a possibility."

Tony nodded slowly. "I'm sure we can manage short-term. Maybe he'll take Scott and me to help, we are family as such."

"Good thinking. Me and Rose can go to the docks, you two head to the gym. Tell him what you've found out," she said.

"You not coming to the gym?" Scott sounded surprised.

"I've been banished until this man has been dealt with." She sighed.

"This bloke will have men watching the gym," Tony said. "If we go, he will know who we are. You phone Tommy Lee, let him know what I've told you, then tonight we can plot up and watch the place, if he's in agreement." He stood. "I'm gonna get to the docks. Let me know what he decides."

"Okay... Can you find out the old man's name and address, too?" she said thoughtfully. "We need to cover all bases."

Rosie appeared with the twins, holding each boy's hand. "Can't believe how much they look like their dad."

The twins ran forward and grabbed Millie, kissed her legs, then toddled off to their toybox.

Millie smiled. "Right, I need to do their breakfast, I'll see yous out."

Tony hovered at the door, while Scott and Rosie left.

"I must admit, it'll be good to get my hands dirty again," Tony whispered before following the others.

***

Tommy Lee placed the phone down then stared at the address Millie had given him.

"What did she say?" Sean Paul asked.

"She's got the name and address of the prick. She also said Tony and Scott are willing to help." He thought for a moment. "Phone around the family. I want this place packed day and night. I'm going to the docks."

He grabbed his keys. "I'll be back as soon as I can, then once the others get here, yous can get off home."

He walked through the gym, nodding at the man at the punchbag. He opened the door, and the sharp chill hit him. It was another bright, cold December day. With just under a week until Christmas, he wondered if this mess would be sorted out in time so he could enjoy it with Millie and his boys. His fingers lingered on the handle of the Range Rover while he glanced up and down the road. Was he being watched like Tony had told Millie? He was jumpy, but then he had good reason. He opened the door and climbed in. Looking in the rear-view mirror, he edged the motor away slowly, watching to see if he was being followed. He was annoyed. He'd always worked alone when dealing with shitbags like this. When the time was right, he would take this arsehole out on his own, the way he always did. Painfully and no witnesses.

The journey was ten minutes quicker to the docks from Romford than Stepney, a swift thirty-minute drive, but he didn't go direct, he took side roads in the town, zigzagging around and almost doubling back on himself. When he was certain he wasn't being followed, he put his foot down and headed off, at speed, to see Tony.

Arriving at the docks, he swiftly jumped out of the motor and headed inside. Tony was sitting behind his desk; Rosie was perched on the corner.

"Morning," he said while taking a seat at the other desk. The one he used when Millie wasn't there.

"Morning. Mil fill ya in?" Tony said.

"Yeah… So you think they're watching the gym?" Tommy Lee asked.

"It's what I'd do. Watch everyone's movements, know who I'm dealing with. That's why you need to do the same, but then I don't have to tell you that, do I?"

Tommy Lee didn't answer that. Tony obviously had an idea how he'd previously earned his money.

"I've got my cousins filling the gym, no one will try anything while that lot are there."

"What about your home? If he can't get to you at work, he might go after…" Tony let the sentence linger, unfinished.

"Shit." Tommy Lee hadn't thought of that. No one he had gone after before knew him, knew where he came from, where he lived. Now he had a family, that left him vulnerable. "She'll have to stay with Duke, in Kent."

"This is Millie we're talking about," Rosie intervened. "She's not really on speaking terms with her parents, not after the twins' birthday, so she won't go there. How about she stays with me. If Tony's gonna be helping get this bloke then I'll be on my own, and no one knows where we live."

Tommy Lee ran a hand over his face and sighed. Millie was not going to like his.

***

The gym stank of sweat and tension. Tommy Lee stood at the centre of it all, jaw clenched tight as concrete, eyes burning into the floor.

The heavy bag swayed slowly from a recent session, the chains creaking in the silence.

"You sure this is the way?" asked his youngest cousin.

Tommy Lee didn't look up. He just nodded.

Mickey Cole had made the mistake of thinking he was weak. That because he was new to the business, he'd be easy money. A few lads from Cole's firm had turned up wanting protection money. Like he was king, and Tommy Lee owed him just for being there.

But he had something more than just loyalty. He had family.

And they didn't bow.

By sunset, the gym was loaded, not with punters, but with Irish Traveller muscle. Cousins, uncles, distant family who didn't need to ask twice why they were there. They filled the place like iron being poured into a mould, strong and silent, drinking tea and checking the locks on the back doors.

Tommy Lee walked among them, nodding, quiet words exchanged. A shotgun under the floorboards. A crowbar taped under the bench press. Blades tucked into boots. The gym was ready. The night would be for something else.

As the moon rose, Tommy Lee pulled John Jo and Sean Paul into the old changing room, where they spoke in low voices under the hum of flickering lights.

"You sure we go to him?" John Jo rubbed his knuckles. "Wouldn't it be easier to wait until he sends more of his men and cut them down here?"

"No," Tommy Lee said, cold. "You don't kill the tail. You cut the head off."

They left after dark, three ghosts slipping through a city that slept with one eye open. Outside the gym, men took positions. Cousin Patrick on the roof across the road, gun in hand. The twins, Seamus and Liam, in the alley behind the gym with iron pipes and silent grins. Everyone watching. Everyone waiting.

He had Mickey's address. A flat out towards the edge of town, half fortress, half ego trip. Word was Mickey kept two men on guard at all times and a pit bull named Razor in the hallway.

Didn't matter.

They took their uncle's van — an old Ford Transit, the kind no one looked twice at. Inside, silence. The kind of silence that felt like the sea before a storm. Tommy Lee ran through the plan again. They'd park two streets down, approach on foot. Masks on. In through the side garden, John Jo takes the door. Sean Paul with the bait for the dog. Tommy Lee? He was the one who would walk up to Mickey and end it.

"You kill a man like Mickey," John Jo said in the driver's seat, "the town changes."

Tommy Lee looked out of the window. "Good."

***

Millie sat with glass in hand, her mind firmly fixed on Tommy Lee. Would he be safe?

Of course he is. He's got all his family with him.

She held on to that thought. She didn't want to think of the alternative.

"This is like old times." Rosie beamed, refilling Millie's glass with lemonade.

She glanced up and smiled. "It is." She held her glass up and clinked it against Rosie's. "Cheers."

Rosie turned the TV over and then nestled on the sofa. "They'll be fine, Mil."

"Will they?" She took a large gulp of drink. Then burped. "Pardon… I've got a bad feeling, like we're missing something."

Cole. The name rang a bell, but she couldn't place it.

Shit.

"Can I use your phone?"

"Sure, you don't need to ask."

Millie walked to the hallway where the telephone sat on a side table. Picking the receiver up, she dialled Finn's number.

"Finn. It's Millie. Do you remember that bloke who got put away for twenty-five years for chopping that woman up? Bits of her body were found in with the pigs. Can you remember what happened to him?"

Millie listened then when finished she tapped the receiver then dialled the gym. "Tony, it's Millie. Did you get the old man's address?"

She listened intently, realising what they had missed.

***

The wind was thin and sharp as they slid down the side street towards Cole's place, footsteps muffled on the wet tarmac. The kind of cold that crept into your gloves, your guts. But none of the brothers felt it.

Tommy Lee led, a black balaclava folded up under his chin, crowbar in one hand, blade in the other. John Jo walked close behind, a sack with tools slung over one shoulder. Sean Paul brought up the rear, the bait for the dog hidden under his coat, along with a bat, the handle wrapped in gaffer tape like it was made for war.

They paused at the side gate.

"Here." John Jo pulled a small bolt cutter from the sack. Two snips, clean, practiced, just like when he was stealing motors.

They were through the side garden, stepping over a broken rake and a rusted kid's bike.

Tommy Lee motioned with his hand: stop. There, in front of the back door, just visible in the night, was Razor. The dog. A beast with eyes like headlights.

Sean Paul stepped forward, calm, and dropped two raw steaks marbled with rat poison onto the ground. Razor sniffed, growled once, then greedily tore into the first. His growls softened to gulps. Then, silence.

The back door was locked, of course. But locks were just ideas. John Jo knelt, jimmied his tools, and twenty seconds later, they were inside.

Stairs led up to the first floor of the flat. They followed them up. The place smelled of money and bad taste as they made their way up the stairs. Fake gold ornaments, marble counters, and photos of Mickey posing beside boxers he didn't train and cars he didn't drive lined the landing. Music played faintly from a speaker somewhere in the distance. Motown. Mickey's favourite?

Tommy Lee clenched the crowbar. They moved along the hall swiftly, without a sound.

Another set of stairs: Tommy Lee peeked through the banister rail; two guards. One in the hallway, eating a sandwich. The other by Mickey's bedroom door, arms folded, face like a butcher's block.

Tommy Lee didn't hesitate.

He surged forward. The hallway guard didn't clock him in time. The crowbar cracked into his jaw with a sound like dry wood snapping. He dropped without a word.

The second guard fumbled at his waist for a piece, but Sean Paul was on him fast. The bat swung sideways into the ribs, then the head. The man slumped against the wall, eyes wide open but empty.

They stood at Mickey's door now. Tommy Lee's heart didn't race. It thudded slow and steady, a war drum. He pushed the door open.

Mickey was sitting on the edge of his bed, barefoot, boxers around his ankles, cock in hand. The room reeked of cigars, sweat, and arrogance. He glanced up, face reddening.

"Tommy Lee, I presume," Mickey said, obviously caught off guard. He seemed to compose himself quickly, standing and pulling his pants up. "You're brave or stupid. I can't tell."

Tommy Lee stepped inside. The silence was violent. The crowbar dripped a line of blood down onto the carpet. "You sent men to demand money from me?" he said.

Mickey smirked. "You think I run this town?" He choked a laugh. "You have no idea what you're letting yourself in for."

Tommy Lee closed the door with a flick of his foot. "I'm a Pavee, that's Irish Traveller to you. And we don't take extortion very well."

He wedged a chair under the handle, then stepped nearer, swinging the crowbar with force, landing it like thunder.

***

They didn't speak on the drive back. Tommy Lee sat in the passenger seat, hands still sticky despite the gloves. The crowbar lay across his lap, with dried blood and flecks of brain matter decorating it.

John Jo drove, gaze locked on the road. Sean Paul sat in the middle.

"So it's over," John Jo mumbled.

"Yep. He's gone, it's done." Tommy Lee sighed. Yet he felt nervous. They had covered their tracks well with the fire, but Mickey's words kept replaying in his mind.

You think I run this town?

If he wasn't the head of the snake, who was?

Pulling up at the gym, the men climbed from the Transit and headed in.

"Done?" Tony met them at the door.

"Done," Tommy Lee confirmed with a nod. He shrugged out of his jacket and continued up the stairs to the office.

"Millie phoned—"

Tommy Lee spun round, heart suddenly thumping. "Is she okay, the twins—?"

"She's fine," Tony said quickly. He raised a hand to stop him. "They're safe. But listen, she did find something, something I missed." He paused. "Cole's old man died in prison."

"And?"

Tony stepped closer and lowered his voice. "His son. Mickey. Real name Michael Cole, same sneer, same attitude, same blood. He's the one who's been making all the moves. But here's the thing…he's never been running this. Not really."

Tommy Lee frowned. "You said he was the front man?"

Tony nodded. "I thought he was, but after talking to Finn, Millie found out the real story. Years ago, when Charlie went away, he gave everything to his right-hand man, Eddie. He couldn't remember his surname but thinks it began with an R. Anyway he was the one his missus was messing with on the sly. Eddie took the reins while Cole rotted in a cell. When Cole died, and many believe he had arranged it, he didn't just keep running things—he *became* him."

"Became him?"

"Changed his name. Took the wife. Raised the son like he was his own. Built the lie so clean people forgot there was ever a switch."

Tommy Lee's gut twisted. "So Mickey allowed himself to be raised by another man; was he really a Cole?"

Tony shrugged. "By blood, yeah. But his head was filled with Eddie's voice, Eddie's values. All this 'Cole' shite? That's Eddie's legacy. Mickey just wore the mask."

"So I killed the son…but the real power's still breathing."

Tony's voice was quiet now. "Yeah. And now you've lit a fuse."

Tommy Lee looked up, eyes burning. "Good. Because I'm going to burn down the whole fecking family tree. Roots and all."

CHAPTER 9

Tommy Lee had everyone in place since the murder of Mickey Cole. Men planted outside, men keeping watch from the inside. Still there was no word from Eddie the Charlie Impersonator. There had been no retaliation. No signs of anything untoward. Not a dickybird.

"Everyone wants to go, it's Christmas Eve." John Jo said while he entered the office. "You can't expect them to be away from their families, not this time of year."

Tommy Lee also wanted to be with Millie and the twins. "Tell them to pack up. You may as well get off, too. I'll see you tomorrow."

He grabbed all the paperwork from the top drawer and shoved it into his holdall. If anything happened to the gym over Christmas, at least he had what he needed to rebuild. From the office window, he watched his cousins and uncles make their way out, all giving him a wave or a nod when they left.

"Everything's locked up at the back," Sean Paul told him. "You ready to go?"

"Yeah." He grabbed his belongings and stepped out of the office. He locked it before making his way down the stairs. "I'll see yous boys in the morning."

They were all spending Christmas at John Jo's this year. The women would cook the dinner while the men chatted and played with the children.

He locked the heavy metal door, then threw his belongings into the back of his Range Rover. John Jo tooted when he drove off. Tommy Lee was now alone. He glanced up and down the deserted road. The only noise came from the pub four doors up. He climbed in, gripping the wheel. First he would go to the house and load up with all the Christmas presents, then head off to pick up Millie and the boys and stay in the Buccaneer trailer at his dad's for the night. He wouldn't stay at the house, that was tempting fate a little too much.

***

Maeve had the fire burning so the trailer was warm for them all. She had also made both the beds with clean sheets and covers. "There, get yourselves settled. I'll put the kettle on. I've got a handsome Irish stew in the pot and a nice bit of crusty bread."

"Sounds perfect," Millie said with a smile, even though it was late.

"Can you bring it in here, Mother, the boys need to go bed, they're exhausted?" Tommy Lee asked.

She huffed, nodded, then left.

"Your mum's just excited to have us staying," Millie said quietly while laying Duke in the bed.

"I know, I'm also excited at getting to sleep with my wife for the first time in six days. Feels like my balls are going to burst if I don't make love to you soon." He grinned, placed his son down, and covered him over. "I want you naked, in that bed, in five minutes."

"You can wait until your mother's left." She playfully slapped his arm.

With out thinking, he grabbed her arse, pulling her tight against his throbbing cock. The door opened, and his mother stepped in with a tray.

"Here you go." She glanced at Tommy Lees hands gripping Millie's bottom. "Guess I'll leave you two lovebirds to it." She placed the tray on the side then stepped back out, the door shut firmly behind her.

"You were saying?" He wiggled his eyebrows.

"Fine." Millie walked to the other end of the trailer and started to strip.

"You're a right feek," he groaned, his face flushed with excitement, his gaze roaming her body.

Millie stopped and stared at him blankly. "What's a feek?"

"It's a pretty girl. You're the prettiest I've seen, and, may I add, you're mine." He lunged towards her, pushed her back onto the bed. His lips met hers. All thoughts of the gym and upcoming war forgotten.

***

Eddie sat sipping an expensive glass of cognac. He glanced at the clock. It was now three-thirty a.m. He should have been tucked up in bed, dreaming about the festivities that the new day would bring. Christmas Day had always been a day of celebration with his wife and son, Mickey, the son he would no longer see, and the wife who was so high on medication she could barely function. He threw the glass across the room, splintering it into tiny pieces as it hit the wall, his temper burning inside.

"Fucking pikeys."

Headlights illuminated the room. He stood and turned to the window. His men were back. He strode to the door, pulling it open to find his men standing there.

"Well?" he barked.

"There were too many of them to follow. The main one, Tommy Lee's his name, we lost him. He knows what he's doing, boss." His gruff voice grated on every nerve in Eddie's body, all seven trillion of them.

"So you're telling me you have no addresses?" he roared.

Another man stepped forward. "One lot we followed, they're camped up in a lay-by, just outside Billericay. Three caravans."

Eddie sighed. "Take them out, all of them."

"B-but there's kids there, boss," he stammered.

It had always been an unwritten rule, you never touch women or children. But fuck it, his child had been taken, so what if he was forty and not his flesh and blood. Mickey was still the son he'd raised, his boy.

"I'm not going to repeat myself. I want them all burning in Hell. Now do the fucking job I pay you to do, or do I need to find myself more men?"

"Yes, boss."

With that, the men returned to their motors, all with an uneasy feeling.

***

Tommy Lee awoke to the sound of his sons' tiny footsteps. They were heading towards him, giggling and calling, "Daddy!" He turned to face them. Millie was behind them, on all fours, crawling.

"I'm coming," she growled.

He smiled. He wished he were. The three times they had made love through the night just wasn't enough. They did, however, need sleep. Throwing the covers back, he snatched the twins up and plonked them onto the bed next to him.

"Is Mummy going to join us?" He grinned.

"Mummy needs to get breakfast." She hauled herself up onto the bed and kissed him on the lips. "Merry Christmas."

"Merry Christmas, darling." He swung his legs out of the bed and reached into his jacket pocket. "Here."

She took the present, grinning like a child. Peeling the wrapping off, she lifted the lid. "Oh my God, it's beautiful."

She took the locket from the box; it hung on a solid gold rope chain.

"Open it."

She slid her nail into the locket and gently prised it open. Tommy Lee had put a picture one side of the twins, and on the other, Millie and himself.

"It's beautiful." Her eyes glistened.

"Let me put it on you." He took the chain and clipped it around her neck.

"Do you want one of your presents now?" She examined herself in the mirror.

"I told you not to buy me anything. I've got you and the boys, I don't need anything else."

"Not even another child?" she quizzed.

"What?" He studied her. "Are you…?"

"I am." She winked. "Baby number three has been growing for the last two months."

He jumped out of bed and picked her up. "That was a present I wasn't expecting." He kissed her gently then placed her down. "You're going to need a bigger locket." He laughed.

"And you need to cover that up." She pointed to his growing cock.

"Take the boys in, let Mother feed them. You come back here, you can give me another present."

"I'll take the boys into your mum's with me, while you get dressed. Your family will be waiting for us. There's hot water in the bowl to wash with."

"It's Christmas, woman, am I not allowed a little fun?" he said.

"Later you can have all the fun you like. Now up." She grabbed the twins and left.

***

Tommy Lee tapped on the door then let himself in. The smell of eggs and bacon hit him immediately. "Merry Christmas," he called, stomach rumbling.

"Merry Christmas, son," Maeve greeted. "Take a seat, food's ready."

Millie appeared in the doorway, a smile lighting up her face. She gave him a nod.

Clearing his throat, he began. "We've got something to tell—"

The shrill ring of the phone stopped him mid-sentence.

Paddy snatched the receiver up, mumbled, then held it out. "You're going to want to hear this."

Tommy Lee took the phone and listened, then slammed it down. "We need to get over to John Jo's."

"What's happened, boy?" Maeve clutched her chest.

"Cillian's trailer caught fire. Apparently the gas bottle exploded. They were lucky to get out. If they'd been sleeping at the other end they would have been blown to pieces." He shook his head. "This is him. Eddie."

Millie placed her hand on his arm. "Are you sure?"

"His cousin, Eoghan, said he woke at the sound of gunshots. Cillian pulled his family out just before it went boom. Eoghan reached for his gun and started firing, must have scared whoever it was off before they blew the rest of them up." Tommy Lee rubbed his brow. "So he's played his first hand."

"Do you think we should all stay at John Jo's?" she asked. "Safety in numbers and all that."

"You're going back to Rosie's. Tony can watch you and the boys." His tone was final. "Father, hook the trailer up. You and Mother can stay there."

"I've got me horses to tend, I can't just go off," Paddy snapped.

"We'll make sure the horses are looked after. Watch the twins while we load up the motor. Millie." He flicked his chin towards the door.

They stepped outside into the cold December air. He moved with purpose. Opening the boot, he then headed into the trailer. "Get your stuff."

Millie stopped and turned to him. "I don't want to leave you here with this shit to deal with."

"It'll be okay. I've got a plan." He sat on the bunk and tapped the seat next to him. "This is what I want you to do."

***

Tommy Lee got back to John Jo's at midday. He had a plan, and the wheels were beginning to turn. They first headed to the remnants of the burnt-out trailer. The wind cut sharp across the ground where it sat, twisted and blackened. Someone had cleaned up, placing the torn-off parts back onto the chassis. It still stank, melted and scorched plastic. His imagination went into overdrive, the screams in his head echoing as if real. He had to remind himself no one died, not this time. A victory for the trailer's occupants. This was Eddie's work, he was responsible, not him personally, but one of his thugs. Tommy Lee had seen war, real war, before the gym. Before Mickey. Before this life. And something inside him now shifted back to that old rhythm. Cold, efficient, unmerciful. He would make Eddie, and everyone associated with him, suffer, before killing them all.

While dropping Millie off at Tony's, he'd phoned around his old army buddies. Some would arrive tomorrow; Robbo would be here in three days, once he had a flight. Then they would be here, ready for the final step in his plan. Meanwhile, he had Millie finding every business the filthy prick had a finger in. That was step one. Hit him on all fronts, keep his men busy while Tommy Lee took them out, one at a time. Then it would be time to hit Eddie, and he planned to hit him hard.

He scanned the ground. The trailers were set up at the back, another two were pulling on. Family always came when trouble was brewing.

Joining him, PJ thrust a cup of tea under his nose and handed him a plate. "This should warm you up. Mother's making tea and sandwiches for everyone."

"That woman's always good in a crisis." Tommy Lee nodded.

"Crisis! Don't you mean war?" PJ sighed. "Are we going to be safe here?"

"Yes."

"Then why aren't your wife and kids here?"

"Because I can't protect you lot while they're here. I need to be focused… You know what Millie's like, she'd be the first one to grab a gun and start shooting."

PJ kicked at the ground. "But Marina's here, I don't want her put in danger or hurt."

Tommy Lee stared at him, hard. "You wasn't worried about her getting hurt when you were sneaking off with men, or have you stopped all that?"

"That's in the past, I don't need you keep bringing it back up. This." He pointed at the trailers pulling onto the ground. "Is all your doing. You should have just paid the man the money."

"You know, I remember a time when we had to save you from those men. Remember what they did to you? I could have walked away but I didn't. I found you and then I made them pay. That's what families do. They protect one another, they make things right."

"But I didn't start that," PJ said.

Tommy Lee's voice lowered to a growl. "Yes you did, by going off to those seedy bars. You caused that by your actions. John Jo, Sean Paul, and I sorted that mess, and then I made sure they would never do it to anyone else… Now fuck off back to your wife, as you care about her so much."

PJ hovered; he obviously had no comeback.

Tommy Lee glared at him, standing there with a scowl on his face. At what point had his little brother become so selfish? Had he always been like that? The baby of the family, given every opportunity there was. Excuses made for him. Alibis given for him.

"Go, I have work to do."

"I hope you know what you're doing, otherwise we're all dead." PJ marched back to John Jo's, tail firmly between his legs.

CHAPTER 10

Millie jotted down the last business that her men had found Eddie to be associated with. Five in all. A pawnshop, that was probably a front for stolen goods. A secondhand car lot. A backstreet boozer were he had a meeting room upstairs. A massage parlour, that was certainly a brothel, and the farm. Apart from the farm, which he owned outright, the other businesses he owned a fifty percent share of. She doubted very much that he had gained those by legal means. More than likely he had taken the shares as way of payment.

'Give me half your property, pay up in full or die.'

She could have written the script herself, as she would have done the same. It was standard practice in the criminal underworld. The lesson being, always pay your debts.

She knew what Tommy Lee wanted her to arrange, and she had no problem doing it, but her conscience pricked. These people would lose everything, caught up in a war they had no hand in. They didn't deserve that.

Don't be soft, he would kill the twins without blinking. It's your family or him.

She shook the thought from her mind. "Tony, I need to give Tommy Lee a list of the businesses," she called out over the noise coming from the front room.

Rosie was playing with the twins, and their screams of excitement were deafening. Millie pulled the door shut and picked up the phone.

***

PJ sat on the arm of the sofa, listening in on the conversation. Tommy Lee hadn't spoken to him since the argument earlier. Should he apologise? He wasn't sure. Every word he'd said had been true. He'd always been the one covering for him. Not John Jo, not Sean Paul. Him. Every time PJ had cocked up, Tommy Lee had been the one to put things right.

Tommy Lee ended the call and set the phone down with a dull click. "Millie's got a list of all the businesses," he said, not looking at PJ. "She's going to arrange her men to do the honours when I've got everything else in place."

He turned to Sean Paul. "Have you rung around all the others, told them to stay sharp?"

"John Jo's talking to Billy now. That's the last of them," Sean Paul confirmed.

"Good." Tommy Lee marched towards the door.

PJ jumped up and followed. "Tommy Lee, can I have a word?"

"If you're going to give me more shite, then no."

"No. I wanted to apologise... You're right, you have always looked out for me. And I know it's hard for you being away from Millie and the twins, especially at Christmas. I overheard you on the phone, you know, telling her how much you miss her... Look, I want to help. The quicker this is sorted, the quicker you get back to them and we get back to normal, so what do you need me to do?"

He left out the part about him being able to sneak off to meet men.

"We need to set up guards around the camp, in the trees, and across the road. We need to see them coming. Then they can be dealt with before they can get to us." Tommy Lee pointed to the boundary. "A pair on each corner should do it, another couple across the road."

"Okay, sounds like a plan." PJ focussed on the road. "What if they come by car?"

"We're blocking the road to the left with a fallen tree, so there's only one way in. Right, I need to get ready. You pair up with John Jo, he's got the guns." Tommy Lee strode away, leaving PJ standing open-mouthed.

Guns?

***

Eddie set his knife and fork down. His housekeeper had made him a lovely plate of cold meats with bubble and squeak. A proper East End Boxing Day dinner. He screwed the lid of the pickled onion jar back on then glanced at the clock. His men would be here shortly, ready for his orders.

He took his glass of Shiraz and headed into the lounge, lighting a cigar as he went. A loud thump on the ceiling had him cursing under his breath. His wife had obviously risen. The medication must be wearing off. He sat in his normal place by the window.

"Sir, the leftovers are ready for the pigs," his housekeeper informed him.

He gave her a nod then placed his glass down. Rising, he headed towards the kitchen, pulled his boots on, and grabbed the bucket of slop. He marched outside. Loud grunts rang out around the yard; he heard them long before he reached them. They were telling him they were hungry. He threw the leftover food into the pigpen and watched them squeal and fight for it. A nasty scowl covered his face.

"Yous are going to taste human flesh again very soon." He grinned. "Pikey flesh to be more precise. I just hope you don't catch nothing nasty from it."

The sound of a car caught his attention. Heading back to the house, he threw the bucket down outside the kitchen door, tugged off his boots, and sauntered back into the lounge where his men were waiting.

"I think it's time to hit the gym, boys. I want it burnt to the ground," he told them. "And don't fuck this up."

"When do you want it done, boss?" Gruff asked.

"No time like the present," he said. Why did he employ idiots? Hadn't he just said?

"But it's daylight—"

"I said I want it done now," Eddie bellowed. "This will flush the prick out. I want him alive. I want him here, and I want him today."

***

It was just after four p.m. when the grey sky cracked open with freezing drizzle. The streets around the gym were quiet. Festive decorations still clung to the windows of shuttered shops, unaware of the war simmering in the background. In an alleyway two blocks down from the gym, four men moved low and fast, dressed in black. One carried a full petrol can, the contents sloshing around inside. They didn't get far.

A blacked-out old Transit van cut across the mouth of the alley and screeched to a halt. Before any of them could reach for a weapon, six of Millie's men burst out, silent, gloved, brutal. In under a minute, the four arsonists were down, tied, their heads covered, and dragged into the van like bags of meat.

Within the hour they were at the lock-up; it was a mechanics' yard on the edge of the estate in West Ham, long abandoned but still locked tight from the outside. Inside, a single flickering bulb lit the grime-streaked walls and oil-stained floor. The four men were tied to office chairs, heads bare now, sweat glistening despite the cold.

Millie stood with her arms folded, eyes sharp beneath her hooded coat. Her men kept guard at the doors, two of them smoking by the shutter, calm as ever.

Tony moved from foot to foot, nervous. "He's not gonna like this, you being here," he warned her.

"I know," she said with a sigh. "But the gym is still standing, and we're in a better position now we have them." She flicked her head to the prisoners.

Tommy Lee arrived ten minutes later, boots stomping through the slush outside. He was still wearing the same clothes, his jaw clenched tight. When he stepped inside and saw Millie standing there, his temper flared.

"What the feck are you doing here?" He slammed the metal door shut behind him.

Millie raised an eyebrow. "You're welcome."

"I told you to stay away."

"And I ignored you. Because if I hadn't, you'd be picking through the ash of our gym right now." She dropped her arms to her sides.

He turned his focus to Tony. "Did you know about this?"

Tony shook his head. "Not until I got the phone call."

Tommy Lee glanced at the four tied-up men, or was that boys? They looked like teenagers, bruised, scowling, one with blood drying on his lip. Then back at her.

"You shouldn't be here," he said, lower now. "Not in person."

She stepped closer, voice softer. "I'm not made of glass, Tommy Lee. And those four bastards were five minutes from torching everything we've built. My lads followed the tip-off, waited, and jumped 'em clean. No one even saw it."

He studied the four, all bound and gagged. "Have they talked?"

"Not yet. But they're scared. One of them pissed himself. That one." She pointed. "Thinks Eddie is going to rescue him."

"Eddie can't even save himself now." Tommy Lee moved closer to the tied-up men and crouched in front of them. "You were gonna burn my gym. Kill anyone inside. So here's how this goes: you talk, or I start cutting pieces of you off."

"I've got places we can bury them," Millie added.

Tommy Lee looked over his shoulder. "You really shouldn't be here."

She met his gaze. "But I am."

For a second he was pleased to lay eyes on her, know she was safe, in touching distance. But she had to go and go now. "Tony, take Millie home, please."

"What?" she snapped. "Why won't you let me help?"

He grabbed her arm and marched her to the door. "I don't want you to see this. Go back to the twins and give them a kiss from me."

"Fine. But one thing to think about. When this is over there'll be a new face running Romford, so why not put in place one of his men, see if that will coax any info out of them."

"Okay. Now out… Tony, make sure she gets back safely, and don't let her out of your sight." Tommy Lee watched her leave, just to make sure she actually went.

"Right, fellas, where were we?" He grinned then began to pull down their gags. "Who wants to go first?"

No answer. Just the sound of the rain spitting against the tin roof.

He yanked a stool towards them and sat with his elbows resting on his knees. "I was in a situation like this before… Only there were six pricks, tied up in a row. Do you know what I did to them?" He didn't wait for an answer, just continued. "I asked for information. The first four said no, the fifth lied, and the sixth…tried to run."

He let the silence sit for a minute.

"I caught him. Took his kneecaps out with a crowbar. Dumped him on the M11, crawling like a dog, until he got run over and mangled to shreds under the wheels of a truck… The others, well, they didn't live to tell the tale either."

His voice never rose above a murmur.

"Now I'm giving you the chance they never had: you talk, you live." He finished. He stood and walked outside, giving them the chance to mull over his words. He watched the rain drip from the tin roof, pooling on the ground. Sauntering to his Range Rover, he opened the boot and took out a bag. It contained his chosen tools. He lifted it and threw it over his shoulder, then marched back to the building ready for the finale.

Dropping the bag onto the floor in front of them, he bent down and unzipped it. "So lads, what's it to be?" He picked up a pair of pliers.

The younger man was the first to speak. "They told us it was just a scare job. Empty building. No one would be in it. Get in, splash the stuff, light it up, run."

"Who told you?" Tommy Lee asked.

"Guy named Dennis. Said it came from higher up. From the boss himself."

"What's your name?"

"Robert."

Tommy Lee stood. "So Eddie's sending kids to do his dirty work now."

"Not just kids. He's got others. Older lads. Proper hitters. We're just the distraction," Robert said, almost proudly.

Tommy Lee stepped closer, face inches from the youngster. "Distraction for what?"

Silence.

He slammed his hand on the back of the chair. "For what?"

Robert flinched. "They're planning something bigger. Another fire. Somewhere else. Not the gym. Somewhere you wouldn't expect."

Tommy Lee grabbed the face of the young man next to him. "That true?"

"Yes," he muttered. "Some boozer in Stepney. Millie's name came up. They said hit it hard. Send a message."

He looked at Millie's heavy who stood by the shutter. "Make a call to Finn. I want his place locked down. Then you lot get over there."

"What about this lot?" the heavy asked.

"I'll take care of them." Tommy Lee grinned. "And after that, I'm going to make sure Eddie knows what happens when you poke the wrong fecking family."

CHAPTER 11

Millie sat cross-legged on the living room floor, towel-drying the freshly bathed twins as they giggled and wriggled around her. Her hands moved on instinct, but her thoughts were elsewhere. Tommy Lee…and the barn. Had he dealt with them? Was it over?

"You should really eat something, Mil," Rosie said gently. She lowered herself onto the floor beside her. "You're eating for two now, remember?"

"I'm not hungry," Millie murmured, eyes still distant.

From the hallway, Tony called out, "I've got to nip out. Won't be long."

Millie stood quickly and followed him to the door. "What's going on?"

Tony turned, meeting her eyes with the same mix of loyalty and unease that had been hanging over them for weeks. "Tommy Lee said you're to stay put. And yes," he held up a hand to cut her off, "I know you sign my paycheques, but this is bigger now. It's serious, Mil. And with you being in the family way…you're safer out of it."

She opened her mouth to protest, but the words didn't come. He was right. As much as it hurt her pride, her baby deserved to be safe. She wouldn't dream of putting the twins in harm's way, so why would she risk this one?

With a tight nod, she let him go and wandered back into the lounge.

"Some fucking Christmas this has turned out to be." She collapsed onto the sofa. Her eyes drifted to the little tree in the corner, its multicoloured lights blinking softly against the wall. It should've felt warm, festive, but all she felt was the tight swell of tears pressing behind her eyes. Not the quiet kind either. The kind that made you want to break apart completely.

"I'm sure it'll all blow over soon," Rosie offered. "Things will go back to normal… Have you looked at any more houses lately?"

Millie sighed. She knew what Rosie was doing, gently steering her away from the edge. But it wouldn't work. Not this time.

"No," she said, almost a whisper. "I haven't."

Because right now, no place felt safe. Not even this one.

"I'm gonna take the boys up to bed," she said.

"Mil, Finn's gonna be okay."

"Finn… What's Finn got to do with this?"

***

Finn loaded up Bertha, his trusty shotgun that he kept under the bar. Just in case there was ever trouble in the pub. He hadn't used it for a few years. In fact, Millie was the last one to fire it…

Fin spotted Millie coming into the bar; she was met with arms and fists flying everywhere. Flo was in the corner whacking anyone who came near her with an ashtray. Millie appeared angry, like she was going to burst. She grabbed the shotgun from underneath the bar, cocked it, and pointed it towards the ceiling. She squeezed the trigger twice in quick succession. The two shells hit the ceiling, plaster falling like it was snowing, and the four people standing underneath ducked away. The sound continued to ring inside the bar. Everyone stopped and gawped at her.

"Enough…. I've had enough," she'd screamed.

Two fecking great big holes, she'd blasted, in the ceiling. He stared up and smiled. You couldn't see them now. Paul Kelly, her late husband, had fixed them for him, or was that for her? It had been a shock when they had split, but then Paul had changed. He'd become reckless, thinking he was untouchable. And the women he'd been seen with, that must have hurt Millie when she'd found out. Should Finn have told her before? No. Never interfere in a man and woman's marriage.

The hit-and-run that had killed Paul had sent shock waves through Stepney and left Millie running his empire. Her empire. Finn worried about her, that time had been dark. Still, she was happy now. Happy with Tommy Lee and her little family.

He glanced around the pub. All the regulars were in for their Boxing Day pints. Men slipping out, leaving their wives to clean up and sort the children. He was here with Brenda, looking forward to closing up and putting his feet up with her. But not now. When one of Millie's men had phoned and told him what was happening, his temper bubbled. He peered over when Tony and another couple of Millie's men walked in.

"Anything?" Tony asked.

Finn shook his head. "I know everyone in here."

"I've got men outside on look out. You two keep an eye out from the upstairs windows, one front and one back."

The men rushed into the back.

"What do you want me to do?" Finn asked.

"Just act normal, we don't want to alert them," Tony said. "It's been a while since we've all been in here."

"I would say it's like old times, but everything's changed. We've all got older and moved on with our lives… How's Rosie?" Finn asked, nostalgia clouding his mind.

"She's good. Right, I'll go and guard the back window."

Finn rang the bell, time for everyone to leave. "Drink up, folks, time to get home to your lovely wives." He was sure a few groans came from the punters. They would be only too pleased to leave if they knew what was coming.

"Goodnight," he called to the last to leave, then locked and bolted the door. Before he had made it back to the bar, the pub shook with the first impact, a bottle crashing through the front window, flames licking up the curtain before Finn stamped it out with a blanket.

Tony rushed in to help, smoke curling across the room. He crouched by the window, gun drawn. "They didn't waste any time."

Finn wiped sweat from his brow, breathing fast. "You reckon they're gonna push through the front?"

"They want us looking this way," Tony muttered. "But I've got a feeling this ain't about the Artichoke. Eddie knows we will come running to protect this place. He's done his homework, obviously knows more than what we first thought. Millie, this place. Reckon he knows everything."

Finn listened. Silence. No. This was too clean, too obvious.

He crawled to the window beside him as one of Millie's men came running in from outside.

"I got one shot off, think I injured him. They've driven off. Should we go after them?"

"Wait," Tony said. "This is a show. They're keeping us busy."

He stood, walked towards the back room, grabbed the phone, and dialled. "Come on, come on…"

The line clicked.

"Tommy Lee. It's a setup. They're trying to draw us away. The pub's just bait—they're going for the site. The one you're staying at. John Jo and Sean Paul's ground."

He was met with a long pause.

Tommy Lee gripped the handset, his knuckles white. "I know." He slammed down the phone.

***

Tommy Lee had everyone in place. Lookouts on all corners of the ground with a couple over the road. "Get all the women inside and tell them to stay there. Have all the gas bottles been planted along the lane?"

"Yeah," John Jo said with a sharp nod. "Hidden in the hedgerow like you said."

Tommy Lee took his rifle and climbed on top of his father's horse box, positioning himself ready. It was the best vantage point to pick off any intruders with little chance of being spotted.

"There's a van up the road," Sean Paul called up to him, holding a pair of binoculars in his hand. "No plates on it."

"Can you make out the passengers?"

"No, it's too dark. Maybe a second car trailing behind, low lights. Could be as many as ten in total. If the van's full."

"Good," Tommy Lee replied.

Sean Paul glanced up at him. "Good?"

Tommy Lee finally smiled. "Means they're confident. Overconfident."

The van slowed nearer the ground, brakes squealing slightly as it stopped only yards up the road. Tommy Lee aimed the rifle, slowly squeezing the trigger, almost caressing. The moment the doors went to open, a single shot rang out, clean, precise. It hit one of the gas cylinders, blowing the side of the van off. The car behind turned and drove away at speed. He had just given them a warning, Tommy Lee style.

CHAPTER 12

Eddie sat frozen, his mouth slightly open, trying to process what he'd just heard. Eight men. Taken out with one fucking shot. And the four youngest lads—still missing.

Fuck.

He ran a hand over his face, jaw clenched tight. "I want everyone here. Guarding this place," he said. "Men on every boundary and inside the house."

"Boss," Gruff muttered, "there's only five of us left."

He turned sharply, eyes narrowing. "Then get more."

"We've tried. Word's out… Soon as they hear it's a pikey you're at war with, they're not interested."

Eddie waved him off with a grunt, but the words stuck. He faced the window, staring out. His remaining men were huddled near the shed, heads close, murmuring, casting nervous glances towards the house.

Are they talking about me?

He stormed across the room, yanked open the old gun cupboard, and threw the door wide. His fingers wrapped around the cold steel of the rifle, his mind already ticking through worst-case scenarios. He pulled a box of shells down from the top shelf and began to load, slow and deliberate.

Whoever the bastard was, whoever thought they could take what he'd built, was about to learn exactly what kind of man he really was.

Let them come.

*****

Tommy Lee finished cleaning up the road. All gas canisters had been returned to the trailers, and every piece of metal and rubber, from the van, had been cleared and disposed of, along with the bodies, before the gardai had arrived. His excuse, a cylinder had exploded when it dropped off the back of a truck. They seem pacified, for now. The next stage of this war would have to be fought at Eddie's. Tommy Lee couldn't bring anymore unwanted attention to his brothers' ground.

It was a little after midnight that he'd welcomed his army buddies with hugs and slaps on the back. Maeve had fed them a hearty meal of leftover stew, and he'd showed them to his trailer so they could rest up, ready for tomorrow. He only had Robbo to wait for, and he should be arriving by five p.m.

"So what's the plan?" Stevie asked.

"We go in, take out his men, then I finish him. But we'll discuss it more when Robbo's here."

"How is that mad fucker?" Stevie grinned.

"Still as fecking crazy as a box of frogs." Tommy Lee laughed.

He stood and left them drinking beer. He wandered out into the cold night air and patrolled the ground. He didn't think anything else would happen tonight, Eddie had taken a big hit today.

After Tony and the others had left earlier, Tommy Lee had set to work getting the truth out of the young men. It was quick, none of them had any pain threshold, and within thirty minutes he had the real plan. Then he had cut them up and discarded the bodies. Did he feel guilty? No. If they were old enough to play with the big boys, they were old enough to take the consequences.

John Jo joined him, falling in step by his side. "Do you think it's over?"

"No, but it will be tomorrow," Tommy Lee assured him.

"What's happening tomorrow?"

"He won't be a problem anymore. Life can get back to normal. I will be in bed with my wife, and everything will be right with the world." Just the thought of being back with Millie lifted his spirits.

"What happens when another tosser comes to run Romford?"

"Then I will deal with him, like I dealt with this." Tommy Lee pulled his keys from his pocket. "Stevie is going to watch the place for a few hours. I've got some business to take care of."

***

Tommy Lee knocked on the door, stood back, and waited. It was late, he knew that, but he needed to come.

A bleary-eyed Tony opened the door. "What's happened?"

"I need to see Millie."

"You'd better come in then." He stood back, door fully opened. "She's in bed."

Tommy Lee marched up to her room and opened the door gently. The table lamp illuminated the corner where she lay. She sat up, alarmed.

"Shh, it's me," he whispered.

"What are you doing here, is it over?" she asked, wrapping her arms around him when he got in beside her.

"Not yet, but it will be soon." He brushed his lips against hers. "I needed to see you."

83

He pulled his top off and lay down, bringing her with him, his hands wandering her body. "I've missed this," he mumbled into her neck.

He yanked her nightie over her head, his breathing heavy. Kissing her shoulder, he continued down her body.

Millie gasped while he kissed her thighs, her breathing as heavy as his. Easing her legs apart, he slipped his tongue in, licking and sucking while she fell into rhythm with his movements.

He stopped, wanting to tease her, so, moving back up, he tugged off his jeans then positioned himself ready to take her. Her groans of pure delight egged him on, and he drove himself inside her, unable to wait. Harder, faster he thrust until the glorious moment she climaxed, pulsating around his cock. He shook, his pent-up energy left his body, and he crumpled on top of her.

"I love you," he murmured.

"I love you, too," she whispered back.

He rolled off and pulled her to him, wrapping his arms around her. He kissed the top of her head. They lay together, the only sound their thudding hearts.

"I need to get back."

"I know." A sadness tinged her words.

"I'll be back, to pick you and the twins up soon as it's over," he assured her.

He slid off the bed and walked over to where his boys were sleeping. They looked so peaceful, unlike when they were awake, tearing around like little psychopaths. He grinned, recalling his mother's words 'boys will be boys.' He wanted to protect them, protect Millie, and he could only see one way of doing that.

He turned to face her. "John Jo reckons someone else will take over Romford when this is over."

"He's right, it will be open season, ripe for the taking," she agreed.

"Then how about we take it?"

"Do you want that life, always looking over your shoulder, not knowing who to trust?" She sat up. "You'd need good men at your side, men who know the game."

"I'm sure John Jo and Sean Paul would be up for it, and let's not forget my cousins."

She nodded. "Sounds like you've already decided... You could give Eddie's fifty percent shares back to the owners as a sign of fairness, then charge them protection money... I think they would be eating out of your hand after that."

"Sounds like you've thought about it, too," he said, perching on the edge of the bed.

"It would be a lie if I said I hadn't." She shrugged. "Are you sure, though? It may not be as easy as it sounds."

"If I put my mind to something, I get it. You should know that."

"Should I?" She frowned.

"I saw you, wanted you, and conquered you." He chuckled.

Millie grabbed her nightie and threw it at him. "Bighead."

He caught it and grinned. "So we going to do this?"

A smile spread slowly across her face. "Why the hell not."

***

John Jo leaned back on his motor and surveyed the ground. There were seven trailers dotted around, including his mother and father's. The place looked messy. The ground was churned up, thanks to the rain, and everyone was scared, thanks to Tommy Lee.

He had seen a side to his brother he never knew existed. It was like he thrived on war, on killing. Maybe that was what the army had taught him. Meanwhile, Sean Paul and himself were losing money by sitting here waiting for the coast to clear so they could continue stealing motors. He'd had one lined up, ready for the taking, one that would earn them a small fortune, and then this had happened. Tomorrow he would put that right. He'd phone his contact and arrange everything for the following night. Tommy Lee was now preoccupied with Eddie; he had his army mates to help him now. John Jo felt pushed out. It annoyed him, although he would never let on.

He spotted headlights and moved into the shadows, watching. Tommy Lee drove in, Stevie heading to meet him, rifle resting on his shoulder.

"Everything all right?" Stevie asked.

"All good, mate," Tommy Lee said. "Had conformation from Robbo; everything's set for tomorrow night." He then headed in.

So they would be busy. John Jo grinned. Perfect.

A low rumble caught his attention, followed by headlights. A car was turning in. He marched towards it, but Stevie beat him to it, already opening the door and dragging the driver out.

Tommy Lee appeared, his face taut. "Who the feck are you?"

The man shrugged out of Stevie's grip, holding his hands up in surrender. "I'm not armed."

"I said who the feck are you? Answer the fecking question." Tommy Lee growled.

"My name's Dennis, I work, or rather did work, for Charlie Cole."

"You mean Eddie." Tommy Lee snapped.

"He hasn't been called that for a few years, but yes, Eddie." He agreed.

"Bit fucking stupid coming here, Dennis," Stevie added, taking the safety catch off the rifle.

"Eddie's always been a crazy bastard, but now…he's lost the plot. I can't work for a man like that, a man who's happy to kill women and children."

"So why are you here?" Tommy Lee asked. Was this a trap?

Dennis sighed. "The minute he wanted me to kill that family, I knew I'd had enough."

"You blew up the trailer. You fecking prick. There were two little children in there, as well as their parents," John Jo roared. "Kill him."

"Wait!" Dennis stepped back. "I shot over the caravan, to warn them. It wasn't until they were out that I did what Eddie ordered. There were others with me, so I had to make it look good." He shook his head. "I think Eddie had an idea, though, cos he ain't shared any information with me since."

"What did you think you'd achieve by coming here?" Tommy Lee asked. "You must know I'd be foolish to trust you."

"Of course, trust needs to be earned… I've been in this game all my life, I don't know anything else. When this is over I want to work for you. I know everything about the business, I could be an asset."

Tommy Lee stared hard at Dennis, his instincts telling him this man was speaking the truth, but if he could turn on one boss he could turn on him.

Dennis continued. "I knew the risk was fifty-fifty coming here. You either believe me and give me a chance, or I end up dead, but I know him better than anyone. I know the layout to the farm and the house, and I know he's waiting for you."

CHAPTER 13

Night had fallen. Tommy Lee and his army buddies, Robbo, Stevie, Ghost, Marsh, and Denny, all dressed in combat gear with blackened faces, laughed and joked as they always did before a mission. The guns had been loaded, and they sat in the Buccaneer, waiting to head off. Dennis had given them the information they needed, including a hand-drawn diagram of the farmhouse and outbuildings. The only thing he couldn't confirm was how many men Eddie now had. He wasn't sure if he had managed to recruit more men or if he still had the handful from the previous day. After the briefing, he had been tied up and placed in one of the stables. Just in case he was a plant. Sean Paul, John Jo, and PJ took turns guarding him.

"This is like old times, fellas." Robbo grinned.

"I'd be lying if I didn't say I missed this," Stevie said. "Even working with you, ya mad fucker."

Tommy Lee laughed. Robbo was mad and missed in equal quantities.

"D'ya remember that newbie, what was his name?" Robbo scratched his head. "Grey... Brown—"

"White," Tommy Lee cut in. "Peter White."

"That's the one," Robbo continued. "When he was showing of with his rifle, dropped it and shot a hole in his foot."

All the men roared with laughter.

"That put paid to his service," Ghost said, aptly named because he could disappear without trace.

"You don't mess around with guns, he learnt a valuable lesson that day," Stevie said seriously.

John Jo joined them inside, perching on the edge of the bunk, his face a picture when he saw their attire.

"How's Dennis?" Tommy Lee asked.

"He hasn't stopped fecking talking," John Jo said. "I think I know more about the crime world now than I do breeding the cobs."

Robbo laughed. "That'll come in handy when your brother takes over."

John Jo's face scrunched into confusion. "Can I have a word, outside."

Tommy Lee sighed. He hadn't told his brothers that bit of information.

Shit.

They stepped out into the crisp, cold night air.

"I was going to tell you. When this was over." Tommy Lee placed his hand on his shoulder.

"Well, that's all right then." John Jo shrugged his hand off. "We're brothers, Tommy Lee. Blood. Don't you think you should have told us first?" He appeared hurt.

"Let me get tonight over with, then we'll sit down, and I'll explain."

"Save it for them in there." John Jo pointed to the trailer. "They seem to be more your family than we are." He stormed away.

"Wait," Tommy Lee called.

But he never got a reply.

***

Sean Paul appeared shocked. "You want us to steal a motor tonight. What about guarding that man?" He pushed his fingers through his hair. "Jaysus, John Jo, Tommy Lee will have a fit."

"This has nothing to do with him. He's not interested in us no more. We should be the one's going with him tonight, not that lot." John Jo roared. "We have families to look after, bills to pay, and that comes first. Now are you in or not?"

***

The van rolled slowly down the country road, headlights off, the gravel crunching beneath the tires. The air smelled of damp earth and manure, the cold biting deep even through thick jackets. Inside, no one spoke. They didn't need to. Tommy Lee sat in the front passenger seat, rifle across his lap. His mind was steel. No hesitation. No second thoughts. This was the endgame.

In the back, Robbo checked his magazines. Stevie tightened the straps on his gloves. The other three, Denny, Marsh, and Ghost, kept their eyes locked on the windows, scanning for movement. Eddie's farm sat at the end of a long, rutted track, squat and ugly under the half-moon. A fortress once, maybe, when he had an army. But now? Now it was just a place to die.

Ghost whispered first in disgust, "Two men at the gate. Smoking. Piss-poor discipline."

Tommy Lee nodded. "Let's go introduce ourselves."

He stood at the tree line, watching the farmhouse. The windows gave a creamy glow of light; he knew Eddie was inside. Hiding. Waiting.

They hit the gate fast. Stevie took the one on the left, knife sliding clean into his ribs, hand over his mouth before he could even grunt. Robbo grabbed the second, spun him into the mud, and snapped his neck with one sharp twist. Tommy Lee dragged the bodies into the bushes. No alarms. No sightings.

They stalked forward, low and silent.

The farmhouse sat dead ahead, lights still on. A barn to the right. Pigpens stretching out beyond it, the filthy grunting of animals thick in the air.

Denny reappeared. "Three inside, front room. One in the kitchen. Eddie's in the back."

Tommy tightened his grip on his rifle. "No survivors."

Stevie was first through the door, suppressed shots spitting into the first two men before they even knew what hit them. The third scrambled for a gun. Robbo put one between his eyes.

Denny kicked open the kitchen door. The guard inside barely had time to turn before Ghost took his throat out with a blade.

Then the house was silent again.

Tommy Lee prowled through the hallway, slow and steady. At the back of the house, a door stood slightly ajar. He pushed it open. Eddie sat in a wooden chair, whiskey in one hand, rifle on the table. His face twisted when he saw Tommy Lee.

He stood. "You f—" he began, not finishing the sentence.

Tommy Lee fired. Not to kill. The bullet took Eddie in the thigh, sending him sprawling to the floor with a howl. Tommy Lee strode forward, pressing his boot down hard on the fresh wound. Eddie writhed, blood spreading under him.

Tommy Lee crouched. "You had a good run."

Eddie gritted his teeth. "Go on then…finish it."

Tommy Lee smiled, cold and empty. "Not yet." He nodded to Robbo. "Take him outside."

They dragged him across the dirt, kicking and gasping, to the edge of the pigpen. The pigs stirred, their fat, filthy bodies shifting in the slop. Robbo and Ghost held Eddie up against the pen, his arm held firmly in place.

Eddie coughed, spitting blood. "You think this scares me?"

Tommy Lee stood beside him, pulled out a katana, then without a word he hacked off his hand. Eddie screamed. Tommy Lee held it up, then flicked it over the fence. The pigs went for it instantly, squealing and snapping, fighting over the fresh meat.

Eddie's breath came in ragged, shuddering gasps.

Tommy Lee leaned in close. "I'm taking you apart, bit by bit. Like you tried to do to me."

He grabbed his other hand next, slicing off the fingers. More screams, more blood. Another flick into the pen. More pigs diving in.

He grabbed Eddie's head and shoved his face towards the squealing pigs. "I want you to watch this, your pride and joy munching on your flesh."

He sobbed now, shaking uncontrollably. Tommy Lee wiped the blade clean on Eddie's shirt.

"You spent your life feeding off people," Tommy Lee said softly. "Now look at you." He glanced at Stevie. "Take an ear."

He stood back and watched as he hacked it off then threw it in.

Tommy Lee drew Eddie's face towards his. "You made one fatal mistake...you never feck with the Travellers."

Robbo looked at him. "You want any more bits cut off?"

Tommy Lee shook his head. "Let the pigs have the rest of him. We need to clean up; dump the rest of the bodies in with the pigs, it might be a while before they're fed again."

They turned, leaving him whimpering in the mud, pigs closing in. They walked back to the house, screams echoing around the yard.

Tommy Lee didn't look back. It was over.

CHAPTER 14

January 1979

It had been a week since Eddie's demise, and things were pretty much normal again. All the trailers had now left, back where they came from, Paddy and Maeve had gone home, and John Jo and Sean Paul were pinching motors, and the money was building up nicely.

They had just delivered the latest stolen car to the destination given. It was driven straight into the back of the lorry. After receiving the money, they headed back home.

John Jo checked the envelope with a smile. "It's good to be back in business. Reckon we should go and see the farmer about the field next to us. We could move the cobs onto it."

"And the chickens, the noisy feckers," Sean Paul confirmed with a nod. "They have me awake at the crack of dawn." He scratched the back of his neck, then added, "I was thinking about Mother and Father. Mother seems down since they went home. What if they move on with us?"

"That woman will be watching our every move," John Jo said, instantly regretting it. "But I guess it would make sense…after the trouble with the gym."

"Mother can help with the children, Father with the cobs. If we manage to get that next field we'll have more than enough room."

"We could stash an old motor up the road," John Jo said. "That way we could still sneak out without them knowing. Let's go see the farmer tomorrow and see if we can have a deal, then we ask Father."

Sean Paul nodded in agreement. "What's on the new list?"

John Jo pulled a folded piece of paper from his pocket and squinted. "Can't see a thing, it's too dark. We'll have a proper look tomorrow, see what motors he's after, then we can have a scout about over the next few days." He shoved the list back into his pocket and smiled. "Things are on the up, boy."

***

PJ moved through the backstreet discreetly, hands in his pockets, head down. It was late, and the area was deserted. But you could never be sure there weren't prying eyes about. The alley off Runwell Street was exactly as he remembered, narrow, damp, unmarked. Only those who needed to know, knew. It hadn't been that long since he had been there, but it felt like an eternity. An eternity since he'd had male companionship.

At the end of the alleyway was a rusted iron door. A single knock. Then three more in rhythm.

A hatch slid open. A pair of painted eyes peeked through. "Password?"

"Dragon," he murmured.

The latch clicked. The door creaked open. Inside, the music hit him like a wave, bass heavy, full of soul and sweat. The club was buried beneath a shutdown tailor's shop, the air thick with cigarette smoke, cologne, and something darker, something exciting. A sea of bodies swayed in rhythm to the music. Laughter and chatter came from a group of men in the corner. PJ didn't speak to anyone at first. He just ordered a whiskey and let the beat roll over him. His eyes adjusted to the dark. He scanned the area, then he saw him.

Tall, wide smile. Shirt unbuttoned, blond hair curling around his face. Their eyes met, then again. With a flick of his head, PJ led him into the back room.

They sat behind a purple velvet curtain. It smelled of sweat, dust, and lust. Nothing new, but everything he craved. There were no names, no pasts, just hands gliding over each other's bodies, unbuttoning shirts, pulling down zippers. He could hear the men in the next room, their groans of excitement. PJ spotted a face, staring from a gap in the curtain, watching. He smiled; if it was a show he wanted, then he would give him one.

Two hours later PJ was home, satisfied, but for how long? He climbed into the trailer, tiptoeing to the bed. Marina was asleep, one arm over her head, hair wild across the pillow. He stripped, then climbed in, careful not to wake her. He lay with his hands on his chest, trying to steady his rapidly beating heart. The excitement he had felt tonight had been exhilarating. He couldn't explain it, there were no words. It was just sex, he assured himself. He glanced at Marina, then the guilt took him. He was disgusting, not fit to be a husband or father.

You are going to Hell.

"I know," he whispered.

But what could he do? This life he lived, one for them and one for himself, was tearing him in two. How much longer could he go on?

***

Millie lay baby Duke back in his cot and hushed him. At one a.m. the little sod had decided it was playtime. Luckily, Tommy boy never woke, he could sleep through anything, which was a blessing. She tiptoed out of the bedroom and joined Tommy Lee back in bed. His arms immediately reached for her. She nestled into him.

"So tomorrow," he began. "I'll go see the people who Eddie stole the businesses from and get them signed back to the owners."

"I think that's the best idea. A show of good faith, then offer your services," she mumbled into his chest.

"If they say no?"

"Then make sure they know they're on their own." She pushed herself up. "Are you sure you want to do this?"

"It's better I take control than go through all that shite again with someone else," he said firmly. "I will not have you and the twins put in danger. Not ever."

"Okay." She glanced down at him. "What about your other line of work, are you giving that up?"

"I gave that up the day I got with you. I'm building a future for us and the boys, one that keeps me in our bed every night." He grinned, then grabbed her back down while twisting on top of her.

"One more thing before you ravage me," she muttered on his lips.

He drew back, sighing. "Go on."

"You'll need good men working for you, men you can trust."

"I've got three brothers. We may argue from time to time, but I trust them with my life. With them by my side, I can't fail." He yanked her nightie up over her head. "Now, where were we…"

***

Paddy finished feeding the horses and stomped back towards the mobile, placing the bucket down next to the step. He climbed in and was handed a cup of tea.

"Thanks, darling." He placed it on the table and shook off his coat. "I might have to sell a couple of the cobs."

"Why would you do that, they're your pride and joy?" Maeve asked, a little shocked.

"It's getting too much for me. Me fecking back is playing up. Ten is a lot for one man to care for." He glanced at the window. "Who's that?"

"It's John Jo and Sean Paul." She grabbed two more cups.

"Morning, Mother. Father," John Jo said with a grin. "We got a question for yous."

Paddy stared at both boys. What were they up to now? He sipped his tea and pointed to the chairs. "Take a seat."

"We wondered what you'd think about moving onto our gr—" Sean Paul began.

"I've got ten horses here, they won't all fit in your paddock, not with yours," Paddy grumbled.

"We've just bought the field next to us. The horses will go on there, leaving plenty of room for your mobile," John Jo said.

Paddy glanced at Maeve. Her eyes were glistening with hope, but he remained silent.

"We'll get a base done this week," Sean Paul continued. "And the fencing done in the new field."

"I don't know," Paddy said. "We've lived here a long time. It's our home."

"You can sell this ground, buy more cobs, buy a new mobile, whatever. Think about it, yous ain't getting any younger... You'll have help with the horses, Mother can help with the grandchildren and watch them grow up, and yous won't be lonely."

Paddy sighed. They had a point. "What do you think, girl?"

Maeve sat at the table and placed her hand on his. "I'd love to be with my family, but if you want to stay here, then we stay here."

He smiled wearily; she'd spoken like a true Traveller's wife. "Give me a couple of days to think about it, boys. It's a big decision."

"Okay, in the meantime, we'll get the paddock sorted and the stables so it's ready for when you say yes." John Jo grinned.

Paddy caught him winking at Maeve, her face lighting up with a smile. She was a beauty to him, always had been, always would be. "Yous do that. We'll come over in a couple of days' time."

"We best go, got lots to do. Thanks for the tea, Mother," Sean Paul said, and placed a kiss on her cheek.

John Jo did the same, and then they left.

"So...you'd like to move?" Paddy asked her.

"You was only saying earlier about selling a couple of the cobs. This way you get to keep them and have help looking after them. You could teach the grandchildren... Plus, it would be nice to get a new mobile," Maeve reasoned. "But as I said, it's your choice."

"Get your coat on, girl, let's go have a look at the mobiles." He smiled when her face lit up again.

"See you, Paddy Ward, I loves you more with every day."

***

Paddy and Maeve turned into the gravel lot off the A130. The tyres crackled over loose stone, the scent of damp grass and diesel hanging in the air. A crooked wooden sign swung above the gate. The place was a dump.

The wind rolled cold across the open yard, kicking up dust and rubbish as Paddy stepped down from the Transit. Maeve followed, buttoning her coat tight over her cardigan and then stuffing her hands deep into her coat pockets.

"These all look ready for the crusher," Maeve said, her voice full of dismay.

The man running the yard came waddling over, thick coat, cap down low, chewing on a bit of ham like it was gum. "Morning. Levi said yous were coming. I've got a beauty round the back."

They followed him across the yard, boots crunching over broken glass and gravel. Paddy glanced around. There had always been money in old shit, and judging by the amount of it here, this bloke must be a millionaire.

"Here you go, had this in yesterday, only two years old." He beamed and pointed at the mobile.

Maeve didn't wait. She was already at the steps, her trained eyes scanning every detail. The paint was fresh. The trim wasn't peeling. She pushed the door; it opened smoothly. Inside, it smelled of nothing untoward. No must. No mould. Just clean air and the faint scent of pine polish. The layout was the same as their old one. End lounge, middle kitchen, bedrooms at the end with a bathroom in between.

"This is it, Paddy," Maeve said with a tone of certainty.

"Right then, let's make a deal," he said to the man standing waiting outside.

They haggled, of course. You had to. The seller wanted too much for it, as they always did. But Paddy was sharp and stubborn. They walked away once, even got in the van. By the time the seller knocked a hundred off and threw in delivery, they were shaking hands.

"Right, girl, we best get over and tell them boys to build the base." His eyes creased with amusement at the excitement on Maeve's face.

"How long do you think it will take?" she asked.

"It's gonna be a week, girl, for the cement to dry, but we can stay over in the Buccaneer while we shift the horses and sell the land."

With that said, they set off to their sons'. This would be the next chapter in their lives. Maybe even the last.

CHAPTER 15

Tommy Lee stood outside the pub. Should he have taken muscle with him? No. He was the muscle. He had never relied on anyone in his life, other than his army buddies, so why start now?

He stepped in and glanced around the bar. The man at the end was passing a small packet to a customer, other than that it was quiet. Good.

"Can I have a word with the landlord," Tommy Lee said to the barmaid.

"Can I help ya, mate?" The rough voice came from the end of the bar. A man in his fifties, large frame, a scowl on his face, sauntered towards him.

"I think I can help you. Is there somewhere we can talk. In private." It wasn't a question, which the landlord seemed to pick up on.

"Follow me."

He led the way to the back and up the stairs to what Tommy Lee presumed was Eddie's meeting room. It smelt musty, obviously hadn't been used for a while.

"If Cole's sent you, I had the money, but no one turned up."

"He didn't send me, in fact, no one did. And just between you and me, he won't be sending anyone again." He watched the emotions change on the man's face.

"I don't understand." His face was now blank.

"What's your name?"

"Bob."

"Okay, Bob, let me spell it out for you. He thought he could demand money from me, I said no, he messed with my family, so I killed him and all his men." Tommy Lee let the information sink in before continuing. "I think it's only fair that you get your business back, but be warned, others will come, unless…"

"Unless?" Bob asked eagerly.

"Do you know the other businesses that he took?"

"Yes."

"You get them all here tonight, say seven p.m., and I'll explain your options." Tommy Lee turned and left the room. He had said all he would for now; he had been taught never to reveal your hand straight off, and that's what he intended to do.

***

Millie sat with Maeve, listening to her go on and on about the new mobile. The woman was so excited it made Millie smile. "So when will you be moving?"

"As soon as the base is done, although Paddy said we can go once the horses are settled over there."

"Well, I think it's wonderful news. Just think of all the fun you'll have with your grandchildren." Millie snatched Tommy boy away from the plate of biscuits. "Maybe we should put these out of his reach. Honestly, he's got a bottomless stomach like his dad." She grabbed the plate then watched in horror as her son threw a temper tantrum.

"All my boys have good appetites," Maeve said proudly. She had to shout above the screams.

"What's going on?" Tommy Lee walked into the lounge. He picked up his son and threw him over his shoulder. "Need some help?" He glanced at Millie.

She wanted to laugh and punch him at the same time. "He wants more biscuits; he's already had three."

"I'll take them out to see their pony." He picked up baby Duke, and after putting their coats on, left.

"He's a good father." Maeve watched him leave. "Never thought I'd see the day, you know, with him working away."

Millie nodded. He was a great father, and husband, but she knew he needed excitement. Maybe taking over from Eddie would be a godsend. "I'm gonna go see the pony with them."

She marched to the paddock where he stood holding the twins. The air held a chill to it. Everywhere appeared grey. The trees, naked without their leaves, looked as cold as she felt. "Hey, how did you get on at the pub?"

"I've got a meeting with all of them at seven p.m. Thought it easier to tell them together." He handed her one of the twins.

"Great idea, can I come?" She waited for a no.

"Yes, I'd like you there." He placed Duke on the pony and walked along with him.

"You would?"

"Why do you sound so surprised?"

He walked along the edge of the paddock, and she followed on the safe side of the fence.

"You know about this stuff. You might pick up on something I don't," he reasoned.

When they reached the end, he took Tommy boy from her then handed her baby Duke.

She smiled. Tommy boy giggled and reached for the horse's mane.

"They love riding," she said. "So I'm to keep quiet and observe?"

"Well, I've never known you to keep quiet, but yes, if you can." He turned to face her, his smile melting her heart.

"I'll do my best," she agreed.

He took baby Duke and pecked her on the lips. "I know it's going to be hard for you, but please try." He laughed. "I'll get Mother to watch the twins, and you never know, we might find time for a bit of loving."

"Jesus, Tommy Lee, I actually think your sexual appetite is bigger than your grub one." She gasped.

"It most definitely is, and don't you forget it." He walked by her side, their boys resting up on each of his shoulders. "Oh, and before I forget, I've found a house."

***

The atmosphere in the room was thick with nervous energy and unanswered questions. The men around the table all wore the same expression: fear. Tommy Lee sat at the head of the table with Millie sitting next to him. She still had the hump with him. He should have known committing to buying a house without her seeing it first would be a problem, but it was too good to turn down. He glanced around the table. Everyone was seated.

Bob was the first to speak. "Can you tell us why we have been summoned here, mate?"

This got his back up, a bit of respect wouldn't go amiss. Millie must have picked up on that because she answered before he had time.

"Gentleman," she said. "Firstly, you will address my husband as Mr Ward. And secondly, this is for your benefit, and it will do you good to listen."

Tommy Lee cleared his throat. "As I have already told Bob." He pointed to the landlord. "I had a visit from the man that's been extorting money from you. He thought he could demanding money from me. I said no, he didn't like it, so I sorted him."

Murmurs went up from the men sitting around the table.

"Silence," Millie bellowed.

Tommy Lee smiled. He knew she wouldn't be able to keep her mouth shut. "I understand he took half of your businesses—"

"So now you own them," a short, seemingly frail man said.

"No, I don't take what's not mine...you will get them back." He picked up his glass of scotch and studied it, the liquid golden, swirling around the glass.

"What's the catch?" the landlord asked.

"There is no catch," Millie answered. "But you know as well as I, others will come."

"So we sit here waiting for our livelihoods to be taken away again?" another tall, slender man asked.

"You could, or you could have my protection." Tommy Lee stood and placed his hands on the table. "You'll get your businesses back, they were yours to start with. You can have protection for a price, or not. This isn't a demand for money, it's a service. If you don't want it then fine, go."

The short, frail man stood. "I don't need protection with him gone. I have handed enough money over to crooks," he sniped.

"And what business do you own?" Tommy Lee asked.

"I own the pawnshop, it's been in my family for years." The man stood then left the room.

"Jacob's a proud man," Bob said. "It crushed him when that piece of shit took half his business."

"And yet his type prey on vulnerable, desperate people all the time." Millie glared at him. "People who can't afford to feed their children or pay their rent. The likes of him take more than they should from people with nothing. In my book it doesn't make him much better than the likes of Cole, who by the way is really called Eddie."

"We know the story Mrs Ward," Bob muttered.

"Well use his proper name then," she snapped.

"Never mind what Coles real name is or isn't. The main point is it's Jacobs business, Mrs Ward," another man chipped in.

"It is, but from what I can make out, Eddie targeted you lot because you're dodgy so less chance of yous going to the old bill. You." She pointed at Bob. "I'm guessing you supply drugs, and don't deny it, my husband saw you earlier today, and the one with the pawnshop is a fence. You." She nodded to a tall man. "What do you own?"

"My name's David, and I own a respectable massage parlour."

She rolled her eyes. "You own a knocking shop. And you, what do you own?"

The last man stood. "My name is Richard, Richard Lewis. I own the car lot, so tell me, Mrs Ward, what's my dodgy sideline?"

"That's simple, you sell ringers." She smiled when his face turned pale.

Tommy Lee laughed loudly. She was good.

"Why are you laughing, Mr Ward?" the landlord asked.

"I'm laughing because yous need help protecting your businesses. Jacob will probably end up either dead or penniless." He grabbed Millie's arm. "I think we've wasted enough time with this lot, let them learn the hard way."

"Wait!" Bob sounded nervous and desperate. "I want protection."

Tommy Lee sat. "Anyone who's interested stay here, the rest feck off." He waited, but none left. "Good, now let's talk business."

**

Tommy Lee pulled the twins' bedroom door to, then descended the stairs. "They're out for the count."

He entered the lounge and flopped down onto the sofa. Millie placed a cup of tea on the coffee table then sat next to him.

"They take after you, able to sleep anywhere and at the drop of a hat." She blew into her cup to cool it. "So are you going to tell me about this house?"

"It's everything we want. Four bedrooms, large garden, and best of all, only a ten-minute drive to the gym. We'll go see it tomorrow. If you don't like it then I'll tell them I've changed my mind and get the deposit back."

He glanced at her; she seemed deep in thought.

"I'm sure it'll be fine," she muttered and placed her cup down.

"It went well tonight," he said, his focus still on her. "I'll speak to John Jo and Sean Paul in the morning, let them know what's happening."

"D'ya think they'll be up for it?" she asked, her voice laced with doubt. "They weren't happy about you going after Eddie without them; in fact, have you spoken to them since?"

"We're brothers, Mil, blood comes before anything." He picked up his cup and gulped the hot liquid down.

She had a point. He had never fallen out with John Jo before, and he wasn't talking to him. Not properly. The only conversation they'd had since the farm had been strained. He would speak with him and make peace. Tommy Lee had been brought up that family was everything, and he'd remind his brothers of that.

The shrill tone of the phone cut into his thoughts.

"I'll get it." He jumped up.

He snatched up the handset, his father's panicked chortle on the other end. Tommy Lee listened while silently cursing. After the short conversation, he returned to the lounge.

"What's wrong?" Millie asked, her question hushed but urgent.

He ran a hand across his face. "John Jo and Sean Paul have been arrested."

CHAPTER 16

The air in the interrogation room was stagnant. Fluorescent lights buzzed faintly overhead, casting a lifeless glare over the scratched table and worn chairs. A battered tape recorder perched at one end. John Jo had his back towards the door, a position that made him uncomfortable. He had been taught to always face an entrance so you could see who was coming. A plainclothes police officer and a uniform hulked opposite, his eyes flicking from one to the other. He prayed Sean Paul would stick to the story they had cooked up weeks ago if ever things were to go tits up. It was a drunken wager. Two brothers egging each other on, nothing more.

The older copper cleared his throat, a man somewhere north of fifty, red-faced, balding, his gut pressing against the buttons of his suit jacket. "I'm Detective Inspector Brown," he said, his voice rough, maybe from cigarettes or shouting down lads like John Jo.

111

He nodded towards the uniformed officer, a leaner man with slicked-back hair and a predator's stillness, and paused while he gave his name.

"I'm Police Constable Parker."

Brown leaned forward, fingers drumming the edge of the table. "Can you state your name for the benefit of the recording?"

"Not until I see my solicitor." John Jo smirked. He'd told his father to phone Tommy Lee and get Mr Barrett here. Millie's brief. He'd got them off last time, and John Jo hoped he would do it again.

Parker glared. "You've been caught driving a stolen car. I don't think he will be of any use."

"I'm not talking until I've seen him." John Jo crossed his arms. He sat back and returned the prick's glare.

With a sigh, Brown clicked the recorder off. "No point wasting time here then. You can make yourself comfortable in the cell while we go home to our warm beds." He shoved back from the table and stood, planting both hands on the scratched surface. "You've been caught red-handed driving a stolen car. Even God himself won't stop you going down for this." He sidestepped the table and left the room with Parker staying.

Another officer entered immediately after. "Okay, lad, on ya feet."

He grinned; they were scared of him, that's why there had been two in the interview and now two to take him down.

He stood without a word and followed the coppers through the echoing corridor. His boots scuffed over the concrete floor, the walls closing in with each step. They took the stairs down, steep, narrow, the air growing colder the deeper they went. No windows down here. Just concrete and iron. The cell door clanged open, and John Jo stepped inside. It was little more than a tomb, one slim bunk, a toilet in the corner, and a flickering light that didn't so much illuminate as expose. He slumped down onto the hard bunk, kicked his legs up, and folded his hands behind his head.

There was nothing else to do now. Just wait.

His thoughts drifted, as they always did when it got quiet. To Gypsy. Would she be safe if he went to prison? Who would build the new paddock? Then there were Mother and Father to think about and moving them onto the ground. He would have to give Barrett a message for Tommy Lee. He and PJ would have to sort everything. Not that he thought he would go to prison, he'd always seen himself as invincible. The lad who never got caught, the one with luck tattooed on his bones. But maybe that had been the problem all along.

Maybe that would be his downfall.

***

Millie placed the phone down, sighing loudly.

"What's up?" Tommy Lee placed his arm around her shoulders. He guided her back into the lounge.

"Barrett wasn't happy about being woken at this ungodly hour." She perched on the edge of the sofa. "But he said he'll be there within the hour. Once he knows what they've been charged with, he'll let us know."

Tommy Lee blew out slowly to contain his temper. "You should get back to bed. I'll wait up for Barrett."

"Okay." She stood, kissed him, then left the room.

He sat, the small table lamp dimly lighting the room, the clock on the mantelpiece ticking loudly. He rubbed his temples, trying to massage the tension away, but it was futile. The weight of worry lay heavily on his shoulders while each passing second felt like an eternity.

He sat there for two hours, his mind racing, temper building. What had the two fecking eejits done this time?

The phone rang out, disturbing his thoughts. He almost ran to answer. "Hello."

"Mr Ward, it's Mr Barrett, I have news of your brothers' arrests."

The knot tightened in Tommy Lee's stomach. "What have they done this time?" he asked.

"John Jo was caught stealing a Jaguar motor vehicle. Allegedly, Sean Paul was following behind and tried to prevent the police car from chasing."

Tommy Lee cursed under his breath. "Have they been charged?"

"Yes, I'm afraid so."

113

"What about bail, I'll put up what's needed."

"The police have said no. We can make an appeal to the magistrates court in the morning, however, they were caught red-handed and then tried to resist arrest. I'm afraid it's not looking good."

"Jaysus fecking Christ, I swear I'll murder the both of them... So what do we do now?"

"I will meet you outside the court at nine-thirty a.m., then we can discuss options, and before I forget, John Jo has a list of things that need to be done on his land, but we can discuss that tomorrow, or rather in a few hours."

Barrett yawned loudly, the noise grating on Tommy Lee.

"I'll see you then." He slammed the phone down.

He wasn't much of a drinker, but right now he felt he could drink a pub dry. His brothers had been foolish, greedy even, and now they expected him to pick up the pieces. Like he didn't have his own problems or family to look after.

Fecking cheek.

But he would do what was needed. He always did.

***

Tommy Lee sat with his father in the front row of the small magistrates court, his heart pounding as he watched John Jo and Sean Paul stand in front of the judge, the reality of the situation now hitting hard. A few murmurs came from the spectators sitting behind them. Both brothers were dressed in suits, hair combed to perfection.

He could see they were nervous. John Jo fiddled with his top shirt button while Sean Paul moved from foot to foot. Despite knowing they were wrong and probably deserved a prison sentence, he prayed they would get off with a hefty slap on the wrist. After all, wasn't this punishment enough, being on show, destroying the family name? Mother's face said it all that morning, she was crushed.

The magistrate, a stern man with sharp features, glanced down at his papers.

"You are charged with stealing a vehicle, specifically a Jaguar, and resisting arrest. How do you plead?"

"Not guilty, Your Lordship," John Jo called.

"You will address me as Your Honour... And you?" the magistrate asked Sean Paul.

"Not guilty...Your, erm, Honour."

Tommy Lee could see under the bravado; they were both worried, and so they should be. This was real life. This was what happened when you fecked up.

The prosecutor stood, a sharp man with a neatly trimmed beard and a briefcase set at the side of him. "Your Honour, the evidence against the defendants is clear. They were caught in the act of stealing the vehicle and attempted to flee when confronted by the police. They showed no regard for the law or the safety of others."

The knot in Tommy Lee's stomach tightened. It was hard to listen to the prosecutor's words without feeling the sting of disappointment.

"Objection!" John Jo shouted, breaking Tommy Lee's thoughts. "We weren't trying to hurt anyone. It was a stupid drunken prank, a mistake that wouldn't have happened if we were sober."

Barrett's face flushed red. He turned to John Jo and placed his finger against his lips, obviously telling him to shut up.

The magistrate raised an eyebrow, clearly unimpressed. "Being drunk does not justify criminal behaviour, young man. You must understand the seriousness of your actions."

"He needs to stop talking," Paddy whispered to Tommy Lee. "If he don't, they'll definitely go down for this."

Tommy Lee nodded to his father in agreement.

When the magistrate finally spoke, he was firm. "I am going to adjourn this case for further consideration. You both will be remanded into custody until your next hearing."

Remanded into custody.

The words echoed in Tommy Lee's mind. The gavel struck, signalling the end of the session. Tommy Lee stood, catching John Jo's and Sean Paul's eyes. He gave a nod to let them know things would be taken care of. Then they were led away.

Paddy stood beside him. "We best get home and let your mother and the girls know."

"I need a word with Barrett, here." Tommy Lee handed his father the car keys. "I won't be long."

They made their way out of the court in silence. Tommy Lee waited just outside the entrance. Mr Barrett wasn't far behind.

"Mr Ward." He nodded. "It's not looking good. We had a slim chance before, but now…"

Tommy Lee cursed silently. "There must be something you can do?"

"I'm a solicitor, Mr Ward, not a magician. I specifically told your brothers not to say anything for a reason."

"So they'll go down for this?" He knew the answer but had to ask.

"I'm afraid so. The best we can hope for is a lenient sentence, if John Jo can keep his mouth shut while I defend them." He glanced at his watch. "I need to go, I have another client to see. Good day, Mr Ward."

Good day? I doubt that.

"When will I be able to see them?"

"They will be taken to HMP Chelmsford where they will need to go through processing and assessments. That can take a few days. I will be in touch when I know more. Now I really must go."

Tommy Lee turned and headed towards his Range Rover. He now had to prepare the whole family for the worst.

CHAPTER 17

Everyone sat in Gypsy's mobile, comforting each other. She looked wrecked, her face a picture of worry and heartache, and Shirley Ann, although putting on a brave face, appeared equally as troubled. Tommy Lee had explained everything in detail, and still his mother thought they would get off.

"I'll give Billy a ring, get him to round up a few of the cousins to help build the stables and fence off the paddock," PJ said thoughtfully. "Should only take a week or so."

"I'll get the base sorted," Tommy Lee said.

"What about the gym?" Paddy asked. "Shouldn't you be there, son?"

"Millie's taking care of that, she's got Scott with her, freeing me up to help PJ get everything sorted here." Tommy Lee glanced at

117

Gypsy, her swollen belly reminding him John Jo would miss the birth of his second child if he got sent down.

"Where are the twins?" Maeve asked, obviously put out because she wasn't minding them.

"Millie's friend, Rosie, is at the house with them. I'll head over to the gym once we are sorted here, so Millie can get back to them," he assured his mother.

"Shall we make a start then?" PJ stood. "Best to keep busy."

They left the warmth of the mobile and trudged to the new field.

Tommy Lee was the first to speak. "How's things with you?"

"Okay...and you?" PJ kept his eyes forward.

"Okay... How's things between you and Marina?"

PJ stopped dead and turned to his brother. "Why don't you ask what you really want to know — am I still chasing men?"

"I didn't mean that."

"You meant exactly that... I'm behaving, doing what you all expect of me. Happy?"

"I want to know how you and Marina are. You're having a baby, and I'm taking an interest, so stop being fecking touchy." Tommy Lee pulled the hedgerow apart and walked through.

Surveying the land, he made a mental note of where John Jo wanted the stable block then mooched towards the far boundary.

PJ fell into step next to him. "How's the gym doing?" he asked, a swift change of the strained conversation.

"It's doing well. Actually, I wanted a word about that. I need help collecting payments, wondered if you'd be interested. Pay's good."

"That's not really my line of work, is it, I'm only interested in the horses. They take up all my time as it is." PJ paused in thought for a second. "One day I'll have me own cobs, on me own ground, that's what I'm working towards."

"Well, if you change your mind the offer's there. It's evening work so wouldn't interfere with the horses. Anyway, I need to get back to Mil, I'll catch you later." Tommy Lee headed back.

Had PJ turned over a new leaf, or was he touchy because he was still up to his old tricks? Tommy Lee knew time would tell, because you couldn't keep a secret like that buried for long.

***

It was later than Tommy Lee had expected when he walked into the gym. He took the stairs two at a time and grinned when he spotted Millie behind the desk, jotting numbers down in the ledger, her blouse unbuttoned just enough to remind him what was underneath.

She glanced up, returning his smile. "How's Gypsy and Shirley Ann?" Concern saturated her voice.

"Bearing up. Mother and Father are there, so they ain't on their own. Father's taking the Buccaneer there in the morning." He yanked her up, kissed her, then sat in the chair, tugging her back down onto his lap. Squeezing her arse in the process.

"This is not the time or place for your shenanigans, Mr Ward." She squirmed followed by a loud giggle.

"This is the exact time, Mrs Ward. Now give me a kiss, I need it."

She shoved him away, face now serious. "Wait."

"What now?" he muttered.

"Have you seen the paper? It's saying about six missing men. Police are appealing for information."

Tommy Lee glanced down at the article. "They can appeal all they like, they'll never find them or the rest of them. Now as your husband, I demand a kiss."

"Mil," Scott yelled up the stairs.

"Jaysus fecking Christ, he has the worst timing." Tommy Lee helped her up. He stood then opened the office door and glared at Scott who was standing at the bottom. "What is it?"

"Someone's scratched Millie's car, right down the side." He winced.

"I just walked past it, it was fine." Tommy Lee ran down the stairs. He walked out onto the pavement and stared at the thick scratch that ran from the back of the motor all the way to the front.

"It looks deliberate—" Scott began.

"Of course it's fecking deliberate." Tommy Lee breathed out slowly to contain his temper.

Millie appeared next to him, her hand clutching her chest. "What the…?"

"Reckon they thought it was mine," he quickly said to reassure her. "They look similar."

"Maybe," she whispered.

"Go in and put the kettle on, I'm gasping for a drink. I'll check this and follow in a bit." He motioned to Scott to stay with him.

Once she had disappeared, he bent down and inspected the scratch. It was deep, too deep to have been a key. "Have you seen anyone hanging around the gym, anyone you're not sure of?"

"No, it's all the usual crowd inside, and I don't come out here unless I'm nipping to the shop," Scott said. "You don't think this has anything to do with Eddie?"

"We wiped him and his men out, unless someone else fancies their chances, but why target Millie?" Tommy Lee stood and scanned up and down the street. "Unless they're playing games with me, go after the wife to get a reaction."

"There was definitely no one else at the farm?"

"No, we combed the buildings and the area after clean-up. There wasn't a soul there, not even his wife. The place was left spotless, no blood, no bodies, and nothing to point to us."

"It could just be kids, some of 'em are horrible little bastards these days," Scott said, but Tommy Lee could hear the doubt in his voice.

"Well, whoever it was will end up sorry when they get the same treatment." He turned and entered the gym, glancing around the men in there. Seeing if any of them were acting strange. He could do without this now John Jo and Sean Paul were out of the picture for the foreseeable. He would need to be here and leave PJ to sort out the land.

CHAPTER 18

12th February

A few weeks had passed, and all had remained quiet. No little surprises at the gym or at the brothers' ground. The paddock had been fenced off, and two large sets of stables built. Paddy and Maeve were now in their new mobile, and Gypsy and Shirley Ann seemed to be coping without their husbands, albeit it had only been a short time. Maeve's sister, Lena, and her husband, Joseph, had pulled onto the land to help out while the boys were away, along with their son and his family.

Today the family headed to court for the trial. The children were left with Lena, and Millie had left the twins with Rosie. They were all there not only to support the girls but also to support the men.

The courtroom was brightly lit, the air thick with tension as John Jo and Sean Paul sat side by side on the hard wooden bench. Their youthful faces, once filled with bravado, now bore the weight of uncertainty and fear. The judge, a stern figure in a black robe, presided over the proceedings with an air of authority. He glanced down at the papers before him, the details of their case laid bare for all to see. The courtroom was filled with a mixture of onlookers, journalists, and other family members, all eager to witness the outcome of this case.

"Court is now in session," the clerk announced, and the room fell silent.

The prosecutor stood, presenting the case against the two young men. "Your Honor, the defendants, Mr John Jo Ward and Mr Sean Paul Ward, are charged with theft, specifically the unlawful taking of a Jaguar motor vehicle which upon capture resulted in the vehicle being damaged. Their actions have not only resulted in significant mental strain and financial loss to the victim but have also contributed to a wider issue of crime in the community."

Tommy Lee's chest tightened as he listened. He exchanged a worried glance with Paddy, who sat beside him, his brow furrowed in concern.

The prosecutor continued, detailing the events leading up to their arrest, describing how the brothers had been caught red-handed attempting to steal a high-end motor vehicle.

"These young men have shown a blatant disregard for the law and the consequences of their actions, and it is imperative that the court sends a clear message that such behaviour will not be tolerated."

Next, it was the defence's turn. John Jo's lawyer stood, attempting to paint a more sympathetic picture of the young men. "Your Honor, while my clients have made a grave mistake, they both work extremely hard rearing horses. They pay taxes and were, with the exception of this drunken moment of stupidity, upstanding pillars of the community, regularly attending church. They both express remorse for their actions and wish to do better."

After both sides had presented their cases, the judge leaned forward, his expression serious. "Gentleman, you are both young men who have made choices that have consequences. The law is clear, and it is my duty to uphold it. However, I also recognise the importance of rehabilitation and the potential for change in your lives. Having taken into account all of this, the sentence will reflect that."

The judge paused, allowing his words to sink in.

The courtroom was silent, the tension palpable. Tommy Lee glanced at his mother, her face pale. He gripped Millie's hand tightly for comfort. This wasn't looking good, and judging by his brothers' faces, they also realised it.

The judge coughed to clear his throat before continuing. "Taking into account the circumstances surrounding your actions and the remorse you have shown, I am imposing a custodial sentence of two years for each of you. You will serve this term concurrently."

The gavel struck, resonating through the room. Two years. It was both a relief and a crushing blow. Tommy Lee stared down at John Jo and Sean Paul, who both stared blankly ahead. Were they processing the weight of their fate?

"Additionally," the judge continued, "I want you to think long and hard to address the underlying issues that led you to commit this crime. Upon your release, it is imperative that you seek support and guidance to ensure you do not fall back into a life of crime."

The gavel struck again, signalling the end of the hearing. The two men were led away, their heads hung low, the reality of their situation settling in. Tommy Lee glanced at Gypsy; she was sobbing uncontrollably, Maeve comforting her.

As the courtroom emptied, Shirley Ann turned to Tommy Lee. "What will happen to them now?"

He wrapped an arm around Millie's shoulders, pulling her close. He felt grateful that he would be sleeping in bed with her tonight, unlike his brothers, who'd be lying on a bunk in a cell.

"They'll be taken straight to the prison," Millie replied.

Could she sense his emotions? He'd always been the strong one, the protector, the fixer, but this was one situation he couldn't fix.

"I'll have a word with Barrett and see if he can get visiting orders for you both, as soon as possible," she continued. "And if either of yous need anything, just let us know."

"Thanks, Millie," Shirley Ann said. She dabbed at her eyes gently with a hanky. "I just don't know what I'm going to do without him."

"We'll get through this as a family." Millie glanced up at Tommy Lee.

Her grip tightened around his waist, bringing him comfort. "I'd be lost without you," he whispered into her ear.

They trudged out of the courtroom, in silence, and onto the street, the day grey, to match their moods. The drizzle soaked them quickly before they had reached their motors.

"Wait here for Barrett," Millie said while climbing in. "He will speak with John Jo and Sean Paul before coming out. He'll let us know how they are and where they are being taken to."

"You seem to know a lot about this kind of thing." Tommy Lee turned towards her. "You haven't done time, have you?" He grinned.

She barked a laugh then playfully punched his arm. "No, and don't you go getting locked up. I don't think I could bear it." She fell silent, the rain pelting against the Range Rover the only noise.

"What are you thinking now?" he asked.

Her face had paled.

"I feel for Gypsy and Shirley Ann. I feel shit, so how must they feel?" She sighed.

"Like you said, they will get through it with the help of the family… Look, there's Barrett. You stay here, no point us both getting soaked."

"Wait, ask him to make sure they get put together on the same wing."

"How can he do that?" he asked.

"Bribery. Tell him we'll make it worth his while, and the screw who assists," she said knowingly. "He will have connections to the dodgy ones."

He leapt out, pushing the door shut behind him, and jogged over to Barrett. "Any news?"

Barrett slid into his motor, leaving the door open. "They will be detained in Chelmsford. They seemed in good spirits, considering. I'll arrange visiting orders for everyone as soon as I can. I need to get going, I have another case in court in an hour. Good day, Mr Ward."

"One more thing before you go. I want them on the same wing, preferably the same cell. Whatever it takes."

Barrett nodded, closed the door, started the engine, and drove out of the car park.

"What did he say?" Millie asked as he climbed back into the motor.

"They'll be in Chelmsford, which is good, not far for everyone to travel. Reckons they are in good spirits considering and he'll get the VOs as soon as able, and I said same cell… I suppose we should go and let everyone know. I'm not staying long, though, I want to get back to the twins, then I'll pop to the gym later." He clipped in his seat belt.

"Why don't we pop in there on the way home, it'll save you coming out again. I'll make a nice bacon pudding for dinner, and you can relax for a bit."

He glanced at her; was she worried about him? "Okay, but only if we have sex for dessert."

"If you insist." She giggled.

"I do." He pushed the gearstick into first and drove off with a smile on his face.

***

PJ, perched on the arm of the sofa, listened to his mother comforting Shirley Ann. Marina had her arm around Gypsy's shoulders, soothing her. Today had been a complete shitshow, not only for John Jo and Sean Paul but also for him. With his aunt, uncle, and cousin now staying here for the foreseeable, it would be harder to sneak out. Marina was easy to escape, gullible. All he had to do was mention he was interested in a horse and she'd be waving him off and wishing him luck. The fact he'd never actually returned with one hadn't registered with her so far. She was so wrapped up in the pregnancy and family that it never dawned on her he'd always returned late at night and empty-handed.

It had been a few months since he'd stopped fighting the urge for male company, figuring that if he was happy, in turn he'd make her happy. That's not to say he never felt guilty, just the opposite. He would look at her, her pretty face, trusting smile, and her eyes that sparkled every time she laughed. Did he make her laugh? He wasn't sure. He knew she was content, he knew she loved him, and he loved her in his sick, twisted way. She was the pillar of their marriage, and she never knew.

"Looks like Tommy Lee and Millie are here," Paddy said, peeking through the window. "Hopefully they'll be able to tell us more." He stood and walked to the door.

PJ sighed.

Good ole Tommy Lee. The son who puts family first.

Well, he hadn't while he was off murdering people. That would be an eye-opener for their parents if they were to find out. But then hadn't his brother always helped him, always fixed his problems, too? Why did he feel bitter towards everyone; was it the lie he'd been living? Probably.

"What did the solicitor say?" Maeve asked and clutched her chest.

Tommy Lee stood in the doorway. Millie stood in front of him.

"They're doing okay. They'll be taken to Chelmsford prison, which is handy for visiting, and he will arrange visits as soon as able."

"They may also be able to get parole after serving a third of their sentences, provided they keep their heads down," Millie said quickly.

"Eight months?" Gypsy asked, her voice edged with hope.

"Yes, they just need to keep their noses clean, and don't forget they will take into consideration the time they have already served." Tommy Lee said. "Right. We need to get to the gym. Let me know if you need anything. See yous all later."

PJ watched them leave without offering a hello or goodbye, his mind firmly set on somehow getting away later and having some fun.

***

John Jo sat on the bunk. The place was a dump. Bunk beds on one side and a table opposite with two chairs that had been fixed to the floor. A single wardrobe and a toilet at the end with a tiny sink next to it. Three shelves were over the table, and a high-up window with bars on shone very little light in over the toilet. The walls were brick, whitewashed and barren. This was going to be harder than he'd thought. Being a Traveller, he'd always been used to open spaces and greenery. The only compensation was that he had a cell with Sean Paul.

"I hope Shirley Ann's okay," his brother muttered.

"And Gypsy, " John Jo said with a heavy heart. "When we get out we'll be concentrating on the cobs, no more motors."

"Definitely no more motors," Sean Paul agreed. "At least Mother and Father are there to keep an eye on things."

"Tommy Lee will make sure everything runs smoothly," John Jo added. "And PJ's good with the horses."

"Yeah, but who'll keep an eye on him?" he asked, raising an eyebrow.

"I think he's passed all that nonsense. He'll be a dad in a couple of months, then there'll be no time to think of men."

Did he believe that? No. A couple of times he had noticed PJ coming home late with little or no explanation. But with that said, it wasn't his place to question his brother. He was a married man now with a child on the way, although he'd let Tommy Lee know, just to be on the safe side.

"Right, shall we go and have a look around, get our bearings?" Sean Paul said. "I noticed a pool table downstairs."

John Jo nodded. "Remember, we need to keep our heads down if we want a chance of parole."

CHAPTER 19

The late afternoon sky had turned the colour of old pewter, clouds sagging low like they were ready to burst. Tommy Lee stopped the motor outside the gym. He was itching to get home. To have Millie all to himself and concentrate on her body, leaving the day's memories behind him. He glanced at her. She sat beside him in silence, her coat drawn tight around her.

Unclipping her seat belt, she said with a smile, "Ready?"

"Always," he said, mirroring her smile. "Don't forget, we aren't staying long."

They stepped out into the cold, the gym's shutter up and the familiar bass thump of a speed bag echoing faintly from inside.

Scott was indoors doing pad work with a lad who moved like he had bricks tied to his feet. He paused when he saw them, nodding.

His eyes flicked from Tommy Lee's face to Millie's, reading them both like a book.

"All right?" he asked, breathless. "What happened?"

Tommy Lee gave a short nod. "They've gone down. Two years each."

"Sorry to hear that, mate." Scott reached out and gave his shoulder a brief squeeze.

"They may get out sooner, if they can keep their heads down, but that's a big if. John Jo's temper is similar to mine; if anyone gives them shit, he's likely to batter them."

"We need to keep positive…for them." Millie said and faced the stairs ready to go to the office.

He gave a faint grunt of agreement and scanned the room. The gym looked decent, clean, warm, busy enough for a midweek afternoon. The odour of sweat lingered in the air, a familiar scent of the gym. A few younger lads shadow-boxed in the corner, and one of the older pros sat on a bench watching them with the odd word of advice. Content, Tommy Lee followed her up the stairs.

"Place is doing well. I wasn't sure when we bought it." He yanked the door to.

"We have a few fights arranged for the next few weeks. I think my dad is fighting this weekend," she said. "Oh, that reminds me, I should phone him, let him know what's happened before he hears it from someone else. I don't need to be in his bad books again."

Tommy Lee moved to the window that overlooked the ring. "I think we should have Scott here full-time. He seems to be enjoying it."

"But what about the docks?" She placed the paperwork down onto the desk and joined him at the window.

"You trust Tony and Rosie to run the place. I can go if needed, and I'm sure you will, too." He tapped the window and motioned to Scott to join them.

"I trust Scott more than I trust Tony, but if that's what you want," she added.

"Let's leave it up to him." He held the door open for Scott to enter. "We've been having a chat and wondered if you'd like to work here full-time?"

Scott glanced between Tommy Lee and Millie. "But Millie needs me at the docks."

"I will take over the docks," Millie said without thinking.

"No you won't," Tommy Lee said. "Have you forgotten you're pregnant and already have twins to look after?"

"No, how could I when you're always reminding me?" She returned his glare. "I'll sort the docks and the children, you, Scott, get to choose, so what's it to be?"

"I enjoy it here, could do with a fresh start, too…" he answered thoughtfully.

"That's settled then." Tommy Lee glanced back at Millie who now had a face like a smacked arse. "We will discuss the docks later."

Satisfied, he turned and headed back outside, Millie trailing behind him, arms folded. He'd need to sweeten her up or there'd be no loving later.

Feck.

He reached into his coat for his keys, then stopped dead.

"What?" Millie followed his line of sight. "Shit."

He stared at his Range Rover. One of the headlights was smashed. Glass splintered across the tarmac, the jagged metal frame twisted inwards like it had been booted.

She stepped forward, eyes narrowing. "That wasn't like that when we got here."

"No. It fecking wasn't." He crouched to check the damage, jaw tightening. "Clean hit. Didn't even scratch the bumper."

"That's deliberate. Someone's watching us."

"I know." He sighed. "First your car. Now this." He glanced around the surrounding alleyways and road, scanning every shadow. "They're not just trying to scare us. They're playing games with us."

"Taunting us," she whispered.

He stood slowly, grinding his jaw. "Let them. They want a war, we'll bring them a fecking funeral."

She looked at him, long and hard. "We should put someone on the door again. Night and day."

"I'll sort it with Scott. We need someone trusted. I'll phone around the family." He headed back into the gym.

Millie turned to follow but stopped. "You think it's Eddie's lot?" she called.

He halted on the threshold for a second. "Yeah," he said finally. "And if it isn't, someone wants us to *think* it is."

Millie stepped closer, resting her hand lightly on his arm. "When people play games they get caught out, but we need to be one step ahead until they slip up."

He nodded, eyes still locked on the darkening sky. The rain was beginning to fall lightly, but soon to turn heavy. "I don't want you to worry, I'll see to everything." He gripped her hand to reassure her and led her back inside. "I'm still looking forward to bacon pudding and dessert." He grinned.

"I've lost my appetite," she said, dragging her feet.

"It's going to be all right, you're not to worry. Understand?" He turned to her and planted a kiss on her lips.

He would be a liar if he said this didn't excite him. The thrill of the chase, the capture, and the execution was all a game he knew and loved, maybe a little too well.

***

The rain had been soft all day, hardly more than a mist, but it clung to everything, dripping off the bare branches, pooling in the potholes outside the ground. PJ stood by the stove in the trailer, staring at the fire but not really seeing it. His boots were clean, his shirt pressed sharp. He'd used his good cologne. He'd combed his hair to perfection. He would slip out in an hour or so and see a man about a horse. Or so Marina thought.

He sighed at a knock on the door. It was like Piccadilly fecking Circus here lately. Marina answered. It was PJ's cousin, Micheal, and then left them to it.

"Evening, boy," Micheal called from the door. "Us men are going to the pub for a couple of beers, you coming?"

"I'm supposed to be seeing a man about a horse, maybe next time." PJ shrugged. "It's too much of a bargain to turn down."

"I'll come with you then, we can call in the pub on the way back."
Shite.

"Dunno how long I'll be. You go pub, and I'll try and pop in after," PJ lied.

Michael raised an eyebrow. "That right?"

PJ forced a chuckle. "You know how it is, the man needs rid as soon as, I'd be a fool not to take a look. I should be back by ten p.m."

His cousin narrowed his eyes but let it go. "You better not be going chasing women, leaving me here in the cold with all the dull ones."

"No woman, I'm a happily married man," PJ lied again. "This is strictly business."

He waved him off and closed the door, taking a deep, calming breath at the same time. The familiar sting of guilt bloomed. He wasn't going to see a man about a horse. He was going to see a man about himself.

***

PJ left in a rush, landing a kiss on Marina's cheek and muttering something about a man with a young cob in Chelmsford, which sounded vague but not unusual. She knew the horse trade came with sudden chances, and if you weren't quick enough you'd miss a bargain. Still, something about the way he hadn't met her eyes stayed with her.

She lingered by the door, listening to him drive away. She closed it slowly, the latch clicking into place, then stood for a moment staring at the fire. A flicker of doubt moved through her. She placed a hand on her growing belly and smiled down at it. Was she being silly? He had been to see a fair few cobs, always in the evenings, but never made a deal. He always had an answer, of course—too expensive, someone had just bought it, the cob wasn't healthy—but

133

out of all the horses he had seen, surely one of them must have been okay.

Something wasn't right.

Was he chasing women?

***

Tommy Lee gazed at Millie as she stood in the doorway of the en suite wearing lacy briefs and bra. "You wore those the first time we met," he said, raspy.

"Didn't think you'd remember." She smiled.

"I remember everything about that afternoon. You wore a black pencil skirt that hugged your hips to perfection and stopped just above your knees, with a pale-blue blouse that skimmed your curves, the top buttons left undone just enough to hint at what lay beneath. Making me want you there and then. Jaysus, I was wound tighter than a spring. I even considered taking you on the table."

Millie gasped. "Well, I'm glad you didn't."

"It was touch and go, I can tell you…and then when we got to the room and I finally started peeling those clothes off, I was greeted with this sexy little number." He wiped his mouth; Christ, was he dribbling?

"And then the condom split, and you didn't have any more," she teased, closing the gap between them.

"I'm guessing that's when the twins were conceived." He reached for her arm and dragged her down on top of him, and then the phone started to ring.

"Jaysus fecking Christ, is one evening without a disturbance too much to ask for?" He rolled her off and stood, naked. "I'll get rid of them," he muttered as he shot out of the door and down the stairs at lightning speed and returned a minute later.

"Who was it?" She nestled under the covers.

He pulled them back and slid in. "Marina."

"Marina. What did she want?"

"You."

"Why didn't you call me?"

"Because this is more important. I said you'd go see her in the morning."

"Tommy Lee Ward, you can be so selfish at times."

"I need you more than anyone else right now. It's a man's right to take his wife anytime he pleases," he said seriously.

"Really, well, I've changed my mind." She attempted to push him away, but he wasn't having it.

CHAPTER 20

Tommy Lee drove through the gates and onto his brothers' land, the gravel crunching under the tyres. In the back seat, the twins were screaming their lungs out, and the noise was drilling into his skull.

He winced and tapped the steering wheel. "What's wrong with them now?"

Millie twisted around in her seat, trying to soothe them. "They probably need to stretch their legs. And they're likely hungry."

"They only just ate," he muttered, half in disbelief, half in frustration. "All right, boys, we're here now," he added, forced cheer in his voice.

That quieted them…for about two seconds.

He pulled up outside his parents' mobile and killed the engine. He sighed. "I'll take them in. You go see Marina."

Millie nodded, grateful for the break, her hand resting briefly on his shoulder before she got out.

Tommy Lee leant into the back and started unstrapping the boys, one at a time, bracing himself for the chaos that always followed them.

"Okay, I won't be long." Millie headed towards PJ's. She knocked loudly on the trailer door.

PJ appeared, his face a picture of sorrow. "Millie, what can I do for you?"

"Thought I'd say hello to Marina. Tommy Lee's just taken the twins into your mother's." She stood awkwardly, waiting to be invited in.

"She's not here," he said.

"Where is she?"

"Gone to stay with her mother for a couple of weeks." He left the door open.

Millie followed him in, pulling the door closed behind her. "What's going on, PJ?"

"She's got it into her head I'm chasing other women." He slumped down onto the bunk, the plastic covering scrunching beneath him.

"Well, we both know that isn't true… I take it you've been out chasing men then." She folded her arms and glared down at him.

"I've been out a couple of times. It's not like I'm going to run off with them, is it? And before you say anything, a lot of men go out chasing a bit of skirt."

"You do realise it's still cheating…you're cheating on your wife and unborn child. You have a family, they should come first, not your lust for cock." Millie bit her lip to hold her temper in check. "You need to keep it in your pants, and while you're at it, go get your wife back."

She turned and left, slamming the door behind her. These fucking Ward boys would be the death of her. She had already phoned Tony this morning to see who they knew serving time in Chelmsford prison in the hopes to get an insider to keep an eye on John Jo and Sean Paul. He was making a few phone calls and getting back to her.

She stormed towards Maeve and Paddy's. A nice hot cuppa was needed to calm her nerves.

Tommy Lee looked up when she walked into the front room. "That was quick."

"Marina's gone to stay with her parents for a couple of weeks." She sat next to him and whispered, "She thinks he's chasing other women."

"I'll go see him. Gypsy and Shirley Ann have gone to the shop; let them know about Tony." He stood and left.

The twins were now happy. They each had a chocolate biscuit which was smothered around their mouths. Millie rolled her eyes at the spoilt little buggers.

"So, Millie, how's things with you?" Maeve handed her a cup of tea.

It made her stop and think; how *were* things with her? "Okay, I guess…haven't really had much time to think about it since the sentencing."

"No, we feel the same. It's been one thing after another lately," Maeve said, obviously dismayed.

"I'm sure things will pick up soon. Hopefully John Jo and Sean Paul will be out in about seven months. I know it sounds like a long time, but it will soon go." Was that the right thing to say? She really wasn't good at this.

Maeve's eye misted over. "Let's hope you're right."

***

Tommy Lee beelined to the stables. PJ wasn't in his trailer, and that was the only other place he could be. "Millie's just told me," he called upon spotting him.

"I don't want to talk about it." PJ grabbed a handful of hay to feed the horses with and traipsed out to the paddock.

"You need to go get your wife back," Tommy Lee said.

He knew PJ was selfish, he always had been. More than likely he thought while Marina was out of the picture, he could play away with the men.

"She'll come back when she's ready." PJ held out his hand. The first horse took a mouthful and munched.

"And what if she doesn't?" The question hung in the air, unanswered. "You're going to lose everything."

"Don't you think I know that? Despite what you and Millie think, I do love her, and this craving male company, I can't help it. It's who I am. I'm being torn in two, and it's killing me."

"Then we need to come up with a plan," Tommy Lee said calmly.

"What, you're going to help your queer brother?" PJ sneered.

"Not with a fecking attitude like that, I'm not." Tommy Lee turned away and stared into the distance. His little brother was being petulant.

"I'm sorry," PJ finally said. "I just don't know how to deal with this."

"How about one night a week, you say you're meeting me, for work. You help collect the money, I'll pay you, and then on the way home you can do…"

He couldn't bring himself to say it. He also felt rotten for giving PJ an alibi, but Marina had to come first along with their marriage.

"The only condition is, you don't go out the rest of the week, unless it's with Father to the pub or out with Marina." Tommy Lee held his hand out. "Do we have a deal?"

PJ stared at the ground. Was he thinking? He looked up and smiled. "Deal."

***

Millie's eye went wide as Tommy Lee continued to explain the PJ situation. "You did what!"

"Listen, he's going to keep sneaking out regardless. This way it will be once a week, and he won't destroy his marriage or hurt Marina," he explained.

"So you've just helped cover for him cheating on his wife," she yelled.

The twins, who had been happily sleeping in the back of the Range Rover, began to cry.

"Now look what you've done," she said.

"You're the one shouting…you need to calm down." He turned into their driveway and parked the motor near the front door. "You told me to sort the situation, and I did."

Not that he was happy about it. He felt dirty himself for aiding his brother's life choice. But what else could he do, he wanted to protect Marina. "Once the baby's born he may change."

"And what if he doesn't?" She unclipped her seat belt and climbed out.

They carried the twins into the house and up the stairs. Once they were settled back to sleep in their cots, they made their way to the kitchen. Millie filled the kettle while Tommy Lee took the cups from the cupboard.

"If you ever cheat on me, whether it's with a man or woman, I'll cut your cock off and make you eat it."

He laughed, then stopped once he saw her face. Her eyes had gone dark; she looked a bit scary. "Duly noted, not that I'd ever want to. You take up all my time in the bedroom with your sexual demands."

"You're the one who has to have it three times a day, minimum." Her face softened.

Good.

"Just so we're clear, it's you I want three times a day." He pecked her on the lips then reached for the sugar.

"I feel sick," she moaned.

"I don't feel good either, darling, but what was I supposed to do?"

"If this comes out, you'll be the one everyone turns on." She poured the boiled water into the teapot.

"Then we make sure it doesn't." He slipped his arms around her expanding waist. "I don't want you to worry, I'll sort—"

The loud ring of the telephone stopped him short.

"I'll get it." He marched to phone and yanked it up. "Hello."

"It's Tony. Can you let Millie know I've found someone on the same wing as John Jo and Sean Paul?"

"Can't you just arrange it?" He didn't want Millie involved in this, despite her setting it up.

"There's a bit of a problem…" Tony said, hesitant.

"What problem?"

"He wants a meeting with Millie."

Tommy Lee's temper bubbled. "My wife is not going to meet with him, I will."

"It's got to be Millie…he wants a job at the docks when he gets out and he wants her assurance."

Tommy Lee went quiet. He needed this man to keep his brothers out of trouble, but he also didn't want Millie going to meet him in a fecking prison. "Why can't you meet with him?"

"I only own twenty percent, he wants the big boss." Tony almost sounded indignant.

That must be a kick in the teeth, only wanting to meet with the big boss. "Will he not meet with me?"

"He's phoning me tomorrow, so I can let him know what's happening. I can ask for two VOs, then you can both go."

"Tell him it's both of us or none at all." Tommy Lee placed the phone down. He wouldn't be dictated to by a fecking con.

He sauntered back into the kitchen. Millie was sitting at the table, blowing into her tea to cool it.

"Who was that?" she asked without looking up.

"Tony. The man wants to meet you, he wants a job at the docks."

"Then we best meet him. This could work out better than I thought, we need more muscle," she said.

"You can't take on a con; you think you can trust him?"

"Your brothers are now both cons, do you still trust them?" She placed her cup down and stared at him.

"That's different. They're family." He sat next to her, studying her face. She looked confident.

"The men you fought with in the army, do you trust them?"

"Of course I do, but they earnt my trust." Where was she going with this?

"And that's what this man will do, earn our trust, and if he lets us down, you can finish him."

***

PJ arrived at Marina's parents. They lived on a Travellers' site on the outskirts of Braintree. There were eight other pitches here, all fenced off.

He felt sick as he climbed out of the Transit. Marina appeared before he got to her parents' mobile.

"What are you doing here?" she asked.

"I've come to take you home."

"Not until you tell me what you've been up to." She crossed her arms and glared.

"I've been trying to build a future for us. Look, things are going to change; in future I'll take you with me when I'm buying a cob, but in the meantime, Tommy Lee has offered me work one night a week, collecting money or something — you can check with him if you don't believe me. The rest of the time I'll be at home." He took her hand and smiled. "I love you, Marina. I want you home where you belong, with me."

"You won't disappear no more?"

"Nope, I promise. I just want to be with you." He pulled her towards him, his heart thumping at the lie he'd just spun.

She stood on tiptoe and kissed him; in return, he kissed her back, her lips soft and warm, but they weren't a man's and they didn't give PJ the same feeling.

CHAPTER 21

Tommy Lee had dropped the twins off with his mother. He and Millie were off to visit Terrence, the con in Chelmsford prison. After working off his tension last night in bed with her, he was feeling upbeat, forgetting all the crap with the mystery man who was taunting him, and the PJ situation that had seemed to sort itself out over the last week. They were both wearing suits, much to Tommy Lee's disgust, but Millie said they had to dress to show they meant business—she in a skirt and jacket, which to be fair made her look sexy, and he in a fitted tailored suit, with a tie. He hated it, he felt like he was going to a funeral. She had told him off three times already for fiddling with the knot.

He pulled into the car park and stopped. "I hate these fecking places," he said, his eyes focused on the tall walls.

"We won't be here long. Maybe we could stop for something to eat on the way back, I'm starving." She rummaged through her bag for the VOs. "Here." She handed them to him.

They made their way to the entrance. He gripped her hand, leading her. Once inside, they were searched, and Millie's bag was placed in a locker. All they were allowed was a bit of money in their pockets for a drink.

They stood outside the metal door waiting to be shown in. Once it was opened, they took a seat near a barred window, Tommy Lee making her sit on the inside so she couldn't be leered at.

The room was lined with rows of tables, each bolted to the floor. Whitewashed concrete walls cast a cold, lifeless atmosphere over the space, while the harsh glare of fluorescent lights was enough to trigger a headache. It felt both sterile and grimy at the same time. Tommy Lee hated it, hated the thought that his brothers were stuck in this miserable place.

"You okay?" she asked.

"Yeah."

He stared across the room when the opposite door opened. A prison guard appeared, behind him the prisoners.

"Do you know what he looks like?" he added.

"No, but he will know us," she assured him. "I'm just glad Gypsy and Shirley Ann are visiting this afternoon and not this morning like us. This would have been hard to explain."

"John Jo would do his nut if he knew." Tommy Lee glanced up at a man mountain looming over him. He stood immediately. This man was as tall and broad as him. A proper bruiser.

"Mr Ward, I presume," he said, his voice deep.

Tommy Lee gave a sharp nod. "Terrence."

They shook hands.

"And Mrs Ward." He slid into the seat opposite.

"Terrence," she greeted.

"You know why we're here," Tommy Lee continued.

"I do." Terrence leaned forward and in a whisper said, "You know what I want."

"Yes, but I have to ask why, why would you want a job when I'm willing to pay you good money?" he asked.

"I'm tired of doing the dirty work for others. You can see where it's got me. All I want is a steady job, and I've heard what a fair boss Mrs Ward is to work for."

"You'd also be working for my husband," she muttered.

"I know, I hear you have a gym… I'm a good bloke to have around. I'll watch out for your brothers. All I want is a chance when I get out. A steady job and somewhere to live. That's all."

Tommy Lee glanced at Millie. She was smiling. "When are you due for release?"

"I've nine months left. I'll make sure your brothers are clean for the rest of their time, then when I'm out, I expect you to hold up your end of the deal."

Millie squeezed Tommy Lee's thigh, a sign to say yes.

"Okay, you have a deal."

"But if you ever fuck us over, the deal will be off," Millie said, all calm.

"Don't worry, Mrs Ward, I'll prove myself useful." Terrence grinned. "Now shall we have a cuppa to celebrate?"

***

Gypsy and Maeve sat opposite John Jo while Shirley Ann and Paddy sat opposite Sean Paul on the table next to them. Jonnie boy squirmed on John Jo's lap, wanting to get free and play with his cousins who were shouting and generally being unruly.

John Jo eyed the screw standing guard at the door and grinned. "Don't think he likes the noise."

"Feck him," Maeve said. "I want to know how you're doing, son?"

"I'm doing just fine, Mother." He put Jonnie boy down so he could run riot then peeked at Gypsy. "The time will go quick enough. Are the cobs okay? PJ and Father managing?"

"Of course we're managing," Paddy shouted over the racket of the children. "Although we wouldn't have to if yous hadn't been stupid."

"Not now, Paddy," Maeve said.

He turned back towards Sean Paul, ignoring her. "Pair of fecking eejits," he muttered.

"I heard that." Maeve refocused on John Jo. "Are they feeding you enough?"

"We are fine, honestly, has —" He was cut short when a loud gasp came from Paddy. Jonnie boy had knocked his arm, and his cup of tea had spilt over his legs.

Paddy leapt up and knocked the boy onto his backside, who then wailed uncontrollably. Gypsy jumped to grab him, nudging an opened bag of crisps onto the floor, the contents scattering like confetti. Maeve found her hanky and, crunching her way through the contents of the ready salted, patted Paddy dry. He attempted to push her away as laughter rose from the other cons.

John Jo rolled his eyes. His son had managed to bring utter chaos to the whole room, and on top of that, he suspected he and Sean Paul would be ribbed about this for the rest of their incarceration.

From across the room, Terrence watched with interest, his lips curling into a smile as the proceedings unfolded before him. He now had to babysit these two lumps who couldn't handle their own children. Tommy Lee had said to befriend them, but they had kept themselves to themselves since they had been banged up. He knew better than anyone you couldn't trust an inmate. He would sort it though, put a plan together and get in with them.

He refocused on his mother. "So how's the old man?"

"He's okay, son…he's going to see about a job at Fords, for when you get out," she muttered. "I know it's a while yet, but best to be prepared."

"It's all right, Mum, I've got myself a job already lined up." He grinned. "And before you say anything, it's legit. I'm going straight."

CHAPTER 22

March

Tommy Lee sat in the office at the gym, his thoughts on the prick who had scratched Millie's motor and smashed his light. Was it someone targeting them, or a freak random attack?

Scott appeared at the door, breaking his thoughts. "Fancy a bit of sparring?" he asked, sweat beading his forehead.

"Maybe later. I promised Millie I'd get this sorted." Tommy Lee held up a piece of paper and waved it in the air. "Actually, I need a word."

"Sure, what's up?"

"After the damage to the Range Rovers, I'm thinking of getting someone to watch the place," Tommy Lee said and placed the paper back on the desk. "The flat across the road is up for rent."

"Above the baker's?" Scott asked.

"Yeah. As you're now here full-time, how would you feel moving in there?"

Scott wiped the sweat from his eyes. "I guess it'll be handy for work... What does Millie think?"

"She thinks it would be a fresh start for you; also, she reckons Dan could move in, too, yous get on well." Tommy Lee leaned back.

Scott turned and looked out of the door. Dan was watching a young lad as he shadow-boxed. He had been working here before Tommy Lee and Millie had bought the place. He was a year younger than Scott, and they did get on well, even going to the boozer a few times together.

"If it's okay with him, I don't see why not." Scott grinned. "How much is the rent?"

"Millie can sort that out, but knowing her it won't be much," Tommy Lee mumbled.

"Where is Millie?"

"Her motor's gone in to get the scratch fixed." Tommy Lee laughed. "She's not happy being without it, but at least I know where she is for a change."

"She phoned me last night." Scott hesitated when Tommy Lee glared up at him. "She asked if I could take her to the docks tomorrow."

"Did she." Tommy Lee sighed. "I'll speak to her later; you come here as usual." He refocused on the paperwork in front of him, signalling the end of the conversation.

***

Terrence spied John Jo and Sean Paul in the mess hall, a large room that was surrounded by cells. Everything here was grey. Grey walls, grey furniture; even the landings that overlooked them had grey railings. They sat at a scratched-up table playing cards, just the two of them.

He stood at the side, leaning against the wall, waiting for his moment to make an introduction. Right on cue, another inmate, called Muggsy, walked past the table and pushed the pile of cards onto the floor. John Jo was up and grabbed the man. Before he was able to strike, Terrence stepped in and pulled the men apart. He then turned to Muggsy, winked, and told him to fuck off.

"Sorry about that," he said while pulling up a chair. "He's harmless, just likes to wind the other inmates up."

John Jo and Sean Paul remained silent.

"My name's Terrence, and yous are?" He held out his hand.

The two men stared at him blankly. After a few seconds, John Jo answered, obviously weighing him up. He shook his hand firmly, then Sean Paul followed suit.

"It's all right in here," Terrence told them. "Most cons keep themselves to themselves. The only ones you need to watch out for is the one sitting over there, surrounded by heavies. He runs the place. Steer clear of him and his mob, and you'll be fine."

"Why are you telling us this?" John Jo said with an air of distrust.

"Just letting you know the order of things." Terrence held his hands up. "Information like this is key to doing your time and getting out of here, trouble-free. Now, you gonna deal me in?"

***

PJ studied himself in the full-length mirror at the gym. He wasn't used to wearing a suit. "Is this really necessary?" he said as he fiddled with his belt.

"You need to look the part," Tommy Lee assured him, who was dressed in similar. "You'll be going with Scott and Dan."

"You not coming?"

"I need to finish up here then get back to Millie. You'll be okay with them, just do as Scott tells you."

"Okay." PJ sighed.

"It's a couple of hours' work, then you can go and do…" Tommy Lee left the rest unsaid.

PJ knew what he meant. Free to go chasing cock. His brother couldn't say it. Not that he could blame him; even though it felt so right, so needed, he also felt dirty every single time he went home. He was a liar, living two lives. He knew eventually one of those lives would crush the other.

"You ready?" Scott asked.

PJ gave a quick nod then followed him and Dan out. The rain had let up, but there were puddles everywhere, highlighted by the streetlamp's dim glow. He climbed into the back of Scott's car and sat there silently. He didn't have a clue what he was doing, having never done this before.

Scott drove to the end of the road and turned left, then stopped outside the King's Head public house. The windows glowed amber, figures visible through the misted glass, drinkers chatting and laughing.

"Right." Scott killed the ignition. "Let's make it quick. He's always good for paying, but he'll talk your ear off if you let him."

Dan, in the passenger seat, adjusted his tie. "He's just lonely, mate. Whole family left him, didn't they?"

Scott laughed. "Yeah, probably 'cause he never shuts up." He was the first out of the motor.

The bell above the door jangled as they stepped into the warmth. A few heads turned. Locals, already on their second pint, clocked them and turned back to their drinks. Everyone knew the score.

Bob, the landlord, was wiping down the bar using a cloth that looked like it hadn't been clean since 1972. He glanced up, forced a smile. "All right, lads."

"Bob." Scott nodded. "You got it?"

He sighed and reached under the bar. "Business ain't what it was, you know."

PJ glanced around the bar. "Seems thriving to me."

"I've had a stranger in this last week, asking questions about Mr Ward," he said with a quick change of subject.

"What questions?" Scott asked.

"If he comes in here, where does he live. Personal questions. Might be something, might be nothing. Thought I'd best tell you. I don't wanna get mixed up in no wars."

Scott leaned in, his tone cool. "You pay us, you don't worry about the rest. Yeah?"

"Yeah, yeah," Bob mumbled and handed over an envelope. "It's all there. Just saying, things feel twitchy."

PJ took the envelope and gave it a quick squeeze. "Feels right," he said, though he couldn't tell one wad of pound notes from another.

Back in the car, Scott took the money from him and dropped it in the glove box. "Right, gentlemen, we need to get this done fast and let Tommy Lee know about this stranger. Let's get to the knocking shop."

They headed off to The Lotus Room, massage and beauty, discreetly tucked between a laundrette and a betting shop. The windows were frosted, the sign a tired pink having seen better days.

Inside, incense masked the sweat and desperation. A receptionist with too much makeup and too little patience gave them a nod. "Sandra's in the back."

They waited near a pink velvet curtain until Sandra appeared. She was sharp-eyed, in her forties, with a smoker's rasp and a clear habit of sizing people up before they spoke.

"You're early." She slipped a bundle into Scott's hand.

"Just thorough," he said. "Any trouble?"

"Had a bloke try it on last Thursday. Big lad thought he could get rough without paying. I sorted it, but you might want to make sure he doesn't come sniffing again."

Scott gave her a nod that promised a follow-up. "You've got a name?"

She smiled, cold. "Of course I do, but I doubt it's real."

"Describe him," PJ added.

"Dark hair, unshaven. Not a beard, more like he couldn't be bothered, and his eyes were small, mean." She shook her head. "He was a nasty piece of work. I'm not intimidated easily, fellas, but he scared me."

"Understood," Scott said, then turned and headed out.

PJ whistled low as they stepped outside. "I don't know whether to be scared of her or impressed."

Dan smirked. "Both's probably safest. Right, last stop, car lot."

The used car lot sat just off the main road, all fluttering flags, washed-out signs, and rusted Escorts. Richard Lewis stood outside with a cigarette dangling from his lips. He'd clocked them as they'd pulled in.

"Evening, gents," he said as they approached. His grin was too wide, too rehearsed.

PJ disliked him on first glance. He was a typical used car salesman.

Scott didn't return his smile. "You got the week's money?"

Richard hesitated. "Listen, I'm a bit short. Had to let one of the lads go, and that Cortina's been sitting there—"

Dan cut him off. "We're not your bank, Dickie boy. You don't pay, you may not be parking cars here next week. Seems there's a new player in town. I trust you're up to sorting him out yourself?"

PJ studied Richard. His smile faded at those words, his eyes widening. Was something else going on?

"All right, all right." He ducked into the Portakabin office and came back with a smaller envelope than usual.

Scott raised an eyebrow. "This better not be light."

Richard shrugged, like he was just a man trying to make a living. "It's what I've got. Next week will be better."

"You had a deal with Mr Ward. You agreed the terms," Dan said. "He may want a word with you."

Again, Richard shrugged.

Scott took the envelope but said nothing. Silence, with men like him, did more than threats.

The men returned to the motor. PJ slid in the back then shifted to the middle. Hands on the front seats, he pulled himself forward.

"Something else is going on here," he said. "That man's carrying a secret, he's scared."

"That's not our business," Dan said, eyes fixed on the road ahead.

PJ sat back. What if this mystery man had approached Richard, too, warned him to keep his gob shut? Something didn't add up. PJ

knew when a man was hiding a secret. He could see it in his eyes —
they reflected his own.

***

Tommy Lee was just finishing off when the men got back. "Get it
all?" he asked without lifting his head.

"Car lot's short again, the others are okay," Scott said as he threw
the envelopes onto the desk.

"I'll pay him a visit tomorrow, find out what's going on." Tommy
Lee opened each envelope and counted the contents, then shoved the
notes into his jacket pocket. "I need to get going."

"There's something you should know." Dan glanced between
Scott and PJ. "Some geezer has been asking around about you."

Tommy Lee glanced up, his body tense, face neutral. "What
geezer?"

"Some bloke was in the pub asking about you, but also Sandra had
a stranger in, roughing one of the girls up and wasn't gonna pay,
could —"

"Something was wrong with the man at the car lot," PJ cut in. "He
was shifty, scared. I think this mystery man could be the one
damaging your motors."

Tommy Lee sat back and sighed. "Did you get a name,
description, anything that might help track him down?"

"Big lump, dark hair, and mean, piggy eyes," Dan said quickly.
"He gave a false name to Sandra. He also asked where you live. Bob
said he didn't know, probably because he doesn't."

"Okay. When you lot go home, make sure you're not followed."
Tommy Lee stood and motioned to the door. "We'll pay them all a
visit tomorrow, see if we can find out more."

CHAPTER 23

The morning stretched grey across the Essex sky, heavy with the remnants of last night's rain. Tommy Lee pulled the Range Rover into the lay-by just across from the car lot, the engine purring before he shut it off. Millie sat beside him, much to his disgust. She had insisted she be there, just in case she picked up on something he missed.

"You ready?" He glanced at her.

She looked triumphant because she'd got her own way.

"Yes." She smiled. "We're not causing a scene. Just questions," she confirmed.

"Just questions," he agreed. "Unless they lie to us."

The car lot hadn't changed. Same row of rusted Capris and Cortinas with For Sale signs written in shaky marker pen. Richard was pretending to buff a wing mirror with a rag that mostly just smeared. He clocked them and stood straighter, clearly nervous.

"He's worried," Millie said. "His posture is stiff."

"Not here to buy, are you?" Richard tried to sound casual but failed miserably.

Tommy Lee kept his hands in his jacket pockets. "No. We're searching for someone. Big bloke, quiet type. Been round here? Might've asked about me or the lads that come collecting."

Richard hesitated, then glanced around. "I don't want any trouble."

"Neither do we," Millie said, her tone flat. "Just a name or face. If there's gonna be trouble, this man is going to hit here, so start talking."

Richard exhaled with a slight shake to his voice. "He came by last week. Asked about you, Scott, and the other one. Didn't say much. Just stood real still. Had that way about him, like he wasn't afraid of anyone."

Tommy Lee watched him closely, balling his fists. Millie grabbed his arm, calming him.

"You give him anything?"

The man shook his head. "Told him I didn't know anything. Which was only half a lie. He didn't press. Just nodded and left."

"Can you give us a description?" Millie said, calm. "Something that may help us find him?"

"He was about your height, Mr Ward, but the thing that stood out was his eyes. They were small, lifeless." He shuddered.

"Age?" Tommy Lee asked.

"Late thirties maybe. I'm not good with ages. Could be early forties at a push."

"If he comes back you call us, understand?" Tommy Lee said with a sharp edge.

"I don't have your number," Richard said, a nervous lilt to his voice.

Millie scribbled on a piece of paper and handed it to him. "You do now."

Next they made their way to the King's Head. Inside, the place smelled of stale ale and bleach. It was empty except for Bob stacking glasses behind the bar.

He saw them and froze. "Thought I'd be seeing you two again."

Tommy Lee stepped forward. "No trouble, Bob. Just a question. Man came by last week. Big. Said little. Asking about me. You remember?"

Bob's hand paused over a pint glass. "Yeah. I remember."

Tommy Lee waited.

"Didn't give a name. Just asked for a pint and then questioned me about you. Said he knew you from years back, wanted to catch up. I told him nothing."

"Did he seem local?" Millie asked.

Bob shook his head. "Didn't sound Essex. Northern, maybe. Hard to tell with his voice so low."

"Description?" she added.

"Six-foot, thickset. Small creepy eyes," Bob recalled. "There was something strange about him from the off."

Tommy Lee leaned in slightly. "If he shows again—"

"I'll ring you," Bob said, already reaching for the same scrap of paper Millie had handed him. "I ain't stupid."

Last on the list was the massage parlour. Tommy Lee opened the door for Millie to enter. Inside, incense clashed with cheap perfume and the smell of sweat. A brunette behind the reception desk grinned when she saw him walk in.

"Well, now. Aren't you a sight," she said, crossing her legs slowly. "Didn't know you were paying us a visit."

Millie rolled her eyes. "We're not here for that. My husband has some questions."

The woman stared Millie up and down then refocused on him. "So what can I do for you, handsome."

He glanced at Millie; she had a face like thunder. If he wasn't careful, she would batter this tart. He ignored the comment, stepping closer. "Big bloke been in? Asked questions about me and the lads who collect?"

The woman tilted her head. "Maybe. You gonna pay me for the memory? I'll accept in kind."

Millie lunged forward and knocked the woman off the stool with one punch. "Talk to him like that again and I'll fucking finish you."

The woman stood, rubbing her arse and cheek. "You're gonna be sorry for that."

Before she had a chance to close in on Millie, Tommy Lee stepped between them and pushed her back down. "You touch her, and I'll fecking kill you."

The brunette smirked, then shrugged. "All right, all right. Yeah. He's been in twice. Asked for Sandra. Didn't want a massage the second time. Just asked questions. Cold type. Like someone who's used to being obeyed. The second time he came in, Sandra got rid of him before he asked too much, warned him there would be trouble."

"Then what?" he asked.

"He laughed, said she should watch who she lets in then. Then he left." She perched back on the stool. She gave Tommy Lee the once-over again. "You don't let much in, do you? Got that 'lone wolf on a rainy moor' vibe. Bit sexy, if you ask me."

Millie's tone dropped. "He didn't."

The woman turned, sass rising once again. "Wasn't talking to you, sweetheart."

Millie sidestepped Tommy Lee, eyes sharp as glass. "Listen, love. This one? He's spoken for, and not by someone who spends her days batting lashes behind a desk or getting her knickers off for the next paying fuck. You're not in his weight class and you most certainly ain't in mine, so don't even try and spar."

The woman appeared stunned, then embarrassed. She turned back to her desk without a word.

Millie stepped outside and took a deep breath. Tommy Lee stood next to her, grinning.

"You enjoy that?" she asked.

"Who wouldn't enjoy their woman fighting over their man." He glanced down at her. "I fecking love you."

"Yeah, well, a word of warning. If I ever hear you've been back in that shithole, we are done."

"Duly noted." He laughed, grabbing her by the hand.

***

John Jo paced the cell nervously. Gypsy was in labour, and here he was, banged up. The governor had called him in an hour ago to give him the news. His nerves were fraught.

"Sit down, brother, you're making me feel dizzy," Sean Paul griped.

"How can I sit at a time like this? I'm about to become a father again and I'm not there... Jaysus, the child will be six months old before I see it."

"You'll see it at visiting." Sean Paul stood and grabbed his brother by the shoulders. "Why don't we go down and have a game of cards, it might help you relax a little."

"Okay," he said reluctantly.

Downstairs, Terrence was sitting at a table on his own, watching the other cons' antics.

"Morning, Terrence," Sean Paul called out as they joined him.

"Morning, lads. You okay, John Jo? You're a little bit peaky." He eyed the man.

"His wife's in labour," Sean Paul answered.

"Oh, congratulations, we'll be celebrating later then."

John Jo grunted then slid onto the seat opposite. He couldn't think about celebrating until he knew Gypsy was all right.

***

Tommy Lee had dropped Millie back off at his mother's, then come back to the gym. He had only just walked through the door when Scott grabbed him.

"There's been trouble at the car lot. Richard phoned, said one of his cars has been torched."

"You come with me. Dan, stay here and keep an eye on things." Tommy Lee turned and left with Scott on his tail.

"This prick's really starting to piss me off," Scott mumbled.

"Piss *you* off?" Tommy Lee rolled his eyes. "He's got us chasing our tails like fecking eejits."

"This seems personal, not like someone who wants to take over, its more…revenge led."

Tommy Lee nodded in agreement. "Yeah, you're right. We need to turn the tables. Trouble is, until we know who he is, there's not a lot we can do." He thought for a moment. "We need faces he doesn't know, men who can sit in the pub and watch for if he comes back in. Then follow him."

"What about Tony?" Scott asked.

"No, Millie needs him to run the docks. I'll have a think who we can use. Right now, let's sort this shit and keep an eye out. This prick is going to be watching from a distance."

***

John Jo was called to the governor's office. He was flanked by two screws. His stomach was in knots as he entered.

"Take a seat, Mr Ward, a phone call should be coming in any minute." The governor beamed.

John Jo sat and nervously wrung his hands, the shrill sound of the phone making him jump.

"Hello…yes, one moment, please." The governor handed the phone to John Jo.

"Hello?" he said.

"John Jo, you okay?"

"Gypsy! Yes, I'm fine. The baby?"

"It's a boy, eight pounds two ounces."

"I'm sorry I'm not there. Are you okay?"

"Yes. I can't wait for you to meet him, he looks just like Jonnie boy," she gushed. "I've got to go, I'll see you soon. Love you."

The phone went dead.

"Congratulations, Mr Ward," the governor exclaimed. "Such heartwarming news, and hopefully you will have a reason to stay on the straight and narrow."

"Yes, sir, I can promise you now, I won't be coming back here, not ever." He stood and was led back to his wing.

How would he cope now, knowing he had another six months to go?

CHAPTER 24

It was late afternoon, and the sky over Romford had turned a pale grey, typical for a damp Essex day near the beginning of spring. The fire brigade had long gone. All that remained now was the stink, the damage, and a lot of questions. The smell of burnt rubber hung thick in the air as Tommy Lee pulled the Range Rover onto the gravel verge outside the car lot. A curl of greasy smoke still drifted up from the blackened shell of a Ford Cortina, its windows blown out, bonnet warped like melted tin.

"That's a bloody mess," Scott said, eyeing the debris.

"Let's see what he has to say, and don't forget, keep a lookout. The prick who did this will about somewhere, watching." Tommy Lee slid out of the motor and marched towards Richard who stood there puffing on a cigarette.

He nodded towards the man. "Anyone see it happen?"

Richard threw the half-smoked fag to the ground. "Not a soul, apparently. Follow me."

They walked across the cracked forecourt, past rows of half-sold motors and broken dreams. A few tyres had melted where the fire spread, leaving puddles of black goo on the gravel. They entered the tiny office. It even smelt of fire in there despite the window being open. Richard looked like he'd aged; frown lines etched into his brow, and the smarmy smug smile had vanished.

"They're taking the piss now," he spat. "Middle of the afternoon! Right out front!"

Tommy Lee stayed calm. "You hear anything? Engine noise, voices?"

Richard shook his head. "I was in the loo. Came out and saw the motor lit up like Guy Fawkes night."

Tommy Lee left the office and walked towards the burnt-out vehicle. He crouched by the scorched frame. His eyes caught something, barely there. A bit of cloth snagged in the fence behind the lot. He walked over, tugged it free. Dark, torn, singed at the edge. Looked like nylon. Maybe part of a jacket sleeve.

He held it up. "Could be nothing or could be someone in a rush."

Scott raised an eyebrow. "Rushed arsonist. Smart."

"It's burnt, and there's blood on it. Reckon whoever it was injured themselves. Might make it easier to identify them." Tommy Lee handed the scrap of clothing to Scott. "Just so we're sure, you upset anyone recently? Turn someone away, make them feel small?"

Richard's laugh was bitter. "I sell old cars to people who can't afford new ones. I upset everyone… Look, I pay you money for protection, so what are you gonna do about this?"

"I'm sorting it, and just to be clear, you haven't paid what you agreed, so pipe down." Tommy Lee turned to Scott. "Whoever is playing these games, burning cars in broad daylight, he's getting bolder. This is why he's slipped up… I reckon he's done with this place, next time it'll be the pub or massage parlour."

Scott nodded. "Or it could be the gym."

Tommy Lee's eyes darkened. "Then we best make sure we are ready for him."

***

Millie lay on the sofa. The click of the door woke her from her snooze. "Tommy Lee, is that you?"

He appeared before he answered. "It's me." He grinned.

"What's the time?" She swung her legs round and sat up, glancing at the clock. "Ten; you're getting later and later," she complained. "I've made boiled bacon, cabbage, and potatoes. I'll heat it up for you."

"I'll do it, you stay there, I want you refreshed ready for bedtime." He winked, then left the room.

Regardless, she followed him into the kitchen. "There's a nice bit of crusty bread in the bread bin." She motioned while sitting at the table.

"I expected you to be in bed." He grabbed the bread knife. "Was going to have fun waking you up."

"I needed to speak with you."

He stopped and turned. "Am I going to like this?"

"I think so. I found a house. I know we had to let the other one go because of all the trouble with that prick, Eddie, but this one is up the same street, so layout, size, and garden should be the same." She stood and reached into the cupboard for a large bowl for him. "I'd like to get settled before this one makes an appearance." She pointed to her small but growing tummy.

He grabbed the bowl and pointed to the seat. "Sit... I'll put in an offer tomorrow, haven't got time to view it, unless Rosie can go with you?"

"I'll phone her in the morning and let you know... I mean, it's okay if it needs decorating, we can do that, can't we?" Peeking up at him, she noticed for the first time how tired he seemed.

"If it's what you want, we'll buy it." He buttered the bread and laid it on a tea plate.

"You going to tell me what's happened?" she asked. "Because I can see you're worried."

He turned and placed the bowl and plate on the kitchen table before taking a seat next to her. "It's nothing."

"Oh, it's something. Why won't you tell me?"

"Because you're pregnant, Mil, I want you to have a normal, stress-free pregnancy." He shoved the spoon into his mouth and yelped. "Feck, that's hot."

"I worry about you." She placed her hand on his. "And I worry more when you shut me out. Let me help, even if it's only giving you ideas or problem-solving."

"Fine. This prick set fire to the car lot, or one car. He's making me appear stupid, and because I don't know who it is, I can't fight back," he finally admitted. "He fucked up today, left a piece of his jacket on the fence, scorched and with blood on it."

"His getting sloppy," she said thoughtfully. "Do you think it's because you haven't really reacted?"

"What do you mean?"

"Well, he's been going around asking about you, trying to get information, but it hasn't got him anywhere, so maybe keep a low profile, let him think you're not bothered, and he might make more mistakes," she explained.

His silence told her he was thinking. Good.

"You could be right. So you think do nothing?" he confirmed.

"Let him think you're doing nothing. In the meantime, get men into each business, so they can be your eyes and ears." She smiled.

"You're not just a pretty face." He smiled back. "Fancy giving me some advice in the bedroom?"

"Mr Ward, you definitely do not need any advice in that department." She stood and sauntered towards the stairs, stopping at the bottom.

He was there, already behind her.

***

The pub was in complete darkness. The man, all dressed in black, reached for the crowbar and jimmied the window. This would be another warning for that Irish pikey, before he dealt the final blow.

He enjoyed taunting him, making him squirm. This part of the game had been his favourite. The scratched car, the smashed headlight. He was only just getting warmed up. Tonight the pub would suffer, tomorrow the massage parlour, and if he could sort out the gobby bitch who ran it, that would be a bonus. He could rape her, but that would be too quick; he'd have to think seriously about her punishment. Something more fitting. He grinned. He knew exactly what he would do to her.

He climbed in, careful not to make a peep, then headed for the bar. To him, fire was the ultimate weapon, something he was taught as a youngster by his stepdad. Not that he had ever really wanted to know him, he was only concerned with getting his mother's knickers off. And as for his real father, he had tried to build a relationship with him, but he wasn't bothered. No, he preferred someone else's kid to raise and love. But still, he was his father, even though there had never been much interaction between them. He would blindly call for justice as his father had asked. After all, wasn't that what the perfect son would do?

He reached out to the optic and pressed the bottom. Whiskey spilled onto the shelving. Next, he did the same with the brandy. Once he thought it was enough, he pulled the matches from his pocket and struck one. The flame burned brightly in the darkness. He stood back a bit and dropped it. The flames spread quicker than he had thought. In his haste to escape, he knocked over a table, piled with glasses, resulting in a loud crash.

"Who's there?" Bob called, slowly edging down the stairs, but by the time he entered the bar, the mystery intruder had gone.

Grabbing a tablecloth, Bob began dousing the flames, smoke catching in his lungs. He ran it under the tap and continued, a pointless exercise. Within minutes he heard the distant ring of sirens. Help was on its way.

CHAPTER 25

1st April

Tommy Lee stood with Bob, surveying the damage. It was now three a.m. The bar was badly smoked-stained, and the fire, although small, had ruined the back shelving and optics, which had burst with the heat. The stench of smoke lay thick in the air.

"Lucky I woke up," Bob mumbled. "They could've been lifting me out in a body bag."

Tommy Lee remained silent. This prick, whoever he was, was really starting to grate on him.

"So, Mr Ward, what are you going to do now? You promised us protection, and yet we've lost more now than before. Looks like Jacob was right not to get involved with you."

"First, I'll get someone in to clean this up and then I want to put men in here, so they can watch in case this man returns," Tommy Lee said, even though it was too little too late. "You didn't see him in the pub yesterday?"

"No. Haven't seen him since last week." Bob sighed.

"Right, I need to go. Someone will be here about eight to fix this, but I wouldn't worry, he won't be back here now. In fact, I know exactly where he'll go next." Tommy Lee left and made his way home. He would get some men in place at the massage parlour and gym. They were the only two targets left.

***

Millie placed the last of the breakfast things into the dishwasher and closed it. The twins had eaten and were now tearing around the house like tiny, possessed demons. She glanced at the clock when she heard the door click. Keys were thrown onto the sideboard, and footsteps approached. Tommy Lee was home at last. With screams of "Daddy!" bellowing from the twins, she walked to the front room where he knelt on the floor, hugging them.

"Where have you been, I've been worried?" She placed her hands on her hips.

"I went to the gym after the pub, just in case he tried something there. Scott turned up at six a.m., then Dan at seven a.m., so I came home." He sighed. "The fire damage wasn't as bad as I thought."

"I'll put the kettle on." She turned and made her way to the kitchen. "Why don't you get your head down for a couple of hours?" she called back.

"No, I've too much to do," he answered from behind her.

She filled the kettle then grabbed the cups. "Do you want a bacon sandwich?"

"Yes please, darling... I need to get men into the businesses." He took a seat at the table.

"You can't put Travellers in them, he'll know... I know a couple of brothers from Liverpool, Tony's dealt with them before. How about you ask him to contact them? They may be your best bet, and you could use a couple of men from the docks?"

"You need your men there," he said wearily.

"There's more men I can call on, and I've been thinking, I know a woman, Maggie, she came to our wedding. She would be ideal to put in the massage parlour."

"What happened to you relaxing and enjoying this pregnancy?" he huffed. "I don't want you —"

"To worry," she finished. "Well, I do worry about you." She jumped back as the twins charged in. She continued frying the bacon and buttering the bread. "I don't want anything happening to you…it would kill me…" Her last words lingered.

He stood and placed his arms around her waist. "Nothing is going to happen to me, I promise." He kissed her neck.

"Let me help. Please," she said as he continued kissing down her shoulder.

He pulled back and spun her around. "Okay, but only from a distance. I don't want you anywhere near the gym or these other businesses."

"Okay." She smiled. "You phone Tony after you've eaten, and I'll phone Maggie. This arsehole is not going to win."

"Forget about that for now. What time are the twins due their nap?" He grinned.

"Do you think about anything else other than sex?" she mumbled and placed the plate onto the table.

"Nope." He winked.

***

HMP Chelmsford was a dump, John Jo decided. The place was overcrowded, the screws were nasty bastards, and the amenities were pretty non-existent. The only upside was that Sean Paul was with him. The card games filled most of their time along with eating the shite food and the scant amount of exercise they got when outside. They had taken to doing press-ups and sit-ups in their cell. It helped pass the time and kept them fit. Terrence had become an acquaintance; they wouldn't class him as a friend, they never trusted anyone outside their own community, but he had proven useful, telling them who to avoid whether it was a con or a screw.

"Morning, fellas," Terrence called as he joined them in the mess hall.

"Morning," John Jo mumbled. He could never understand how this man was always happy. What exactly did he have to be happy about?

"I'll join yous in a bit, just need a word with someone." He walked past them and sat with another con.

John Jo refocused on his brother. "Wonder how the cobs are doing."

"There'll be okay with Father and PJ," Sean Paul muttered. "When we see them next we can check. Anyway, shouldn't you be wondering about your wife and children?"

"I wonder about them all the time. I can't wait to see Gypsy again…" His mind wandered.

"Watch out." Sean Paul nudged him. "We've got company."

A weaselly man approached. He had two men flanking him. He stopped in front of them, a cocky smile on his mush. "Heard yous pretty boys are pikeys, is that true?"

John Jo balled his fists. "We ain't fecking pikeys, Ferret Head."

The man stiffened. "Think it's time yous were taught a lesson in manners." He nodded to his two sidekicks.

Before the men closed in, Terrence swooped in, blocking their way. "Have we got a problem here?" His voice was low in warning.

Ferret Head pushed his men apart and stepped forward. "I don't know, have we?"

Terrence grabbed him by the neck and flung him against the wall, holding him in place. "You might not have, but now I do. Take your pathetic army and fuck off out of my sight."

The man held his throat, taking in gulps of air. "It was just a bit of fun."

"Fun? You want fun? Okay, let me bash you, and you can tell me how much fun you're 'aving," Terrence said. "Now yous." He pointed to the three men. "Listen and listen good. If I see yous doing that again, I'm gonna do more than batter ya. I'll fucking put yous in a body bag. Understand?"

Ferret Head nodded then skulked away with his men following.

"Sorry about that, lads." Terrence grinned. "He's one of life's opportunists, though I reckon yous would 'ave pummelled him into dust."

"Why did you step in?" John Jo said. "We could 'ave handled them."

"I know you could, boys, but yous are out in five or six months. If you'd 'ave bit, you would be serving the full two years."

"How do you know how long we've got?" Sean Paul asked warily.

"News travels fast in these places, there's not much else to do other than gossip, and while I don't, you can't help hearing what people say." Terrence shrugged. "Right, I'm off to do me chores. I'll catch you lads later."

John Jo waited until he was out of earshot. "Have you noticed how he's always there when anyone confronts us?"

"Yeah, what do you reckon's going on?" Sean Paul replied.

"I don't know, but something isn't right. It's like he's our guardian angel." John Jo watched Terrence slip through a door.

Why would a stranger protect them? There had to be a reason — and a price.

***

After two hours' kip and an hour quickie with Millie, Tommy Lee now felt refreshed. He dried his hair with a towel and flung it on the bed. He kept his eyes on Millie as she dried herself and dropped her towel to the floor.

"Do you reckon we've got time for another one?" He said and ogled her body.

"The twins will be awake any minute, and besides, you have important work to do." She pulled a t-shirt over her head.

He lunged forward and tugged her back onto the bed. "This is important business."

Right on cue, a loud "Mummy!" came from the twins' bedroom.

"They have the worst timing," he said. "Later, we continue this."

He pecked her on the lips then dressed quickly, putting on jogging bottoms and a sweatshirt and rushed down the stairs.

He had phoned Tony and arranged for the two Liverpool lads to come down and meet with him, hoping that they would be here about four p.m., give or take an hour.

Millie appeared with the twins, one under each arm, wriggling to get free. "They weigh a ton now." She panted and placed them down.

"They take after their father," Tommy Lee said proudly.

The twins wrapped their arms around her legs.

"Yeah, needy." She laughed.

"Better we need you than someone else." He winked. "Right, darling, I'll get going. See you later." He knelt down and kissed the twins goodbye, then stood and kissed her.

***

Millie had driven to the massage parlour with Maggie. Two of her men followed behind, from a distance, watching to see if she was followed. When she parked, before getting out of the motor, her men did a sweep of the area.

"All clear, Mrs Ward," Pat said.

She climbed out of the Range Rover and stared at the shabby premises. "Okay, follow me."

Inside, she was hit with the same disgusting smell of cheap perfume. A couple of scented candles burned on the desk. If they were meant to mask the odour of desperate men, they weren't doing the job.

"Can I help?" the receptionist said, peering up. "Oh, well, if it isn't Her Ladyship."

Millie gave a tight smile. "Still here, eh? I thought they'd have upgraded the décor by now."

The receptionist leaned forward, eyes full of spite. "Some of us don't get to swan around playing gangsters…and on the subject of gangsters, where is that hunk, Tommy Lee?"

Millie was already moving forward, fist clenched, drawn back ready to knock her into next week. With a loud thud, the woman dropped to the floor.

"What the hell is going on?" Sandra rushed through the curtain. "This is a business, not a bloody street corner."

"You remember me?" Millie asked.

"Yes, I know who you are." Sandra looked down at the woman on the floor and groaned. "You don't knock out staff in my place." She stepped between Millie and the desk, hands raised like a traffic warden. "You've made your point. Now tell me what the hell you're really here for."

Millie folded her arms. "Firstly, you talk to me with a bit of respect, secondly, two fires. Car lot and the King's Head. Same job, same pattern." She paused while she studied the woman. She was hard-faced, like she'd fought all her life just to get by. "This place is next." She turned and walked to the door. "Good luck," she called over her shoulder. "Come on, you lot, she don't need our help."

"Wait!" Sandra said with a sigh. "What do you need?"

"I want Maggie on the reception, and these two will be behind the curtain." Millie pointed towards Pat and Roger. "They will grab him if he comes in during business hours. I will send a couple more men for when you close; they'll guard the place, front and back, just in case this prick decides to light another fire."

Sandra sighed. "Okay, but what should I do with her?" She jerked her head towards the woman on the floor.

"That's your problem, but just so we're clear, if she comments on my husband again, I will slit her throat." With that, Millie turned and left.

Maggie and the two men followed her outside.

"Right, yous all know what to do. You've got my number and the gym's. Any problems, let me know, and boys, I really wouldn't sample the goods in there, unless you want a dose of the clap."

***

Tony introduced the two scousers. "This is Jamie." He pointed. "And this is Barry. They're brothers."

Tommy Lee shook their hands. "Tony's filled you in, I take it."

Jamie started speaking. The only word Tommy Lee understood was yes. He glanced at Tony who stood there, grinning.

"Yes, they know what to do. I'll take them over to the boozer now and get them settled. Does the landlord know the plan?"

"Yeah, he'll be waiting for you," Tommy Lee said, still trying to work out what Jamie had said.

"Wait for me outside, fellas." Tony waited for them to leave. "Have trouble understanding him, did ya?" He laughed.

"Never heard a fecking accent like it," Tommy Lee said.

"You should hear them when they've been on the beer. Even I can't understand them then… Right, I best be off. With Rosie babysitting, I need to sort these two, then get back to the docks."

"What do you mean, babysitting?" Tommy Lee's voice lowered. "Please don't tell me it's for the twins."

"Millie had some errands to run, thought you knew." Tony shrugged.

"No, I didn't." Tommy Lee's mood dipped. If she'd been anywhere near the massage parlour, he would be having serious fecking words with her.

CHAPTER 26

Brian stepped out of the meat wagon. He was still cursing himself for getting banged up. A stupid drunken fight, which the other man started. Now he was looking at six months. Obviously, the judge was a fucking prick and had taken a disliking to him. Six fucking months when things were going so well.

He was led through to the reception area. Then they strip-searched him, including two fingers up the arse. Dirty fucking scumbag screw. His few possessions were taken, and he was given a drab uniform. It itched and scratched like a motherfucker. After his mugshot had been taken, he was assigned a prison number, then it was off for a medical.

When he was finally led through to the wing, he'd just about had enough of being told what to do, his temper bubbling. He was shown to his cell; he would be sharing with another inmate. Great.

He placed his things on the shelving and sat on the bottom bunk. The top bunk had already been taken.

The screw looked at him with disgust. "Make yaself at home, I've got a feeling you'll be with us a while."

Brian remained silent. He wouldn't let some jumped-up, two-bit prick wind him up. He had a plan. He would be out of here in six months. All he had to do was keep calm and behave.

He'd done this before and knew the drill. Wakeup call at six a.m. Headcount seven a.m. Breakfast seven-thirty a.m., that's if you could call it breakfast. It would be cereal, toast, and tea, which tasted like dishwater. It wouldn't have surprised him if that was what they used. eight-thirty until twelve p.m. work duties, consisting of either laundry, which he hated, kitchens, which was okay apart from clearing up after, sewing, and cleaning. He wasn't keen on any of them. They were all women's jobs as far as he was concerned. At twelve-thirty p.m. it would be lunch, one-thirty until three-thirty a.m. more work, or if you were lucky, recreation time. Dinner was always at five p.m. and then lock-up at six p.m. It was the twelve hours locked in a cell he didn't favour. All that time stuck in a box and always with someone you didn't like.

After putting his things in a cupboard, he made his way down to the mess hall. This was where he'd be tested by the other cons. He would need to gain respect. Not that he normally had trouble in that department. His build and looks normally kept people from approaching him.

He eyed a table of three men playing cards and decided to sit in and watch. "Afternoon, gents," he slurred in his thick Brummie accent. "Don't mind if I watch, do you?"

The men shook their heads but remained silent.

"I'm Brian, by the way. Just got sent down."

"Terrence, and this is John Jo and Sean Paul."

Brian held his hand out and shook Terrence's. "Nice to meet you, fellas."

"What's the bandage for?" John Jo asked.

Brian glanced at his arm, tugging his sleeve down to cover it. "Got burnt in an accident."

***

Tommy Lee danced around the ring, working off his frustration. Two weeks it had been, and still no sighting of the mystery man. It was like he had disappeared into thin air. A wolf whistle came from behind him. He spun around to see Millie grinning.

"I told you not to come here," he said.

"I'm not staying away forever…oh, I think you should bring that little outfit home with you tonight," she continued. "For bedtime."

"Too much information." Scott yanked the gloves off. He climbed out of the ring. "I'll leave you two to it."

Tommy Lee joined Millie and led her to the office. "I don't want to be disturbed," he called over to Dan. He closed the door behind him and locked it.

"What are you doing?" Millie asked as he rolled all the blinds down.

"I want to see if it's worth bringing this lot home." He grinned.

"What, here?"

"It's not like we've never done it here before." He threw his gloves down and grabbed her.

"But no one was here then, there's a gym full of men down there now. They'll know," she said and shoved him away with no effect.

His mouth pressed firmly against her. He lifted her onto the desk and yanked down her panties, discarding them onto the floor. He surged into her; this was the release he needed. He thrust harder and faster, and within minutes, it was over.

"I fecking needed that." He groaned. Standing, he drew up his shorts and handed her back her underwear.

"I guess that was perfect timing then," she panted. "Still bring them home, though, for round two."

He didn't need telling, he'd already decided he would. "Where's—"

"The twins? At your mother's," she finished. "Anyway, we need to discuss the pub and massage parlour. It's costing money having the Liverpool brothers here. Do you think we should put our own men in there?"

"What men? You've already taken four from the docks. You can't afford to lose more." He sat on the chair and popped her on top of him. "It doesn't make sense, he's disappeared."

"Maybe he's seen the men in place and knows he can't hit yet?" She ran a finger down his chest.

"You do know I can't think properly when you do that." He adjusted her on his lap as his cock started to harden again.

"Sorry… What if it's something else, like he's been injured? He could be in hospital or dead even?"

"That would be wishful thinking. I've still got an uneasy feeling he's about somewhere, it's just finding out where." He helped her up. "I'm going for a shower. I would invite you, but there'll be other men in there, and if they see you naked, I'd have to kill them and end up in Chelmsford nick, with John Jo and Sean Paul."

"Don't even joke about that. I'll head off to your mum's. Meet you there?"

"Give us a kiss before you go." He walked to the motor with her then watched while she drove away, checking the road for any prying eyes.

***

Terrence kept a sharp eye on Brian. He'd taken an instant dislike to the man, the sort who crawled under your skin without saying much. Brian was all surface charm and empty answers but asked far too many questions in return. He had that look about him, too: beady eyes, too close together, full of spite. The kind of man you wouldn't trust with your worst enemy, let alone your mates. The kind you warned the boys about.

"So, where do yous boys come from?" Brian asked, casual like, but Terrence heard the edge behind it.

"Kent," John Jo said sharply. "And you?"

"Originally Birmingham, as you can tell by the accent," Brian said with a smirk. "Was just passing through when I got banged up."

"That's rough," Sean Paul muttered. He nudged his brother. "Come on." He stood, his chair scraping back against the concrete floor with a sharp screech.

Terrence winced. It sounded like fingernails dragged down a blackboard.

"Something I said?" Brian laughed.

"We got letters to write to our families," John Jo said while moving his chair back, ready to go.

"I'll keep ya company, Brian." Terrence nodded to the boys to head off. "So, you've not told us much about yourself."

Brian shrugged, shifting in his seat. "There's not much to tell. Been in and out of nick all my life. Came down this way for a job, had a fight, and got banged up for six months. End of story."

Terrence leaned in slightly. "What kind of job?"

Brian's grin thinned. "Ah, come on, you know better than that. You don't ask a man about his business, especially not if it's the dodgy kind." He glanced towards the corridor the boys had disappeared down. "Them two boys look familiar. They got a brother?"

"I don't know… You seem very interested in them. Is something else going on you're not telling me about?" he said, body tensing.

Brian held his hands up in mock surrender. "Whoa, just curious. Like I said, they seem familiar."

Terrence stood without another word. "I've got things to do." He walked away, his mind racing. He'd seen types like him before, smiles like razors and too many questions. Whatever Brian was up to, Terrence would get to the bottom of it. He wouldn't have anyone ruining his plans.

CHAPTER 27

3rd May

Another three weeks had crawled by. Still no sign of the mystery man. No notes. No messages. No more fires. Just silence, and that was worse.

Tommy Lee had lost patience and sent the Liverpool brothers packing. They left without complaint, but not without a few choice words about "southern chaos" and "northern sense." Millie watched them go without blinking. She'd done the same with Maggie, sending her and her heavies back to the brothel and the docks. The air around them still felt like it could split open at any second. Everyone was on edge. Back at the gym, there was a strange kind of calm, unnatural. The sort of calm that sits just before a storm, holding its breath, waiting to strike. The regulars noticed it, too. The music wasn't as loud. Laughter didn't last as long. Everyone seemed to be waiting, watching shadows that hadn't moved yet.

Millie sat in the office with her feet up on the desk, her feet aching from the growing pregnancy. She hated waiting. Hated silence even more. It meant the bastard was thinking. Planning. That whatever was coming next, it wasn't going to be small.

"Where the hell are you?" she muttered to no one.

Tommy Lee came in, stiff-legged and scowling. He'd been to all the businesses and asked again if anyone had seen the man. "Still no movement. Not a whisper. It's like he vanished."

She didn't answer straight away, instead choosing her words carefully. "This makes no sense. He was escalating, so why stop now?" She swung her legs round and planted them on the floor. "What if he was forced to?"

"Forced to stop?" Tommy Lee sighed. "That makes no sense either. The man was clearly on a mission."

"Exactly. So what would stop someone from following through with their plans?" She stood and walked to the window. Peeked down at the men boxing. "I think we should widen our search but tighten our circle. No more outsiders. No more favours. We sit and wait for when he slips up, then we take his head off."

Tommy Lee nodded slowly.

"Because he will slip," she added. "They always do."

***

The bastard had disappeared. No more fires, no more threats. Just a false name no one knew. A silence crawled under Millie's skin like rot. But she wasn't one to sit still. If this ghost thought he could vanish, he hadn't met a woman like her. Hadn't she got where she was in life by fighting back?

She placed the receiver down and glanced up at Tommy Lee. "Okay, I've found an artist who said they could do a mock-up of this man. I'll go see Bob first, he can give a description, then I'll show it to the others, see if they agree on the likeness."

"Take Scott with you, I still don't like you driving around here on your own. I need to get going for visiting," Tommy Lee said.

"I wonder why Terrence wants to see you?" she muttered.

"Don't know, darling, I just hope my brothers are behaving." He picked up his keys and pecked her on the lips. "I'll see you later, at my parents'."

She waited for him to leave then reached for her bag and coat. The weather had brightened up the last few days. Spring had sprung and along with it her stomach. The baby was moving more, kicking like a goal-scoring tiny footballer, obviously another boy. Which reminded her, they hadn't picked names. She waddled down the stairs, Scott ready and waiting at the bottom.

"You need a hand?" He giggled.

"Fuck off." She led the way to her car and then wedged herself behind the wheel. "Don't think I'll be able to drive much longer."

"We can take my car," he offered.

"No, I wanna make the most of my freedom while I still can." She pulled out into the traffic and continued the short drive to the King's Head, her mind flicking back to baby names.

The trouble she had with deciding was that she worked in a man's world. She liked the name Daniel, but Dan worked at the gym, and then again would it have to be a double-barrelled name like Tommy Lee. Tommy and Duke only had one name, she reminded herself.

Stopping outside the pub, she decided she would discuss it later with Tommy Lee. He should get a say in this child's name as she'd chosen the other two.

"Ready?" Scott asked.

She gave a swift nod and slid out of the Range Rover. "He said he'll meet us here at nine-thirty a.m."

Scott rapped on the door loud enough to wake the dead.

"All right, all right. I'm coming," Bob called. Then the sound of bolts drawing back followed. The door opened, and so did Bob's mouth.

"What ungodly hour do you call this?" he asked.

"We have business to attend to." Millie swept past him and eyed a half-drunk glass of whiskey on the bar. "And I'll need you sober…

I've got an artist meeting me here any minute. You are going to describe the mystery man to her so she can sketch a likeness. You do remember the man?"

"Yes, yes. Of course I do, but did it have to be so bloody early?" Bob muttered.

"I wanted to catch you before you got shitfaced. Now open the curtains so she can see what she's doing."

***

Tommy Lee had made his way to Chelmsford nick. He'd parked, been searched, and was now sitting at a table waiting for Terrence. He had dressed down for this meeting, making himself look like any other visitor. The door clicked open, and the screw escorted the cons in.

Terrence gave a curt nod when he joined him, sliding into the chair opposite, a polystyrene cup with hot tea waiting, and three Mars bars, as he had requested.

"How's John Jo and Sean Paul doing?" Tommy Lee said, hoping they had stayed out of trouble.

"They're fine," Terrence said. "Keeping their heads down…they're nice lads."

Tommy Lee breathed a sigh of relief after anticipating the worst.

"There was someone else, though." Terrence leaned forward slightly. "A man came through here a few weeks back. Said he recognised the boys. Asked too many questions. About family. Where they're from. Who they know."

Tommy Lee's jaw tightened.

"Ugliest bloke I've ever seen, looks like he's been put together with clay, and badly, I might add," Terrence said. "Didn't trust him. Neither should you."

"Me?"

"He was asking if the boys had a brother. It might be nothing, then again it might be something." Terrence scanned the room.

"Name?"

"Brian. Brian Ramblin… Said he was down this way for a job. Got caught fighting and sent to this dump. Six months, he got. When I questioned him on his job, he clammed up."

"What do you mean, down this way?"

"He comes from Birmingham. I fucking hate that accent," Terrence said. "Look, the geezer's a wrong 'un. I'll do my best to find out more, but he's cagey. And I've warned your brothers to not tell him anything."

"When you find out more, send me a VO, and if I have any questions I'll contact your solicitor. Don't leave him alone with my brothers." With that, Tommy Lee stood. Had he found him? "Don't forget, this visit never happened."

***

According to Sandra at the massage parlour and Richard at the car lot, the sketch was perfect. So much so that it sent a shiver down Sandra's spine. Now armed with the drawing, Millie trawled the high street, discreetly asking people if they had seen the man. After an hour, she slipped into the Lamb public house, in the marketplace, for refreshments.

"My sodding feet are throbbing." She kicked her shoes off. "Should have brought me slippers."

"What you 'aving?" Scott gazed at the barmaid.

"Just a lemonade, please." She handed Scott the drawing. "May as well ask while we're in here."

She pulled her right foot up and massaged it, getting little relief. She stopped when Scott and the barmaid approached.

"You're gonna wanna hear this, Mil." Scott grinned. "Tell her." He nudged.

"This bloke was in here about a month ago. Had a fight with one of the locals, beat him up real bad. Police came and took him away, and he got sent down. Hang on." She turned and ran back to the bar, returning seconds later. "Here, that's him."

Millie scanned the article. Six months he'd been given. She grabbed her chest. "Shit."

"What?" Scott asked.

"He's in Chelmsford nick." She slipped her shoes back on. "Come on, we need to let Tommy Lee know."

***

Tommy Lee was already back at the gym, his mind firmly on this Brian. The clatter of Millie's heels on the stairs leading to the office alerted him that she was on her way. Standing, he greeted her at the door.

"I've found him." She panted. "I know where he is."

"Chelmsford nick," they said in unison.

"What?" Millie handed him the newspaper and sketch. "How did you know?"

He lay the paper on the desk and studied the photo. "That was what Terrence wanted, to let me know a stranger was asking John Jo and Sean Paul about me. He also described him; it was the small eyes that gave it away." His eyes flicked to the article. "I've told Terrence to guard them. On the plus side, we know where he is. The downside is my brothers know nothing about it. I've asked Barrett to get me an emergency VO. Forewarned is forearmed and all that."

"Good." She sucked in her breath.

He looked up from his desk. "Mil?"

She took two shaky steps forward before her knees gave way, and she dropped, catching herself on all fours.

"I don't feel right," she gasped.

He was beside her in seconds. "Jaysus, Millie."

"It's my stomach," she said through gritted teeth. "Oh Christ, I think I'm going into labour."

"It's too early?" he said, pulling her up.

"It's stopping…thank fuck." She sighed.

"You've been running yourself into the ground over all this," he muttered and held her steady. "That's enough now. I'm takin' you home and calling the doctor."

"But—" She mumbled.

"But nothing, no more of this. No more trawling streets. We've found him, now you rest, from here on out."

He reached for his coat and keys.

Millie nodded weakly, one hand still pressed to her side.

The hunt could wait. The baby couldn't.

Taking her hand, he helped her down the stairs. "Scott, watch the place, I might not be back."

"Is everything okay?"

Tommy Lee ignored him as he guided her out and into the motor. "When I get my hands on this prick, I'm going to rip his head off and shit in his neck."

CHAPTER 28

Millie had been confined to bed rest for two weeks on the advice of the doctor. She had moaned non-stop for the last three hours. Tommy Lee wanted to pull his hair out. So much so he had ended up phoning for backup.

He lay back on the bed with her, stroking her cheek, while the twins sat on the floor with their toys. "Look, darling, this is what's best for you and our baby. Now please stop moaning."

"But what about this man? You can't deal with all that and this on your own, and then there's the cooking, cleaning, and let's not forget the boys, you know what a handful they are. This simply isn't practical." She sighed.

"It's all in hand, help is on the way." He stood. "I'll make you a nice cup of tea."

"Wait, what help?" she called.

Tommy Lee was already out of the door, choosing to ignore her. He knew she'd have a fit if she knew what he'd planned.

He filled the kettle when a knock came from the front door. He jogged to open it, standing back. Connie, holding Nelson, barged through with Duke following behind with their cases.

"How is she?" Connie asked.

"I've managed to get her into bed. She hasn't stopped moaning, though, reckons she's a burden." He took the cases from Duke and set them down in the hallway. "Mind the door when you go up, the twins are up there, too."

Duke followed Tommy Lee into the kitchen. "How long does she need bed rest?" he asked anxiously.

"A couple of weeks, but the doctor's going to come out and check her before allowing her to get back to normal." He tipped the boiled water into the teapot. "We've bought another house, too. I suppose it's too much for her to deal with."

"You have?" Duke sounded surprised. "I didn't think she'd go through with it."

"Yeah, she wants to be moved in before the baby arrives. I've been given the third of June as a moving date. Not sure if I should put it off, though."

"I wouldn't, get her away from here as soon as possible. A fresh start will do her good," Duke said. "Do you all good… So where is it?"

"Outskirts of Romford, ten-minute drive to the gym and nearer my family… You not thought of moving back this way, like Essex? Some lovely countryside there." Tommy Lee handed him a cup. "Be nice for Mil to have you nearer." He picked up Millie's cup. "I'll just take this up."

"I'll take it." Duke took the cup from him and left the kitchen.

Tommy Lee smiled. He'd planted the seed in Duke's head again, now all he had to do was see if it grew.

***

"I'm fine," Millie huffed as her mother plumped her pillows. "Honestly, Tommy Lee is overexaggerating."

"If the doctor said bed rest then bed rest you will have. Now I'll take the boys down so you can have a nap." Connie picked up Nelson and called to the twins. "Come on, boys, let's go play downstairs."

Millie cursed under her breath. This was all she needed. With her mother here it would feel like being under house arrest. She'd have a few choice words for Tommy Lee when he showed his face.

Connie left the bedroom, pulling the door to.

Millie looked up when the door reopened seconds later. "Dad."

"How's my girl?" he said, while he placed a cup on the side.

"I'm okay," she muttered. "I certainly can't stay in here for two weeks."

"If the doctor said bed rest then you bloody well will. Your mother will take care of the house and twins. You know her, she likes to feel needed… I guess we all do," he added.

"It's really good of yous to come, and I do appreciate it, but what about your life? You need to be home with your family," Millie said.

"You are our family… Tommy Lee told me yous are moving. I'll help with that, you do not lift a finger, understand?" he warned.

"Okay… Dad, I'm glad you're here. Tommy Lee's parents are great, but it's not the same as having you here." She smiled.

Duke returned her smile. "There's no place I'd rather be. I'll go down and let you rest." He kissed her on the forehead then left.

Millie pushed back into her over-fluffed pillows, attempting to make herself comfortable. She hadn't realised she missed her parents as much as she did. While things were still a bit awkward with Connie, it was different with Duke. She felt special around him. Like she belonged somewhere before her marriage. Of course she felt the same with Tommy Lee now, he and the twins were her life, but after growing up in a children's home, having her dad in her life was a second chance.

"How you feeling?" Tommy Lee perched on the edge of the bed.

"I could strangle you," she said. "Why didn't you warn me?"

"I thought it would be a nice surprise," he reasoned.

"Oh, it certainly was that. When the door opened, I thought it was you."

"What did you say?" He grinned.

Millie's face heated up. "Sex is off the menu."

He laughed.

"It's not funny, my mum said she was glad to hear it."

"Well, we can discuss sex later. I need to get back to the gym. Duke's coming with me." He pecked her on the lips then left.

Millie stared at the closed door. If she was stuck in here for two weeks, she might just end up killing someone.

***

The Range Rover purred as Tommy Lee and Duke drove along the A12. The sun was shining over Essex, which made a pleasant change. He didn't think the rain would ever let up.

"So you going to fill me in?" Duke stared out of the passenger window. "You told me some, but I've a feeling there's more."

"We found him," Tommy Lee said.

Duke looked over. "Who?"

"The one responsible for damaging the motors. Also the one sniffing round the car lot and the King's Head. He set fire to them, as a warning maybe, I don't know. He's been asking John Jo and Sean Paul questions…about me."

Duke straightened slightly. "He's in the nick?"

"Chelmsford," Tommy Lee said. "Brian Ramblin. Terrence clocked him, said he was asking too much about the boys and me, probing. Like he already knew something and wanted confirmation."

Duke gave a low whistle. "He's got some front. Do your brothers know?"

"No. I wanted to keep them out of it, but now I'll have to tell them. The solicitor is getting me a visiting order, so I can see them as soon as possible. He offered to tell them, but—"

"But it needs to come from you," Duke finished.

"And they need to be able to defend themselves. Terrence is keeping an eye on things, but I reckon this bloke will make a move once he knows he's rumbled." Tommy Lee turned the wheel hard into a narrow side street, tyres crunching over grit as the Range Rover pulled behind the gym. He switched off the engine, letting the silence fall. "If this bloke's digging for the right info," he said, "a warning won't stop him. That kind doesn't stop unless you stop them."

Duke opened his door and stepped out into the glorious sunshine. "All right then. What do you need me to do?"

"Keep an eye on Millie, make sure she does what the doctor said." Tommy Lee strode to the back door, Duke hot on his tail.

"Okay, and the move?"

"She was talking about getting a company in to pack up, but if Connie doesn't mind helping?"

"She won't mind." Duke stepped into the gym. "In fact, she'll be delighted at being able to help... She wants to make up for what happened."

"I'll also get me mother over. There's a lot to pack." Tommy Lee laughed. "Never know one person to have so much shite, and please don't tell her I said that, she'd fecking kill me."

Duke gave a firm nod. "Right, now that's sorted, let's concentrate on the bastard who's caused all the trouble."

vvv

Brian lay on his bunk, hands behind his head, thinking. Whilst he had always held his cards close to his chest, this time he wanted them to know. More precisely, he wanted Tommy Lee to know who he was and where he was, but that would have repercussions. He would be a sitting duck. If they didn't take him out in here they would get him when he was released. No, the best thing was to stay silent and cause trouble. First, Terrence needed to be out of the picture. He hated the man. Swanning around like he ran the place, when all he was really was a guard dog. Babysitting a couple of pikeys.

"Lights out," a screw called, before plunging them all into darkness.

Brian rolled onto his side and grinned. He would sort Terrence, then cause the pikeys problems.

***

Tommy Lee pulled the covers back and slid into bed. He gently moved his arm underneath Millie's head, attempting not to disturb her, then wrapped the other one over her, and snuggled in.

"I'm not asleep," she muttered. "What's the time?"

"It's bedtime, now sleep." He closed his eyes.

"I've been thinking."

He sighed. "About?"

"We haven't got any names for the baby, so—"

"Jaysus, Mil, it's two in the morning, can we discuss this later?" he said.

"Later never comes. Like I was saying before you interrupted, I want you to name him."

"I get to name the baby even if it's a girl?"

"Yes, but I think it's gonna be a boy, so be prepared. Oh, and no stupid names," she whispered.

"I quite like Cuthbert. Bert for short." He sniggered until her elbow jabbed him in his ribs.

"I'm serious," she barked.

"So am I about sleep." He nestled into her, breathing in her scent. She rang every bell in his body. The next two weeks were going to be difficult for him, being so close, unable to touch her. And now he had the added headache of choosing the baby's name, one that she'd agree on. Maybe he should seek advice on that one.

Her hand reached down and grabbed him, gently stroking. She knew him too well, as a wife should.

"I fecking love you," he groaned.

"I know… I love you, too."

CHAPTER 29

The sun streamed through the gaps in the curtains of the mobile home, throwing soft stripes of light across the floor where Jonnie boy sat banging toy cars together. Outside, the sky was a deep blue, and daffodils swayed on the verge by the gravel driveway. A blackbird was singing somewhere nearby, high, clear notes that carried right through the thin windows. This was the time of year Gypsy loved, or used to.

She stood in the kitchen, barefoot, one hip holding the newborn, the other resting against the counter. She hadn't even brushed her hair yet. The baby had been up half the night. There were dishes in the sink, laundry over every chair back, and milk spilled on the floor.

She glanced at the clock; nearly half past nine. She shifted the baby, kissed the top of his tiny head, and exhaled. Then a brisk knock came from the door. She trudged towards it, unlocked, and threw it open. Maeve stood there, smiling.

What the hell did she have to smile about with two sons locked up? What did any of them have to smile about? She breathed deep to hold back her tears.

"Morning, Gypsy."

She smiled, though she knew it didn't reach her eyes. "Morning, Maeve, come in. Excuse the mess." She stepped back.

"Don't you worry about that," Maeve said, waving a hand. "I've come to help; we'll have this place clean and tidy in no time. Have you eaten?"

"I'm not hungry." Gypsy wished her mother-in-law would leave. "And I'll get this place tidied, I just need to get him settled first." She perched on the sofa and nodded at the baby. "Been up most of night."

Maeve sat beside her, eyeing the newborn. "He looks like my John Jo."

"Yeah," Gypsy said softly. "Jonnie boy, too. Same eyes. Same stubborn little mouth."

Maeve reached across and gave her hand a light squeeze. "I know it's hard on your own, but you're doing it, and you've got us, we're all here to help, then before you know it, he'll be home."

Gypsy glanced out of the window. Shirley Ann was pegging her washing out. "How does she cope so well?"

"We all cope differently, Gypsy," Maeve said. "I fall apart each night in bed, then in the morning I put my fighting face on."

The newborn stirred, letting out a sigh. Jonnie boy dropped a car with a clatter and climbed onto Maeve's lap without a word.

"You go have a shower," Maeve said, already bouncing him. "Let the water hit your face. I'll mind the children."

Gypsy hesitated, then nodded. She got up, feeling every bone in her body, then lay the baby in his pram. She walked down the narrow hallway and stepped into the small bathroom. She didn't lock the door. Warm water ran and, stepping underneath it, she let herself cry for the first time since John Jo got sent down.

***

Chelmsford nick didn't fare any better in the sunshine; in fact, it made it appear worse. The grey walls greyer, dirtier, a stark reminder of what lay behind them. Tommy Lee glanced at PJ. He resembled a bulldog chewing a wasp.

"Remember, we get tables next to each other, and for feck's sake, smile," he said. "They've got it hard enough in there without seeing your fecking miserable mush."

"I don't know why I had to come," PJ said. "Shouldn't their wives be here?"

"I already told you, this is private, the women mustn't know," Tommy Lee said, barely containing his temper.

"Well, they shouldn't have done wrong then they wouldn't be in this mess."

"And you've never done wrong?" Tommy Lee gripped the steering wheel, knuckles white. "You deceive your wife every week and don't blink an eye." He climbed out of the motor, checking his jacket pocket for the visiting orders. "Come on, need to get in first to pick the tables."

They made their way through security, which Tommy Lee hated, and then stood close to the door, waiting to be let in. He wasn't looking forward to this, didn't even know how to word it, but this was a conversation that had to be had.

The door opened, and they headed to the seats near the window.

"Grab that table." He pointed to PJ.

Then they sat and waited for their brothers to be led through. Now was the moment of truth.

"Tommy Lee," John Jo said. "What's going on?"

"Sit." Tomy Lee nodded to the seat. "And stay calm... When you got sent down, I arranged for someone to keep an—"

"Terrence." John Jo sighed. "Don't you think we can take care of ourselves?"

"Hold on. Yes, Terrence, but not to babysit you, he was there to make sure yous kept calm and didn't end up serving two years, or longer. We all know what your temper's like." He leaned forward. "Just as well I did, because I've had trouble with a man, scratching

Millie's car, busting my headlight, and then setting fires to businesses that I protect."

"What's that got to do with us?"

"I've been after him." Tommy Lee's voice dropped further. "To kill him, but the trail went cold until recently." He glanced around the room. "He's in here."

"What, in this room?" John Jo spun in the chair.

"No. He's in this prison. On your wing to be precise."

"Who is it?"

"Brian Ramblin, I—"

"I knew he was a wrong 'un, kept asking questions."

Tommy Lee sighed. "Listen. I don't know who he is or why he's targeted me, but now I have a name I'll do some digging. In the meantime, I want yous to act like you know nothing. Understand?"

"Then why tell us?"

"He's gonna make trouble for you and Sean Paul. I want you to stay away from him. I'll have a word with Tony and see if we can get someone else on the inside, safety in numbers and all that."

"We don't need babysitting," John Jo said indignantly. "We're fecking Irish Travellers."

"I know, but Mother said Gypsy isn't coping well without you, so you need to get out on time. Now any problems, you can let Terrence know. He's got someone who can get messages out," Tommy Lee explained.

"Of course he has." John Jo rolled his eyes.

"This is being done for you and Sean Paul, and don't go giving Terrence a hard time. We asked him for help."

"So what's in it for him?" John Jo leaned back. "No one does things for nothing, what's it cost you?"

"A job… That's all he wants. A fresh start when he gets out, and I agreed. Now don't forget, tell no one, especially Mother and Father." Tommy Lee stood. "Who wants a cuppa?"

***

John Jo and Sean Paul sat in their cell discussing the visit. The door was half open so they could spot anyone coming in. It wasn't long before Terrence appeared.

"So now you know."

"We knew something was off. You don't give help like that unless you're family or being paid," Sean Paul said.

"Look, fellas." Terrence held his hands up to stop them saying any more. "I like yous boys, but I hate that prick Brian more… This may have started off as a job, but now it's more than that. I've never caused trouble for a man who didn't deserve it, and him…" He threw a thumb over his shoulder. "He is a man who causes trouble for the fun of it. Now are we good?"

John Jo studied him for a second. He liked Terrence, despite the lies. "Yeah, we're good. But what are we going to do about Brian?"

"Yous are gonna do nothing. Leave him to me." Terrence turned and left the cell.

"Well, that was short and sweet," Sean Paul said with a sigh.

John Jo nodded. "Tell the truth, I'm more worried about Gypsy…she's not coping without me."

"Then all the more reason to do what Tommy Lee asked. We keep our mouths shut and carry on as normal." Sean Paul pulled a pad from the shelf. "I'm going to write to Shirley Ann. Why don't you write to Gypsy, might cheer her up?"

✦✦✦

The dining room table groaned under the weight of food. Steam rolled up from a massive enamel dish of bacon pudding, golden and thick, the pastry cracked just enough to show a glimpse of salty meat inside. Roast potatoes glistened like jewels in goose fat, the carrots were soft and sweet, and the cabbage had been boiled to within an inch of its life. A jug of thick gravy took centre stage, already half-empty.

The twins were in their highchairs, and Nelson sat on Duke's lap. Tommy Lee sat at the head of the table with Millie to the left of him. She had been given a reprieve and allowed to have dinner downstairs on the condition she would go back up to bed after. She had reluctantly agreed; she had an announcement to make, and best it was done with everyone there.

"Can everyone just *listen* for one minute," she said, her voice rising over the general clatter of cutlery and overlapping chatter. "I'm having the baby at home."

The room went quiet for a minute, and then chaos.

Tommy Lee dropped his knife with a clang. "Absolutely fecking not."

Connie looked up from drowning her potatoes in gravy. "Don't be daft, Millie. You want doctors there. Proper ones. With gloves and equipment, just in case."

"I'm not doing it on the kitchen floor with a torch and a bucket, Mother," Millie snapped back. "It'll be in the new place, it's clean, it's private, and I won't have strangers poking around unless they're invited."

Tommy Lee shook his head, already red in the face. "That's what hospitals are *for*, Mil. What if something goes wrong? What if —?"

"*What if* you let me finish a sentence?" Millie said sweetly while she stabbed a carrot with unnecessary force.

Duke, two plates deep and buttering a bread roll like it was a religious rite, leaned back in his chair and said, "I reckon it's not the worst idea."

Tommy Lee shot him a look. "Oh, here we go."

"What?" Duke shrugged. "You've seen the state of them wards. Bright lights, strangers. You need peace for that kind of thing. My Aunt Vi had all seven of hers at home, in a wagon, and never broke a sweat."

Connie snorted. "She also smoked rollies through all of them and named two kids Jasper."

"Not her fault she got confused," Duke muttered.

Millie burst out laughing at the kerfuffle. "Listen," she yelled. "I've made my mind up. The midwife agrees. I'll be settled by then. It's happening at home. Now can someone pass me another piece of pudding, please?"

Tommy Lee buried his face in his hands. "Jesus Christ, it's not a wedding."

"Well, it's not your womb either," Millie said. "Pass the gravy, Dad."

Connie pointed her fork at her. "If you want me there, I'll be there. But I'm not cutting no cords or chanting over bathwater, and I still think it's a bad idea."

"Well, I've told you all now, so you have time to get used to it." Millie glanced at Tommy Lee who had a face like thunder.

He'd come around. With time. She hoped.

CHAPTER 30

24th May

Three weeks had passed, and all had remained calm in the nick. Terrence had guarded John Jo and Sean Paul at every possible minute of the day. A man called Ted had been recruited by Tony also. A five-foot-something man as wide as he was tall, from somewhere in Africa. He stayed glued to them like he'd been welded on.

Ted didn't say much, just grunted now and then, his accent thick and his stare unreadable. But everyone in the wing knew better than to test him. Rumour had it he'd once bitten a man's ear clean off in a queue for dinner. Whether it was true or not didn't matter. His presence alone was enough to make anyone thinking of giving the brothers trouble suddenly change their mind.

He moved like a wall with legs, silent but constant, always positioned between them and anything that glanced sideways. In the yard, at meals, even when they queued for food, Ted was there, arms folded, head swivelling slow like a turret.

Terrence had taken to him immediately. "He's like a bulldog in a bulletproof vest," he muttered once, watching Ted stare down a group of lads loitering too close to the table.

John Jo wasn't sure at first. "Is he gonna watch us while we sleep, too?" he joked.

"If he does," Sean Paul said, "you better not fart, cos that will knock him out."

Even Ted had smiled at that. A rare crack in the concrete.

But underneath it all, the silence felt temporary. Terrence could feel it, like pressure behind a wall. Something was coming. And he wasn't sure Ted, or anyone, would be enough when it hit.

"Come on, lads. Grub's up," Terrence said, slowly rising from his seat. He'd had an uneasy feeling all day. He had shared his concerns with Ted who seemed to double down on the security.

The mess hall buzzed with the usual noise when they entered. Cutlery clinking against metal trays, low mutters, the occasional burst of laughter from the back tables where the cocky lads sat, pretending they weren't counting days till freedom.

John Jo and Sean Paul sat side by side, heads low over their trays. Boiled potatoes, something pretending to be beef, a handful of peas that had most definitely died scared. It wasn't much, but they weren't here for the cuisine.

John Jo dreamed about homecooked food. Gypsy in the kitchen preparing it, him sitting with Jonnie boy and the baby. How he missed home life, and how he missed his family more.

He eyed Ted who stood nearby, back to the wall, eyes moving slowly from one end of the hall to the other. Every so often, he shifted, not a full move, just enough to remind people he was watching.

John Jo smiled, but it was he who wanted to take Brian down.

Terrence stared at Brian in the far corner. He was two tables away, sitting alone, tearing bread into little strips he never ate. His eyes, small and close together in that ratty face of his, were fixed on the brothers. Always watching. Always calculating. Terrence had clocked him the moment they'd entered. Terrence sat across from the lads, his tray untouched. The hairs on his arms prickled, instinct, like a dog hearing something before it happens.

"Don't turn your heads," Terrence said low. He leaned in. "But he's staring again."

Sean Paul didn't move. "That rat-faced gobshite?"

"He's waiting on something," Terrence murmured. "Timing it."

John Jo wiped his mouth with his sleeve. "He's gonna run out of time if he keeps gawping like that."

"Maybe he fancies us." Sean Paul laughed.

Terrence gave a nod to Ted; he'd shifted slightly, hands folded in front of him. There was tension visible on his face. He knew.

"He's been asking questions again," Terrence muttered. "Not just about you two. About who visits. Where you're from. What jobs you had. He's digging."

Sean Paul scowled. "Well, we know who he's searching for."

"No, he knows you're Tommy Lee's brothers. I'd bet my life on it." Terrence picked up his fork at last. "He's waiting to *do* something."

Just then, a crash at the far end of the hall, a tray hitting the floor, loud and sudden. Heads turned. Laughter from a table near the back.

Terrence glared. Brian didn't flinch. He used the distraction to get up, tray in hand, and wandered closer, casual, like he was heading for the bin. Only he veered off slightly, hovering near their table, a little too close.

Terrence stood. Ted took one step forward.

Brian paused, like he'd forgotten what he was doing. Then he smiled, at nothing, and dropped his tray in the bin with a clatter. He walked out without a word.

Terrence watched him go, chewing slow. "He's testing the water."

"Then let him test," John Jo said, jaw tight. "But he best be ready to drown in it."

Ted peered down at them, one eyebrow raised. "Soon," he said, voice deep and quiet. "Very soon."

And though no one said it, they all knew something had just shifted. Brian wasn't circling anymore.

Terrence leaned in and whispered, "He's getting ready to strike."

***

Tommy Lee helped Millie out of the Range Rover. Maeve came bounding out of the mobile to help with the twins.

"How you feeling, girl?" she asked, eyes on her bump.

"I'm fine now, thanks, and thanks for helping pack up the house. Don't think I could have done all that on my own," Millie said.

Tommy Lee unclipped Duke and handed him to Maeve, then walked round to the other side to get his other son. "She's not to do anything," he warned her. "That's why she's here for the day."

"I know," Maeve said. "Come on in. Gypsy's inside, too, she could do with cheering up."

"She still down?" Millie straightened her dress.

"Better than she was. Don't think she'll be right till my boys are home, though." Maeve headed towards the mobile.

Tommy Lee spotted PJ in the paddock with their father. "What are they doing?"

"It's mating season, bloody big job just for the two of them. Why don't you give them a hand?" Maeve motioned.

"No, I think I'll give it a miss." He threw Tommy boy over his shoulder and followed her in.

"Right, I need to get off. I'll only be a few hours." He placed his son down and pecked Millie on the lips. "And please don't overdo it."

"I won't," she said with a sigh.

He walked to the door, Maeve behind him. "Try and talk some sense into her about this home birth shite while I'm gone."

"She wouldn't be the first woman to have a baby at home," Maeve muttered. "You was born at home, on our bit of ground, and you turned out all right."

"She's not having the baby at home, that's final," he snapped. "Also the ground, has Father sold it yet?"

"No, son, with all this going on he hasn't had time. Why?"

"Tell him to hold on to it for now, because I think I might have a buyer."

***

Brian knew patience. It was the one thing he'd learned in every sentence he'd ever done, bide your time, smile when you need to, and strike when the timing's right. He'd watched the brothers for weeks. Watched how that big lump, Ted, shadowed them like a guard dog. Watched how Terrence never let them eat alone. But everyone slipped eventually. All he needed was ten seconds. Just one opening.

It was now Thursday afternoon. Sean Paul was in the showers, drying himself, Ted standing guard. Terrence had been pulled in for laundry duty with John Jo. It was a little after three p.m. when the alarm sounded. Ted bolted out of the shower block, calling for Sean Paul to follow, to find out what was going on. Sean Paul, still drying his hair with a towel, wandered into the corridor, alone.

"All right, sunshine," Brian said casually. He blocked the way. "You and your brother been chatting shit about me, I hear."

Sean Paul looked up, calm, at first. "Get out the way, Brian."

But he was already moving, fast, hand darting from the waistband of his greys. It wasn't a knife, they'd have noticed, but a sharpened toothbrush, wrapped in tape.

Sean Paul ducked, his reaction too slow. The handle came above his right eye, then again to his ribs, catching his clothing.

"Oi!" someone said, one of the screws, distant.

Sean Paul lunged, got a fist in, but Brian's wild swings had momentum. The third blow caught Sean under the eye, and he went down hard, head bouncing off the tiled wall.

That's when Ted arrived. That's when everything stopped.

Brian barely turned before a meaty hand closed round his throat and slammed him into the floor like a sack of meat. Ted didn't speak.

He didn't have to. The crack of Brian's head against concrete said everything.

"Get the medic!" someone yelled.

Within minutes, guards flooded the corridor. Ted backed off slowly, hands in the air. Brian was cuffed, dazed and bleeding, his little plan in tatters.

Sean Paul was stretchered out, barely conscious, his eye already swelling shut, blood leaking from a cut at the back of his skull. Brian grinned. Maybe it had gone better that he'd thought.

Brian was dragged into the segregation unit that same night, a windowless box with nothing but a piss-stained mattress and a toilet that hissed every few minutes. He sat against the wall, muttering to himself. His head throbbed. His teeth were loose. And worse, now he'd had time to think, the one thing he'd never thought of, he'd have a target on his back.

He banged on the heavy iron door. "I need to speak to someone."

His only chance was to get moved to another prison.

***

The steady rhythm of skipping ropes, the slap of gloves on pads, the dull thud of fists hitting heavy bags, all of it washed over Tommy Lee like background noise. He stood in the office above the main floor, arms folded across his chest, eyes locked on the window showing every corner of his kingdom.

Scott stood beside him, arms resting on the edge of the sill. The gym was full of lads, young ones, tough ones, eager ones, but none of them knew the temperature had changed.

"I should have had him taken out as soon as I knew he was in there," Tommy Lee muttered.

"You couldn't have known this would happen," Scott said. "This Brian bloke's a proper nutter—"

"Exactly, and I knew that." Tommy Lee kept focused on the ring, where two boys sparred under red ropes.

The bigger lad was overreaching; the younger one, sharp-eyed and quick, ducked every hook.

"Sean Paul's a fighter," Scott added. "He'll pull through in no time."

Tommy Lee turned, slow and dangerous. "That's not the point. Someone went after my blood. In a cage, no less. That's not a warning, that's war. A war that was meant for me."

The phone rang, breaking his thoughts. He snatched it up. "What?"

"Nice greeting for your wife," Millie said from the other end.

"Sorry, darling, is everything okay?" he asked, worry and guilt prodding him.

"Yes, everything's fine here. Now listen, it was Finn who knew the story about Eddie. Go see him, he may know about this Brian, if he's in any way related. It's worth a shot."

"It really doesn't matter now. He's dead anyway," he said.

"He knows all about you. You might find out something you can use against him. Anyway, it was just a thought. Love you." The phone went dead.

***

John Jo sat at his brother's bedside, staring. Sean Paul's face was badly bruised, his right eye swollen. He had a bandage around the top of his head. The doctor had said the injuries looked worse than they were. Concussion and a laceration above the right eye. John Jo glanced up at the screw by the door, then back at the doctor.

"Will he need to go to hospital?"

"No, he'll be fine here. A couple of days' rest and he'll be back on the wing." The doctor placed a hand on John Jo's shoulder and gave a small squeeze. "It's time for you to return, son."

He stood, then followed the screw along the corridor, through doors that were locked behind him, until he was at the wing.

Terrence approached. "How is he?"

"He don't look good, but the doc says he'll be fine. What happened?"

"Hang on, Ted's here."

John Jo glared at him as he approached. "You were supposed to guard him. What went wrong?"

"Brian arranged for a decoy, he'd paid a couple of the youngsters to cause a distraction. I told Sean Paul to stay behind me; when I looked back he wasn't there, so I ran back and caught Brian beating him… I hit him good. He's now in solitary."

"So this was preplanned," John Jo mumbled.

"He'll try again," Terrence said. "Unless we take him down first."

"There is no we. I'm going to do it," John Jo spat. "I want the names of the decoys. They can have a taste of Traveller vengeance first."

***

PJ stood at the side of the bed, holding Marina's hand. She was in full-blown labour, and the entire labour ward knew it. He felt faint. The delivery room was no place for a man.

Maeve eyed him. "Boy, you've gone pale. Go outside with your father and get some air. I'll stay with—"

Marina's voice echoed off the light-green walls of the delivery room as she gripped the rails of the bed and let out another guttural, primal roar. "I swear to God, if you ever touch me with that thing again, I'll rip it off."

PJ stood dead still, a pale, sweating shadow of the man who'd once survived a broken ankle without flinching. This, though, *this* was different. "I… I—"

"Enough," Maeve said. "Now take yourself outside. This is no place for a man."

"But—"

"Out!" Marina barked. Her glare left no room for negotiation.

PJ, green around the gills, stumbled backwards and over towards the door. He turned just before leaving, and that's when it happened. He caught sight of it. With Marina's legs akimbo, this round thing was poking out of his wife's fanny. His mouth dropped open. He made a sort of strangled honking noise like a goose in distress…and then he dropped like a sack of spuds with a thud.

The midwife turned. "Is he all right?"

"Ignore him, she's the one having a baby," Maeve yelled.

"But he's not moving," another nurse said, crouching beside PJ's crumpled form.

"That's because he's a fecking eejit," Maeve barked, then pointed back towards her daughter-in-law. "Now unless he's crowning, too, I suggest you lot focus on the woman actually having a human come out of her body!"

A porter rushed in and dragged PJ out of the room, closing the door behind him.

The midwife glanced at the nurse then up at Maeve. "Right, yes, sorry."

Marina gave one last tremendous push, and out popped a perfect, wailing baby boy. PJ had a son.

"There we are. And not a man in sight when it mattered most." Maeve smiled.

***

It was early next morning. John Jo had been told Sean Paul was still in the hospital wing, drifting between sleep and pain. He'd sat at the end of his bed for hours, elbows on knees, teeth grinding. No tears. Just silence. Something behind his eyes had gone flat, not grief, not fear, just still. Like deep water before a storm. Terrence sat at the table, also in silence.

Ted entered the cell. Sat on the other chair, hands heavy on his thighs. "I know who helped Brian."

John Jo didn't look up. "Names?"

"Ben and Mark. Bit players. Ran distractions while Brian moved in. Paid in cigarettes."

"I fucking hate those two little pricks," Terrence said, his voice dripping pure malice.

John Jo stood. "Time to pay them a visit."

Ted grunted approval. "I'll cover the halls, keep everyone distracted."

The kettle in the wing kitchen was already steaming by the time John Jo slipped in with the sugar. He poured it in, watching the water thicken to a syrupy lava. The guards on that end of the block were lazy, used to things running smooth on this wing. It would stay that way for the next ten minutes. In prison, revenge wasn't just about rage. It was about sending a clear message.

With mugs in hand, John Jo and Terrence nodded to the screws then sauntered past them. They continued up onto the top-floor landing, eyeing the cells.

Ted stood against the railings and nodded to the half-open door. "In there."

John Jo grabbed the other mug from Terrence and kicked the door fully open. The two men scrambled to their feet.

"What's the meaning of—"

John Jo threw the contents of the first cup. Ben screamed out as he was hit on the chin and neck. Boiling sugar stuck fast. It clung to skin, thick and blistering, crawling with pain deeper than boiling water alone. He writhed, tearing at his shirt, making it worse.

Mark lunged, but John Jo was faster. A second pour caught his shoulder and jaw. He hit the bunk screaming, kicking like an animal set alight.

"You picked the wrong side," he hissed. "You don't touch family."

They left the cell.

Terrence yanked the door shut behind them. "You need to lie low now."

"Do you reckon they'll talk?" John Jo asked. Did he really care? No.

"No. They know better than that." Ted grabbed the mugs. "Go sit in the mess, I'll get rid of these."

Terrence pulled out a chair and sat. "Well, lad, I don't think you'll be getting any trouble from anyone else. By morning, you'll be a fucking legend."

***

216

Millie lay back on the sofa, her feet resting on Tommy Lee's lap so he could massage them. With only a week until the move, the place was looking sparse. The twins were nestled in their cots, soundo, and the pair enjoyed a quiet evening together. It was a rare occasion. However, Millie knew he was keeping an eye on her. She had complained, telling him she was fine now to carry on life as normal, but since the doctor had demanded she rest, he had taken it quite literal. She was fed up. He wouldn't let her lift anything or go anywhere without him. The only place he would leave her was with his mother.

"Are you excited, about the move?" she said, her eyes closed. "God, that feels good."

"I'm looking forward to having our own place. I've never felt right here, you know that."

"I realised that when you bought the new bed and sofa. This—" The phone stopped her.

"Now what?" Tommy Lee lifted her legs so he could stand. He marched out, into the hallway.

Millie tried to listen in, but he wasn't saying much. He appeared a few minutes later.

"Who was it?"

"Barrett. Apparently Brian was in court today charged with Sean Paul's attack. He's been given another six months and moved to a different nick."

"That's good..." She trailed off when Tommy Lee glared at her.

"How is that good?" He paced the floor. "Now he can pop back up when he feels like it and we won't have a warning."

Millie patted the seat next to her. "Sit."

Once he had sat, she continued. "Right, first off, it means John Jo and Sean Paul can't retaliate; we both know that's what they've planned. Secondly, Barrett can find out where he's sent and we can sort someone to take him out or be waiting for when he gets out... There's always options."

"I want to be the one to do it. My brothers will want to be there, too."

"Barrett can give us all the information, it just means you need to be patient." She grabbed his hand and placed it on her tummy. "Can you feel that?"

"Cuthbert's kicking." He laughed.

"He's not being called Cuthbert." She giggled. "He'll be bullied all his life."

"No one will ever bully my boys...their mother would kill them."

"Indeed I would. So, early night?" She grinned. "After all, the doctor did say I need more bed rest."

He stood and pulled her up. "You just can't keep your hands off me."

That was true, but she also knew how to take his mind away from his problems.

CHAPTER 31

3rd June 1979

The day of the move had arrived. The sun was shining and the air warm. Everything was packed, and the twins were in the Range Rover. Millie's car had already been taken over by Scott, who was then heading to the gym. Tommy Lee stood at the bottom of the stairs waiting for her to come down. She'd already checked every room twice to make sure nothing had been left behind.

"Mil, are you ready?" he shouted up.

"Just coming," she called back.

He watched her waddle down the stairs. "You okay, darling?" He wrapped his arm around her shoulders.

She nodded. "Come on, we've got a lot of unpacking to do the other end."

"You're not doing it, not in your condition." He stared at the huge baby bump. With only four weeks to go, he wouldn't let her lift a finger.

"One more quick check?" She gazed into the front room.

"Everything's gone, darling."

"Mummy," Tommy boy called from the motor, quickly followed by a "Mummy," from baby Duke. Now they were walking and talking they were a right bleedin' handful.

"Right, are we finally ready, Mrs Ward?" Tommy Lee asked again.

"Yeah. You lock up." She glanced up at the house. "We've had some good times here."

"And we'll have good times at the new house, just like here," he reminded her. "Get in the motor, we can drop the keys off on the way through." He locked the door then joined her. "Hopefully they'll have everything in by the time we get there."

He glanced at her. She seemed away with the fairies.

"It's good of your mother and father to come and help," he continued. "Millie?" He reached out and squeezed her thigh.

"Sorry, what?" she asked.

"What are you thinking about?" Sparking the engine to life, he reversed the Range Rover out onto the road. "You were miles away."

"Just thinking about my parents moving to Kent… It hurt, when they left."

"I know, but you know why Duke did it."

"Yeah, he thought he was doing the right thing… Anyway, we're gonna be busy for the next few days, getting everything put away and in order." She smiled. "Hopefully all will be sorted by the time this one comes."

Tommy Lee smiled. "I reckon it's a girl." He veered in outside the estate agent's.

"Boy, I reckon, and he's not being named Cuthbert." She glanced around at the high street. "It feels strange to be leaving here."

"We'll come back to visit Finn. What's important is that we're all together. Right, I'll hand the keys in, unless you want to do it?" He jangled them in front of her.

"No, you do it." She pushed them away, then pointed over her shoulder. "And hurry. These two will want feeding soon."

***

When they arrived at the new house, Maeve and Connie came bounding out to greet them.

"Jaysus, the mother and mother-in-law." Tommy Lee grinned. "Looks like you'll be putting your feet up after all."

"I've not even stepped out the car yet and I'm already being managed," Millie muttered. She tried to swing her legs out with the grace of a woman eight months pregnant and entirely sick of being treated like she was made of glass.

Connie and Maeve each helped a twin out of the back, cooing and fussing like it was the Queen's official visit, and ushered them inside with a trail of chocolate, juice, and threats to "mind your feet!" and "stop licking your brother!"

Millie watched on in disbelief. Paddy and PJ where manoeuvring the display cabinet out of the truck and towards the house. Marina stood near the door, baby Patrick cradled in her arms, surveying the madness with the serene exhaustion of a new mother running on two hours' sleep and sheer will.

"Is the whole family here?" Millie asked.

"Yep. All here so you don't need to do anything," Tommy Lee said smugly.

"Oh my God, they're gonna drop that!" She pointed towards the cabinet. Then the noise of breaking glass followed.

Paddy let out a war cry. "Lift, PJ! Lift!"

"I am lifting, you donkey! It's stuck on the lip!"

Then Duke appeared. "To the left a fraction." He motioned.

Millie sighed. "Do you think any of the furniture's gonna make it in unscathed?" She glanced at Tommy Lee. "This is more like a sketch from the three stooges."

Maeve stuck her head out the door. "Tea's on, and tell Paddy if he drops one more thing, I'm dropping him."

Millie turned to Tommy Lee, his face a picture of regret.

"Maybe we should have got proper removals." He shrugged.

Millie burst out laughing. "What, and miss this treat." She roared. "I've never seen anything so funny in all my life."

"But the furniture?" He broke into a smile.

"Fuck the furniture, we'll buy more. Welcome to our new home, what will be left of it, who knows." She giggled.

***

The sun was just dipping behind the flats as PJ turned the corner onto the quieter end of Dagenham, away from the moving boxes and prying eyes of his family. He walked with his hands shoved in his jacket pockets, head down, cap pulled low. He didn't belong in this part of the world, the part where secrets danced heavy in the shadows and the air smelled of aftershave and pipe smoke, where glances lasted too long and names weren't always exchanged. After weeks of ducking out to meet men and one man in particular, PJ had decided to end this sordid way of life. He had a son to think of now, and he would always come first.

That said, it hadn't been an easy decision. He'd had many sleepless nights, tossing and turning, while fighting his demons, but all thoughts led back to baby Patrick. His boy, his namesake, his son.

He spotted the man straight away, leaning against the wall outside the club with a cigarette that hadn't been lit and a stare that could pin a man to his bed. He was dressed in black jeans and a soft grey jumper, shirt collar poking out just enough to appear smart but effortless. He always appeared that way, effortless. Like he knew exactly who he was and had never had to apologise for it. Unlike PJ.

He paused a few feet away.

"Thanks for coming," the man said, calm.

PJ nodded, didn't smile. "Didn't feel right not to."

The club behind them was quiet, the clink of glasses and muffled laughter leaking through the open door. PJ remembered the first night he'd walked into that place. Nervous. Curious. Excited. Needing to feel something that wasn't an obligation. That was when they had met.

"It's been a few weeks," the man said. "Thought maybe you'd just disappeared."

"I've had a lot going on," PJ mumbled.

"I heard… Congrats on the baby." There was no bitterness in his tone, just something tired and worn, almost sadness.

"Yeah. He's perfect," PJ said, and meant it. "Looks like me but got his mother's lungs."

The man smiled.

Then PJ cleared his throat. "I didn't come here to talk about the baby. I came to say it's over, all of it. We can't… I can't do this anymore."

There, he'd said it. It sounded so much more final saying it out loud.

"Because of him?" the man asked.

"Because of all of it," PJ said. "Because I've got a son now. Because I've got a family who, no matter how complicated, love me. And because I've never been the man you deserve. I don't even know if I ever knew how to be."

"You were enough when you were with me," the man said softly.

PJ stared down at his boots. "I was hiding when I was with you." He paused briefly. "I wanted to believe there was a world where both things could exist, where I could be with you and be a dad and not feel like I was tearing myself apart. But I can't. And I won't do this behind closed doors anymore."

"So that's it then?" The man shrugged.

"So that's it," PJ agreed.

"Figures I'd fall for the guy who can't stay." A sigh. "You know you can't fight who you are. Someday you'll need this again. It's in you, it's who you are."

"I'm sorry," PJ whispered. "I need to go."

Then he turned and walked away, heart beating somewhere between regret and relief, already hearing baby Patrick's wail in his memory like a compass calling him home. For once he'd done the right thing, although a little voice at the back of his mind said different.

***

The day had been exhausting. Millie pulled the covers back and slid into bed, Tommy Lee joining her minutes later.

"Today was eventful," She did her best to get comfortable. "Oh fuck."

"What?" Tommy Lee sat up. "Why's the bed wet?"

"My waters just broke...call your mum." Millie scooted over to the edge of the bed, the pain hitting her suddenly.

"But you're not due for another month?" he mumbled.

It took one look from her and Tommy Lee flew out of the door, stark naked. His footsteps clambered down the stairs.

She flopped back, holding her belly. "Hurry up," she yelped.

He appeared minutes later. "Mother's on her way, so is yours." He grabbed his jogging bottoms and yanked them on.

"What? You shouldn't have phoned my mum, it's too far to come." She yelped, the stomach cramps causing her to groan. "Oh God, I'd forgotten how much it hurts."

Tommy Lee rubbed her arm. This was the most annoying thing he'd ever done.

"Stop fucking touching me."

"Jaysus Christ, Mil, I'm trying to help, and keep your voice down, you'll wake the twins." He backed away when her face turned purple, then he paced the room.

"Will you keep still," she growled.

"Where are they?" he muttered.

"Oh no." She squirmed. "The baby's coming."

"What? It can't." He gasped.

"How long did the ambulance say they'd be?" She glanced up at him, his face blank. "You did call for an ambulance?"

"You told me to call Mother—and you said you were having the baby at home!" He swallowed.

"Fucking hell, Tommy Lee, are you the fourth stooge?" she said.

"I'll do it now." He disappeared from the room.

Maeve appeared at the doorway. "What's all the fuss," she said gently. "Come on, girl, you've had twins, you know the ropes."

"Where's the ambulance?" Millie fought another contraction.

"Don't know. Anyway, you wanted the baby at home, looks like you've got your wish." Maeve lifted the covers and checked. "Tommy Lee!" she bellowed. "Get hot water and clean towels, two lengths of string and scissors, this baby is about to make its entrance into the world."

"Oh God, I wanna push," Millie said just as Tommy Lee entered the room.

"Son," Maeve said, "this isn't for men's eyes, wait downstairs."

"Oh no you fucking don't," Millie hissed. "This is the second time you've done this to me, you can stay and bastard well watch."

He stood perfectly still, not even blinking.

"Okay, Millie, when you feel the urge to push, then push," Maeve soothed. "Looks like this one is in a hurry."

With a deep breath, she began to push, only stopping to throw the odd fuck around the room.

"Good, now pant, girl." Maeve did something down below, Millie couldn't see what.

"I need to push again," she whispered, her energy spent.

"Wait until I say," Maeve warned. "Okay, push."

Millie placed her chin on her chest and pushed with such a roar the twins started to cry. "Sorry," she muttered. Another contraction hit, and once it passed, Millie, drenched in sweat, pushed down one more time.

"Baby's nearly here, one more push," Maeve urged.

"I can't," Millie sobbed. "I can't."

"Yes you can, Mil." Tommy Lee stepped forward. "One more push, darling."

Millie pushed with a scream. Then a tiny cry of the newborn sounded.

"You have a baby daughter," Maeve said while tying the cord twice then making the snip. "My first granddaughter." She wrapped the baby in a towel and handed her to Tommy Lee. "Congratulations, son. I'll give you a minute and see to the twins."

He perched on the edge of the bed and placed the baby in Millie's arms. "You did it, darling."

She gazed down and smiled. "She looks like the twins when they were born. Have you thought of a name?"

"Yeah, I'd already picked one," he said, gazing at his daughter.

"Okay, what is it?"

"Millie Mae." He smiled.

CHAPTER 32

It was a glorious summer day in Romford. Finn perched on the edge of the bed, smiling down at Millie Mae. "She's adorable, isn't she, Brenda?"

"The most perfect little bundle," she agreed.

"Right, I'm gonna head downstairs and see Tommy Lee. I'll leave you ladies to gossip, I mean chat," he corrected and edged out of the door.

He continued down the stairs and into the kitchen where Tommy Lee was making the tea. "A woman's work is never done." He grinned.

Tommy Lee laughed. "At least I'm not left with the housework. Connie's been a godsend."

"Where is she?" Finn grabbed the cup that was offered to him.

"Her and Duke have gone shopping. They've taken the twins with them; they're gonna be fecking knackered by the time they get back. I did warn them." Tommy Lee shrugged.

"They'll manage just fine. Anyway, Millie was talking about a man who's been giving you some trouble."

"Yeah, Brian Ramblin. He seems to have come from nowhere and with no reason to target me." Tommy Lee slid onto a chair at the kitchen table. "She thought you may know something, like is he related to Eddie?"

"Jaysus, boy, you're going back before my time here." Finn sipped his tea and thought hard. "Now remember this is just hearsay, speculation, as such. I did hear Eddie had a son. He and his missus moved down here with the nipper when he got a job with Cole. Cole being a major player meant he'd be earning good. Jump forward three years, Cole's banged up in prison and Eddie's banged up in his boss's bed banging his missus. All fecking complicated. Anyway, as I'd already told you, Eddie took over Cole's identity, his business, and his wife. His own wife and child kicked to the kerb." Finn scratched his head. "The nipper must have only been seven or eight when his mother took him back up Birmingham way."

"Birmingham?" Tommy Lee nodded. "That would fit, but why go after me when it's his father who let him down?"

"People with past trauma do funny things, lad. Maybe it's a case of getting the love from his daddy or respect even?" Finn said, "Just remember, men like this are dangerous. They have warped logic."

"You're telling me if he's after love from a dead man."

The front door sprang open, and in flew the twins with a worn-out-looking Duke trying to grab them.

"I've got to say, Tommy Lee, when you said they're a handful, I think you under exaggerated." He flopped onto a seat and exhaled.

"Grandad duties, hey, Duke." Finn laughed. "Anyway, fellas, I'll grab Brenda and get out of your way." He walked to the kitchen door then turned. "Remember what I said, Tommy Lee. Warped."

***

228

The afternoon sun beat down on the men in the yard. It wasn't often they got to go outside, but when they did, all they had to look at was the tall brick walls. Barbed wire ran around the top just in case anyone could scale them. John Jo, Sean Paul, Terrence, and Ted walked back in towards the mess hall, their time slot over. Taking a seat in the corner, John Jo produced the cards.

"Game, anyone?" he said and shuffled.

The men muttered their agreement, and he dealt the hands with methodical precision, the same way he did everything, slow, careful, nothing left to chance.

"Right." He slapped down the deck. "Five-card draw. No looking at anyone else's hand, Sean, you toerag."

"I don't cheat!" Sean grinned, already peeking sideways at Ted's cards.

"You just use creative interpretation of the rules," John Jo muttered with a roll of his eyes.

Ted leaned back in his chair, holding his cards close. "Never mind cheating at cards, you should be more worried about getting beat up."

"Oi!" Sean Paul said. "That was one time, and he caught me off guard, for God's sake."

"Play the hand," Terrence said. "And shut up."

The game carried on in mostly silence for a few minutes, each man focused, eyes narrowed, the scrape of cards and shuffle of sleeves the only sounds. A small transistor radio in the corner buzzed with static and old soul music. Someone down the corridor was singing, off-key and loud, the noise getting louder as the man approached.

"Put a fucking sock in it, mate," Terrence yelled.

The man stopped and whispered in John Jo's ear. Ted stood. The man walked away.

"What's that all about?" Terrence whispered.

John Jo spoke, low and flat. "Tommy Lee's found him... He's in Wormwood Scrubs."

The sound of cards hitting the table followed as each man threw them down.

"We can't do fuck all from in here," Sean Paul said.

Ted coughed. "I know a few lads on rotation down there, one in D-wing. Proper silent type, don't talk unless paid. But if you want something that sticks...we'll need more than a punch in the yard."

John Jo cracked his knuckles. "No. This is a job for us. I want him to feel it. Not just in his ribs... I want him to look us in our eyes when we take him out."

They picked up their cards again, the game resuming. John Jo knew he'd have to speak with Tommy Lee to make sure he didn't do anything before they got the chance.

***

Tommy Lee stood on the edge of the docks, just outside the office. The sun shone low as it began to set, showing long glistening ripples on the River Thames. The smell of the salt air reminded him of his childhood.

Most of Millie's men had packed up for the day with only Tony and a couple left tidying up.

"You fancy a brew?" Tony called from the door of the office.

Tommy Lee turned and followed him in, taking a seat at Millie's desk. One that she wouldn't be coming back to if he could help it.

"So how's mother and baby doing?" Tony said while clanking cups.

"Both doing well. Where's Rosie?" Tommy Lee glanced around. She was always by Tony's side. Tommy Lee used to joke to Millie that they were Velcroed together.

Tony shrugged with a growl. "Fucking driving lessons. Judging by the way she drove off, it's gonna cost me thousands."

Tommy Lee laughed. "Women want to be independent these days... Anyway, you know why I'm here."

"Yeah, so Finn thinks it could be Eddie's son. Makes sense in a twisted way. So what do you want to do?" Tony handed him a mug.

"I've got Barrett checking for the release date. I want men there to grab him. I can't do it myself, he knows me and my brothers." Tommy Lee placed the mug on the desk. "We'll need a van with false plates, four men to nab him, and a driver. These all need to be people he's never seen."

Tony leaned back against his desk. "John Jo and Sean Paul know the score?"

Tommy Lee gave a nod.

"Then when the time comes, I'll make sure you have everything you need. Millie said someone new will be starting here in a few months. Terrence?"

"Yeah, he's been looking out for my brothers. She seems to think he'll be an asset."

"And you?" Tony asked.

"Jury's still out." He drained the rest of his mug then stood. "I best be getting back to the madhouse."

Tony laughed. "That bad?"

"We've got Connie and Duke staying for a few more days, and my mother is over every morning to see her first granddaughter. She turns up with bags of dresses for Millie Mae, and half of them are three- to four-year-old sizes because she's bought all the firstborn, one-year-olds, and two-year-olds. I think she's bought the entire stock of Romford Market. The stall holders must rub their hands together when they see her coming… I'll tell you, that little girl has got everyone eating out of the palm of her hand and she doesn't even know it." He paused at the door. "I'll see you soon."

ʌʌʌ

Duke surveyed the ground. It was a tidy size, with three bases already set, one for a mobile and two for tourers. Electric was run, drainage and water. It was ready to move onto. He glanced over to what would have been a paddock, easy enough to take the fencing out. The stables could be used as storage, full doors put on them. There was one brick shed. He mooched towards it. Inside it housed a toilet, a shower, and was piped for a washing machine. The place was perfect. He'd be close enough to Millie without being too close, and there was room for Jasper and Arron to move on. He knew

Connie would love it. It was bigger and better than the ground he owned now.

He turned to Paddy who stood at his side. "Okay, let's talk pound notes."

***

Duke returned to Tommy Lee and Millie's, a huge smile on his mush. He walked to the back door and let himself into the kitchen.

Tommy Lee looked up when he entered. "How did you get on?"

"It's a nice piece of ground. Bigger than the one in Kent." He paused. "I've bought it. Just got to sell my land and then we'll be moving."

"You shouldn't have trouble selling that. You going to tell her now?" Tommy Lee flicked his head to the door.

"Do you think she'll be happy?" Duke said with a sudden feeling of wariness. "I don't want to upset her."

"She'll be made up, trust me." Tommy Lee grinned. "Go on, she's on her own."

Duke trod slowly up the stairs. He was excited; would she be? He pushed open the door.

Millie sat up in bed holding Millie Mae. "Dad…you all right?" She frowned.

"I've got some news…"

"Blimey, it's been a day for news. Did you know Finn and Brenda are getting married, and Rosie's pregnant?" She smiled. "Hope yours is as good as theirs."

"So do I," he mumbled.

"Go on then, tell me." She patted the bed next to her.

He sat on the edge and took a deep breath then blurted it out as quickly as he could. "We're moving to Essex."

"What, whereabouts?" she asked.

"I've bought Paddy's ground just outside Basildon." He glanced at her then turned away. "I know I left you before, and not a day goes by that I don't regret it, so now me and your mother want to be closer."

"That's gre—"

"I know you felt let down," he continued.

"No, Dad, it—"

"I'm hoping this will make it up to you," he finished.

"Dad," she yelled.

He turned to face her.

"I said it's great news, or I tried to… What happened back then. Can we please leave it in the past and move on, after all, it was as much my fault as anyone's."

His mouth twitched into a smile. "You think it's a good idea?"

"Of course I do."

"You're not annoyed or angry?" he checked.

"Of course I'm not. It will be great to have you both here, and Nelson. I feel like I don't know him well enough, considering he's my baby brother."

"Well, that's a relief." He stretched across the bed to peck her on the forehead. "You do realise Jasper and Arron will be moving with us?"

"Yes, and it will be nice to see them more often, too," she assured him.

"I best go tell your mother then." He winked and left the room.

***

The cell was quiet. Not the good kind of quiet either, not peaceful or still. It was the brittle kind. The kind where every drip from a leaking tap, every cough from the next block over, and every scuff of boots in the corridor made your skin tighten like you were wrapped in clingfilm.

Brian lay on his bunk, hands behind his head, staring at the ceiling where the old paint had cracked into hairline veins. His mattress was thin, the pillow a joke, and the cell too warm even at night. Summer in the Scrubs was a different kind of punishment. But it wasn't the heat keeping him awake. It was the waiting.

He'd kept his head down since arriving. No big talk. No eye contact. His usual bravado replaced with something leaner, more careful. The guards barely noticed him. The inmates didn't know his name yet. And he intended to keep it that way.

He closed his eyes, took a breath, willing sleep to come. Then he heard it. A whisper of movement.

He sat up, muscles tense.

Silence.

He swung his legs off the bunk and padded across the concrete floor. The cell door was locked, the bolts heavy. No shadows under it. But there was something else. Barely visible. A piece of folded paper. He picked it up and held it close to the window so he could see from the light of the full moon. His heart thudded. There were only seven words written on it.

Tommy Lee can't wait to meet you.

Brian stood frozen to the spot for a full ten seconds, reading the words again and again, his mouth suddenly dry. It wasn't signed. It didn't need to be. He staggered back a step and sat on the edge of the bunk. The paper trembled slightly in his grip. He stared at it like it might catch fire or crawl up his arm. He'd been moved. He'd thought he was safe. But somehow, even in this place, behind bars, with walls thicker than history, he had found him. He knew where he was. Not only would Tommy Lee be waiting if he got out, he had someone on the inside ready to do his bidding.

CHAPTER 33

14th August

The Range Rover kicked up a plume of dust as it rolled off the main road and onto the gravel driveway that led to home. The sun was high, glinting off motor roofs and plastic chairs, warming the metal of the trailers and the coloured balloons strung haphazardly between fence posts. It was nearing the end of August, and the heat clung to everything still. By the time the Range Rover doors opened, half the family was already waiting at the gate. Kids ran barefoot on the grass, dogs barked with excitement, and somewhere, someone had a cassette recorder playing country songs.

John Jo was the first to step out. He wore clean clothes and a great big smile. It was good to be home.

The cheer went up instantly.

"Oi, look who it is!" shouted Maeve, charging forward like a kid at a funfair. "It's good to have you home, son." She wrapped her arms around him and squeezed.

He pulled apart and spied Gypsy. She was holding the baby. He rushed forward and held her. "Jaysus, I've missed you."

"I've missed you, too—too much. Don't you go getting yourself locked up again, John Jo Ward, or there'll be trouble."

Sean Paul was lunged at before his feet touched the ground. Shirley Ann and his sons hugged him.

Maeve elbowed through with a tray of sliced bacon pudding. "Eat now, jokes later. You need fattening up before your women start pawing at ya."

As the boys were pulled into hugs, back slaps, and mock arguments about who owed who a drink, it became clear to John Jo the welcome home party wasn't going to be a quiet affair.

He took a cold can from a tub full of melting ice and sat on an upturned crate, soaking it in, the voices, the music, the sound of home. Gypsy sat next to him. There was something about the way the sun hit tarmac and the smell of meat and onions frying that made everything feel familiar again. Like time hadn't passed. Like he hadn't spent the last seven months planning revenge in a room with no door handle.

"Hey," Millie said as she joined them with Tommy Lee by her side. "Glad to have you back."

"Glad to be back," he said. "Gypsy, give us a minute."

He waited for her to leave, then focused on Tommy Lee. "So what's happening with that prick?"

"He's being watched, and taunted," Tommy Lee said. "Barrett will let me know when he's due for release, then I'll get him picked up, taken somewhere, and we can finish him off."

John Jo nodded. "So how's that niece of mine?"

"Mother's got her, showing her off to the aunties. First girl and all that." Tommy Lee rolled his eyes. "Keeps going on how she delivered Millie Mae, like she did all the work and Millie just watched. Think she forgets I were there also."

"At least you didn't pass out like PJ." John Jo laughed. "Talking about PJ...any problems?"

"No, he's knocked all that other stuff on the head, reckons he wants to be the best father possible for Patrick." Tommy Lee glanced at his mother as she paraded his daughter around. "Jaysus fecking Christ, the child's gonna think she's a celebrity."

"I best go and rescue her, she'll need feeding, and that's one job your mother can't do." Millie hurried away.

"So," John Jo began. "This fecking prick is actually going to get his comeuppance?"

"Yeah, it's going to happen." Tommy Lee sat next to him.

John Jo smiled as the sun blazed above, and the smell of bacon pudding, steak, and cheap lager drifted around the ground. They were home. And for the first time in months, no one was counting the days, and the only bars now were on the gate. And as for Brian, until his release, John Jo would plot his end. It would be slow and painful, he was certain of that.

***

Brian sat in his cell, listening, watching. Any sound, any movement, and he twitched. The days were long, the nights longer. He eyed everyone with suspicion. The other inmates, the screws, even the governor. They were all plotting against him.

It hadn't always been like this. When he'd first landed inside the Scrubs, he'd kept his head down, played it smart. But that kind of quiet only made him a target. The cons smelled it on him, fear, uncertainty. They picked at him like wolves circling. It started small. A stolen blanket here. A shove in the lunch line. A whispered threat in the shower block. Then came the real games. Someone had slipped glass into his toothpaste. Not enough to kill him, just enough to shred his gums and make every swallow taste like metal. Another time, they soaked his mattress in piss while he was in the yard. Even the screws laughed at that one. And then he was sure he'd heard Tommy Lee's name whispered in his ear.

Now he counted the steps of the guards as they paced. He memorised the coughs of the inmates on his block. He was moved to a single cell, for his own protection, but the long silences, the loneliness, the lack of sleep, it all made him worse. He was certain they were still watching. From the peephole. From the air vent. Even through the concrete. Sometimes, he whispered threats to the corners, just in case someone was listening.

The paranoia had set in, and it was driving him crazy.

***

Millie approached Maeve, who was now sitting with her sister, Lena, and a few other women. "I'll need to feed—" She paused. "You've changed her dress."

Maeve grinned. "Couldn't resist seeing what she looked like in this. Ain't she handsome?"

Millie grimaced. Her daughter now looked like she belonged on top of a Christmas tree. "Yes, proper handsome, but don't you think she'll be a bit warm in all those layers of lace?"

Maeve waved her away. "She's fine here in the shade."

Millie swooped down and grabbed her daughter. "I'll take her to meet her two uncles then I'll go into Gypsy's and feed her."

She began walking back towards Tommy Lee and John Jo. Sean Paul had now joined them.

"Here she is," Tommy Lee said as Millie handed their baby daughter to him. "Millie Mae, meet your uncles."

"Ain't she a beauty," Maeve called from over Millie's shoulder.

Millie blew out slowly. Her mother-in-law was never far away from the baby. Whilst Millie understood it was her first granddaughter, the first girl born in three generations, and the woman was excited and thrilled, she still needed to back off.

Millie Mae squirmed and let out a small cry. She was hungry.

"I need to feed her." Millie reached for the baby.

"I'll come with you," Tommy Lee said. Had he sensed the tension in Millie's voice?

They walked back towards Gypsy and John Jo's mobile, side by side, in silence. He opened the door and waited for her to go in.

"You okay?" He stepped in behind her.

"Yeah. I don't mean to be grumpy, but your mother is a bit over the top with Millie Mae. Look, she's even changed her dress." She nodded.

"I did notice." He laughed. "Let her have her moment; after all, she's waited years for a girl." He locked the door. "I've got to make a phone call."

"About Brian?" she said and manoeuvred the baby onto her breast.

"Yeah, I want them to leave him alone for a few weeks, lull him into a false sense of security." He turned and headed to the kitchen.

***

It was now early evening. John Jo and Sean Paul sat with PJ, all three munching on a plate of food.

"I'm stuffed." Sean Paul placed his plate down. He glanced at PJ. "So how's life as a father?"

"Best thing ever." PJ wiped his mouth with the back of his hand. "Every time I see his little face my heart does a flip."

"So no more…" John Jo left the last word unsaid.

"No," PJ said firmly. "I've been concentrating on the cobs, building a future for my family."

"That's good to hear." Sean Paul stood. "When do you think people will start leaving? I want some alone time with Shirley Ann."

"You best go and take her indoors, no one will notice," John Jo said. "I've already had Gypsy in the bedroom."

"Give us your plates," PJ said. "I'll take them in." He rose, grabbing the crockery.

Sean Paul waited for him to leave, and when he was out of earshot, he leaned into his brother and whispered, "Do you believe him?"

John Jo sighed. "I want to but…"

"But he couldn't make eye contact. Looks like we'll have to watch him," Sean Paul said. "After all, didn't Millie say it was something he couldn't control?"

CHAPTER 34

Millie sat in the Range Rover eyeing Tommy Lee. He'd been acting weird all morning. She spun around to check the chavvies were strapped in and behaving.

"So this surprise, I'm going to like it?" she quizzed and turned back around. "Is it something you've bought?"

"You do know what a surprise is?" he asked. "Now stop asking questions and put your seat belt on."

He started the motor and reversed out of the drive.

"Where are we going?" She glanced at him; he was smiling but didn't reply. She stared out of the passenger window, the houses a blur as they passed. "Are we going to your brothers'?"

"Millie...just wait," he mumbled. "All will become clear in ten minutes."

She huffed and folded her arms, watching Tommy Lee like a hawk. Something was up. He was tapping the steering wheel like it owed him money and humming along to the radio, which he never did. The kids were quiet in the back, thankfully, with Millie Mae asleep and the twins holding their toy cars tightly in their hands like treasure.

"Ten minutes, you said," she muttered then glanced at her watch.

"Nearly there," he said, eyes fixed on the road ahead.

The Range Rover rolled through Basildon, the way they used to drive to his parents'.

"Where the hell are we going?" She craned her neck to look around. "This ain't your brothers'."

"Millie," he said, while he lowered the radio, "I'm serious. Just wait."

He turned the car onto a familiar gravel road. Ahead, the road opened up into a stretch of land Millie hadn't seen for a while.

Her stomach fluttered. "This is my dad's ground… Is that…?" She gasped.

Tommy Lee nodded. "Yep."

"But that's—"

He grinned, cutting the engine. "They moved on last night. Quiet. Didn't want a big fuss, and they wanted to surprise you. They're finally here. This is their home now, Mil."

Her dad stepped out first, in a vest and joggers, and her mum came behind, wiping her hands on a tea towel.

Millie's throat caught. "I don't believe it. He said he was going to move back, but I didn't believe him."

"Told you you'd like the surprise," Tommy Lee whispered. He kissed her cheek as she wiped a tear from her eye.

She nodded slowly, a soft smile breaking through. "Yeah… I bloody love it."

"Come on in, I've put the kettle on," Connie called. "Second thoughts, let's sit outside, it's starting to warm up in there even with the doors and windows open."

Arron appeared from around the side, carrying his daughter. "Hello, stranger." He grinned and brought Millie into a one-armed hug.

"It's not been that long," she mumbled against his chest. "So the whole family moved?"

"Jasper and Sherry have gone to the shop, they shouldn't be long." Duke placed Nelson down. "Connie, get me a beer, it's too hot for tea."

"Dad, it's only ten-thirty," Millie reminded him.

"When did you turn into me mother?" he groused. "Do you want a beer, Tommy Lee?"

"No thanks, tea will be fine." He winked at Millie. "So, you all settled in?"

"Yeah, got everything fixed last night... The boys are thinking of getting mobiles, so I'll need bigger bases done and more drainage." Duke reached for the beer and took off the top.

"You're definitely staying here then?" Millie asked. "Not gonna take off again in a couple of years?"

"Definitely staying," Duke confirmed. "Especially now we've all got jobs."

Millie glanced at Tommy Lee and then back at Duke. They both acted shifty. "What jobs?"

"I told Duke you needed someone at the docks, and we need some more help collecting monies," Tommy Lee said. "We need trustworthy men, Mil, isn't that what you said?"

"I did, but it would also be nice if I was informed about things first." She sighed.

"How did the welcome home party for your brothers go yesterday?" Duke asked. "Would've come but had this lot to sort."

That was a not-so-swift change of subject. Millie rolled her eyes. "Can you get the pram out? I'll lay Millie Mae down for a bit."

"Let's have a cuddle first." Connie held her arms out. "She's a pretty little thing... Looks like the twins," she added with a loving gaze.

Millie smiled. Yes, she was the image of the twins, which meant she looked like Tommy Lee. It would have been nice to have one child resemble her. "So how have you settled in, Mum?"

"I like it here, more country than Stepney and nearer to you than Kent."

"Hello," Prissy called. She came bounding around the side of the mobile. "How are you?"

Millie hugged her. "All good, thanks. How's everything with you?"

"Same, all good," she said. "Arron, I'll need to go shop soon. The milk spilt in the fridge, and the bread's hard."

"We'll go now," he said. "See yous in a bit." With that, they left.

Millie wheeled the pram into the shade, and Connie laid the baby down.

"She sleeps well." Connie placed a net over to stop any insects from flying in.

"Yeah, she does, only wakes once in the night for a feed, too." Millie sat on a chair next to Duke, with one eye on the twins who were running around like demons. "So tell me more about this work setup."

"I thought your dad and brothers could alternate between the docks and gym. It will also take the pressure off you," Tommy Lee said before Duke had the chance.

"Don't forget Terrence will be at the docks," she reminded him. "And I wouldn't mind giving Ted a job either. Both men have proven themselves."

"Not sure when Ted gets out. I'll get a message to him, see what he says." Tommy Lee nodded.

"What about your brothers?" she said. "I thought you wanted them involved?"

"No. I've changed my mind on that. Your brothers can go with Scott and Dan to collect. Duke can be at the gym full-time, he can help train and keep an eye on things. But in the meantime, they can all help with the docks, just until Terrence is released."

"Sounds like a plan." Duke grinned. "Get us another beer, Connie, seems like we're celebrating."

***

Brian stood in the dinner queue. The clatter of plastic trays and dull drone of conversation filled the canteen with a strange, synthetic warmth. Things had been quiet, too quiet. Had the other inmates now had enough of picking on him? He felt a meaty fist in the small of his back. He lunged forward and hit the con in front.

"What's your fucking game?" the man mountain snarled. He drew his fist back.

"Enough!" A man stepped in between them. "It was an accident...you do know what an accident is?"

Brian watched as the other man backed away.

"My name's Carl," he said, then turned towards him. "You shouldn't put up with shit like that from anyone."

Brian remained quiet, wary.

"Yeah, I get it, you can't trust anyone in these places," Carl continued. He grabbed a tray and held it up for the lunch to be slopped onto. "And they call this food. This is punishment enough for our crimes," he bellowed to the cook.

"If ya don't like it, don't fucking eat it, now move along," the con serving the food bellowed back.

Carl took a seat at a table towards the back of the mess hall, Brian joining him. "So, Mr No Name. How long before you're out?"

Brian sat and as usual began poking at the grey mass that passed for mashed potatoes. "The names Brian, and another four months," he replied cautiously. "How long you got?"

"Three and a half, that's if I make it without trying to kill one of these fuckers." Carl nodded to a table. "See that prick there, he's the cause of most of the trouble in here. Reckons he's untouchable."

They ate in silence for a few minutes. Carl didn't force small talk, didn't ask stupid questions. That alone set him apart from most. Brian had just decided to finish his meal and retreat when the first spoonful of mashed potato hit him in the back of the head.

Snickers erupted from the table behind him. Two boys were watching him like hyenas. Brian tensed, fingers curling into fists.

"Oi!" Carl barked and stood. "You got something to say, say it to me."

That silenced them. For a moment anyway. Brian blinked in disbelief. Carl was standing up for him.

"You his babysitter now, Carl?" one of the young lads jeered, clearly trying to recover.

Carl didn't flinch. "You want to act like a pack of dogs, you can do it somewhere else."

Brian watched, stunned, as the two backed off, grumbling. Carl sat down again and resumed eating like nothing had happened. Finally, he threw his knife and fork down.

"That's me done. Probably have the shits later after eating that crap." Carl stood. "Catch you around."

Brian watched him leave, then followed, keeping back so he didn't clock him. It wasn't until later that he decided to join him at a table.

"Why'd you do that?" He sat next to Carl by the window. "Why did you step in?"

Carl shrugged. "Didn't like the way they were treating you. Simple as that."

Brian studied him. Although Carl seemed genuine, his gut still screamed caution, but just maybe he had found an ally.

***

John Jo sat outside enjoying the sun on his face. He had missed this, the outdoors, the fresh air, and most of all the freedom. He glanced over at Gypsy. She was laying the baby in the pram. He eyed her curves, his thoughts turning to last night. What a welcome home she had given him, lying in bed, bodies entwined. It was a wonder they didn't wake the whole of Wickford, never mind the children.

"Do you want tea?" Gypsy called over.

"Yes, darling, and make us a sandwich." He spun around as the crunching gravel alerted him to a motor driving in. He stood and approached it, smiling when his cousin, Billy, appeared. "Didn't expect to see you so soon."

Billy grinned. "Business stops for no man."

"What business would that be?" John Jo said with a tinge of caution.

Billy pulled out a piece of paper. "I've got a list —"

"No. We won't be doing that no more... I've spoken with Sean Paul, and we're out," John Jo confirmed. "And if you've any sense, you'll do the same."

"Shame when there's so much money to be earned."

"There's more to life than money, Billy boy. Quit while you're ahead. We are going to concentrate on the cobs, there's a good living to be made with a bit of hard work."

"Okay, I can see I won't change your mind. Anyway, I better be going, taking the children to Southend." He dipped back into his car and reversed away.

Gypsy held out a cup of tea and a plate with a ham sandwich and quartered tomato on. "I'm glad you said no," she mumbled.

"I told you, I won't be leaving you again and I meant it. Now give your husband a kiss," he said, his mind drifting to the horses. If it didn't work out with them he could always dip back in the car game.

CHAPTER 35

The summer sun brought a heat to the Scrubs that felt uncomfortable, the lack of air making it difficult to breathe. The stickiness and the smell of body odour seemed to cling to the walls. Brian couldn't stand it.

Days had passed since the incident with Carl, and yet he kept showing up. A seat in the canteen. A shared cigarette in the yard. A word of warning before one of the rats could pull something. Nothing flashy. Just…present.

Brian had watched him like a hawk at first, eyes peeled for cracks in the mask, waiting for the betrayal to come. But it didn't. And slowly, imperceptibly, the tension in his shoulders began to fade. He started to talk more. Not much, not yet — but enough. Jokes. Football. Home. Carl had a sister in Leeds. Brian had once broken a guy's arm outside a pub just outside Leeds docks. Common ground.

By the second week, Carl felt less like a stranger and more like a fixture, someone real in a place where everything felt designed to break you down.

It was Thursday afternoon. Brian sat watching the old television in the mess hall; it was a load of shit on the box but a distraction from time.

Carl joined him, taking a seat beside Brian. "What's this crap they've put on?"

Brian shrugged. "Not really watching it." He glanced at Carl. "What have you got planned, for when you're out? Job, family?"

"Haven't thought much about it other than getting out of this shithole," he said.

"The Scrubs." Brian nodded in agreement.

"No, I mean London… I want to get as far away from here as possible. I know I was brought up here, but it's changed. I might go stay with my sister for a bit, you know, just until I get back on me feet," Carl said. "What about you?"

"Pretty much the same, but first I have a score to settle." Brian grinned. "Gonna hit him fast and hard." He nodded, almost to himself. "I used to think being locked up was the worst thing that could happen to me. But it gave me clarity. Purpose. You ever think like that?"

Carl gave a small, unreadable smile. "Go on."

"This pikey piece of shit took everything from me, things that can never be replaced…" He left out the part that the unreplaceable was a father who wanted nothing to do with him. That didn't matter. Blood was blood.

Carl didn't blink. "And you want payback."

"I don't want revenge," Brian said with a shake of his head. "I want justice."

"Okay," Carl said. "Sounds like you've got this covered… I need a piss, I'll catch you later." He stood and sauntered away.

It pleased Brian that this man asked no questions. He wasn't a plant like he'd first thought. He was a kindred spirit, fed up with the way the world treated people like them. This man he could trust.

***

PJ stood at the till, Marina by his side rocking the pram. He handed over the money and waited for the change. That was when he saw him. His old lover, Pete. He looked away, grabbed the change, and walked out, with one hand on the pram and pushed it faster than Marina could.

"What's the hurry?" She panted.

"Wanna get home, the horses need exercising." He threw a glance over his shoulder and made eye contact.

The smile that appeared on Pete's face disappeared when he spotted Marina.

Shit!

"Thought we were going to have a look around the market?" Disappointment flooded her voice.

"Another day," PJ grunted. His heart beat faster, his mind drifting back to the days he'd spent with him. Carefree and full of fun.

You're a father now. Patrick comes first. He attempted to shove the thoughts away.

Then Patrick began to stir. PJ gazed down at him, his blue eyes and tiny mouth. "You'll always come first," he whispered to the infant.

"What?" Marina muttered.

He took one last look at Pete then turned. "Nothing. Now hurry up, we need to get back."

***

Tommy Lee drove to the docks. He had Duke with him, showing him the ropes. They made their way into the office. The door was wide open along with the windows. Tony sat at his desk mulling over a letter.

"Afternoon," He called out while stepping in. "Seems quiet here. Where is everyone?"

"Gone for lunch… Duke," Tony greeted. "Mil just phoned, said can you pick up some washing powder on your way back."

251

He nodded. "Duke's going to help out until Terrence gets released next month. Did you find out when Ted's out?"

"Not until November. I did ask if he would be interested in a job, said he'll let us know."

Tommy Lee stiffened. "Well, that's gratitude for you." He glanced around the office. "Anything need dealing with?"

"Just these cheques that need signing." Tony handed them to him. "I'll show Duke around."

Tony led him out while Tommy Lee took a seat at the other desk. With only a little over three more months until Brian was released, he needed to find somewhere secluded and out of earshot to take him. It was a job proving harder than he'd thought. Duke had offered his ground, and he knew for a fact John Jo and Sean Paul would let him use theirs, but he wouldn't involve family, not if there was a chance of getting caught.

This needed privacy. Somewhere no one would hear his screams.

***

Brian hadn't trusted anyone in years. Not properly. Was it because his own father had betrayed him? Left him out in the cold while he showered his love and affection on another man's son? No, he never blamed him. In his warped mind he'd always blamed his mum. She was a useless, snivelling mess. No wonder his father had left. It never occurred to him she may have been like that because of him leaving. Leaving her with a young son, no money, no home, nothing. Just a broken heart.

He'd sat on the sidelines for years, watching from a distance. It wasn't until Boxing Day when his father had phoned him, in desperation, that he'd realised he was needed. And needed in his book meant loved.

Carl reminded him of his younger self. Not only willing to fight but knowing when to. He'd slowly grown on Brian.

It wasn't one big gesture. It was the little things, the way he always knew when to show up, the way he never pushed too hard. When the screws hassled Brian for no reason, Carl didn't explode. He just said the right thing to the right person, and somehow the pressure eased. No fuss. No ego. In a place where everyone wanted something, Carl asked for nothing.

They began meeting every evening in the laundry room — quiet, warm, a place forgotten by the prison's usual chaos. They folded sheets and talked. About football. About the outside. About who they were *before* this place. Brian found himself laughing again, sometimes without thinking or forcing.

One afternoon, before lockup, Brian, so no one could hear, whispered, "If I'd met you on the outside, you think we'd have been mates?"

Carl paused before replying. "Probably not. I was a ghost back then. You were noise. But in here? Yeah. I think we're mates."

Brian smiled. Carl was a decent bloke, salt-of-the-earth type, a diamond, a true friend.

Brian passed him a piece of folded paper. "This is who I'm going after. Tommy Lee Ward. Thinks he's a gangster when all he is, is a fucking pikey."

Carl took the piece of paper and scanned the writing. "You need to destroy this, in case someone finds it."

"Good call...just remember that name. If anything happens to me, it will be because of him." Brian took the piece of paper, shoved it into his mouth, and began to chew.

CHAPTER 36

30th September 1979

The air in the discharge room was thick with silence, broken only by the low hum of flickering fluorescent lights. Terrence sat on the hard bench, his hands resting on his knees, calm as stone. He'd been up predawn, wide awake before the screws even came knocking. You don't sleep the night prior to getting out, you just wait for the gates to open.

A heavy-set officer pushed through the side door carrying a clear plastic bag. "Name?"

"Terrence Hill." It had been a while since he'd said that. A reminder of his past.

The officer grunted and dropped the bag on the counter. "Sign for your things."

Terrence stepped forward, picked up the pen with a steady hand, and scrawled his name with the sharp, controlled precision of someone who'd had time, *years*, to think about how this moment would go. Inside the bag: a leather wallet with twenty-seven pounds in it, forty-six pounds, curtesy of HM discharge for resettlement. One silver ring. A chain with a St Christopher medallion. A folded photograph, creased at the corners. Him and Megan, taken five summers ago, back when the lines around their eyes were softer and the streets still felt like home. Back before she'd betrayed him. That was one score he'd settle sooner rather than later.

"You're done," the officer said. "Gate's down the hall."

Terrence nodded. No handshakes. No goodbyes. Just concrete underfoot and steel behind him. He walked through the corridor slowly, gaze flicking along the walls, the posters, the cameras, memorising them like a man who never wanted to see them again. When the final door buzzed open, sunlight spilled through. Outside, Chelmsford Prison looked colder than it had going in. Windy. Flat. But there was life waiting.

A black Range Rover sat idling by the perimeter fence, gleaming under the early September sun. Millie stood by the passenger door, and Tommy Lee leaned against the bonnet. They were laughing. He could see the love they shared, he had spotted it the very first time he'd met them. The way Tommy Lee frequently glanced at her, checking to see if she was okay.

Terrence paused a moment. Then walked towards them. Tommy Lee was the first to spot him, straightening to greet him, hand held out to shake.

"Welcome to normal life," Tommy Lee said while shaking.

"Thought we'd take you for something decent to eat first," Millie added.

Terrence didn't answer right away; instead, he faced the prison. One last look at the place he'd just spent five years in. He turned back and grinned. "Okay, let's go."

***

PJ walked around Romford Market, his eyes peeled. He'd come here on his own today, searching for something he shouldn't. Since seeing Pete last month, he couldn't stop thinking about him. About their time together. He knew he was playing with fire, but just one last time to be in his company. Would Pete feel the same, though? Time had passed. But he'd smiled when he had spotted him, although it had faded quickly. Did he have someone new? Was it any of PJ's business? He ducked into the Lamb public house. He needed a drink.

The jukebox was playing 'I don't like Mondays' by the Boomtown Rats. He wasn't keen on the song but had to agree, Mondays were shite.

"A pint of Guinness, please, mate," he said to the barman.

He paid and then took a seat near to the window. The market was heaving with bargain hunters. Guilt twanged. He'd promised Marina they would come here, and yet he couldn't bring himself to, not with her.

He stared down into his pint. Disheartened. He'd ruined lives before. Tracy, the gorger who he'd got pregnant. Sam, his first lover who'd met his end possibly at the hands of Tommy Lee, although he had no proof. Violet Conners, who he was supposed to marry, her life left in tatters after the farce of a wedding. Pete, who he'd lied to, used and then discarded. But the worst one of all was his son, Patrick. How would he be treated if it came out his father was a poofter? He'd be ridiculed all his life.

PJ looked up when a shadow covered him. Straight into the eyes of Pete.

***

The meal was going down a treat, judging by the way Terrence was ramming it into his gob. Millie glanced at Tommy Lee and smiled.

"This is the best steak I have ever eaten," Terrence said between mouthfuls. "You never truly realise how much you miss something until you have it again, apart from sprouts, I fucking hate

257

them…which reminds me." He leaned forward and whispered, "Any news on Brian?"

"We know where he is, just waiting for his release so we can swoop in and nab him." Millie leaned back against her chair.

"Good… How's John Jo and Sean Paul doing?" Terrence peeked at him.

"They're fine. When you're done here, we'll take you to get settled in at the flat." Tommy Lee studied his watch. "I need to get back to the gym shortly."

"I've got a bit of business to take care of before I start work." Terrence looked between Millie and Tommy Lee. "Personal business."

"That's fine, you'll probably want a week or so to adjust to outside life, I'd imagine," Millie said. "You can get settled into the flat, then when ready, meet Tommy Lee at the gym. Don't leave it too long, though, we've got plenty of men who are after work."

"Understood." Terrence nodded. He placed his cutlery down and grinned. "Okay, let's go. The quicker I settle this business, the quicker I'll be ready for work."

"It's a woman." Millie said, standing. "Can see it in your eyes, they're sad."

"It is." Terrence sighed.

"Don't get caught," she added. Then turned and walked out.

***

The night air was cooler, a typical September evening. The streetlamps were lit, casting shadows along the tree-lined street. Terrence stood at the corner of the Lane, staring at the small semi-detached house that used to be his. Same cracked garden wall. Same uneven path leading to the door. But it wasn't his anymore. Not really. Not since Megan had opened her mouth and fed the pigs the one thing they couldn't get any other way—his name. It had been quiet, that betrayal. No scenes. No shouting. Just a knock on the door at three a.m. and too much detail in the arrest warrant to be coincidence.

She'd given him up, and now she had someone else. A new car on the drive. A new man's coat hung in the window. Clean, ordinary domestic life, like the last five years hadn't existed. Like *he* hadn't existed.

Terrence adjusted his collar and walked towards the gate, slow and steady, the same way he moved inside, like a man with nothing to lose and too much time to think. He knocked once.

Megan answered fast, too fast. Her eyes widened the moment she saw him. "Jesus Christ."

Terrence tilted his head. "Hello, love."

She stepped back instinctively, hand hovering at the edge of the door like she was deciding whether to slam it or not. "You shouldn't be here. I'm not alone."

Terrence moved closer. "I know."

Her hand dropped. Good, she was scared.

He glanced around the hallway. It was exactly the same as the last time he'd seen it, that night he'd been dragged away: same wallpaper, same scuffed skirting boards. Terrence's boots echoed on the laminate as he entered.

Megan stood frozen in the doorway behind him. "You're not supposed to be anywhere near me."

"This is my house, the house I poured my blood, sweat, and tears into, for you. I did whatever it took to make sure you were happy." Terrence spun slightly. "And here we are, you with another fella, living it up."

A man's voice floated down the stairs. "Everything all right, Meg?"

Terrence raised his eyebrows. "He's polite. That's something."

Half shouting up she called, "stay where you are."

The man didn't come down. Smart. Terrence walked into the front room and sat on the arm of the old sofa. The house smelled different now. No smoke. No cheap aftershave. No trace of him left at all.

He sensed her behind him and swivelled.

"Why?" he asked.

Megan stayed near the doorframe, arms crossed tightly. "You know why."

"I want to hear you say it." He stood.

She shook her head. "You were out of control. You think I did it for me? I did it for *you*. To stop you becoming what you are now."

Terrence's jaw clenched. He stared down at the floor. "You know what it cost me? Do you have any idea?"

"I know exactly what it cost you," she said. "And I still did it. Because the man I loved was already gone. We were done then, and we're done now."

He took a step closer, eyes locked on hers. "You think I came here to beg?"

Megan's face changed, went pale. Her mouth opened, but no words came.

"I thought about it every night in there. What I'd do to you. What I'd do to him. But now I'm standing here…"

She flinched, and he pressed closer still, lowering his voice to a whisper. "…I realised you're already dead to me." He stepped back, calm again. Detached. "Let him keep you. Let him rot with you. He'll soon find out what you're really like, money-grabbing bitch."

Then he walked out. No shouting. No blood. No satisfaction.

That would come later, when he'd watch them both burn.

CHAPTER 37

Millie rolled over and glanced at the clock. It was five-thirty a.m. "Wake up." She nudged Tommy Lee.

"What?" he mumbled, still half asleep.

"Somebody's knocking on the door, listen," she said quietly.

Another knock, urgent, loud.

"If they wake the kids up I'll batter them," she said, then grabbed her dressing gown from the floor where Tommy Lee had thrown it last night.

"I'll go." He climbed out of bed, pulled on his jogging bottoms, and ran down the stairs, Millie close behind.

He yanked the door open, ready to clobber whoever it was who had the fecking liberty to disturb him. "PJ?"

"I need your help." He rushed into the house. "I've fecked up."

"Maybe you should start from the beginning." Millie pointed to the front room. "In there, I don't want my children woken."

"What have you done?" he said and rubbed his eyes. "You've got guilt written all over your face."

"I didn't mean for this to happen, I've been good, you know that…it was a mistake, a stupid fecking mistake." PJ flopped into the chair.

"You've been with a man?" Millie said, half questioning and half accusing.

PJ placed his head in his hands and started to sob.

"What the feck is wrong with you? You've got a lovely wife and son. Don't they mean anything?" Tommy Lee said.

"How do you expect us to help?" Millie knelt by the chair.

"I need you to say I was here all night. If you do this, I promise I'll never do it again," PJ begged.

Millie looked at Tommy Lee. Was he going to say yes?

"I can't be a part of this, not no more," she said. "We've covered for you multiple times, hell, Tommy Lee even gave you an alibi for one night a week. You said you didn't want to do it anymore because of Patrick. You do remember Patrick, your son."

"Mil, go put the kettle on," Tommy Lee said finally. "I need a chat with my brother."

He waited for her to leave then pushed the door to. "Did you see that, PJ, the look Millie just gave me, like she's lost all respect for me? And why is that? Because you want me to lie for you again." He paced the room. "I can't keep doing this, your selfish ways are now affecting my marriage."

"This is the last time, I promise," PJ mumbled, shame tightening his words.

"I'm going to leave this decision up to Millie. If she says no, then it's no. Brother or not, you make me feel sick. I'm ashamed to be related to you."

***

PJ parked his pickup in a lay-by and then lifted the bonnet. He ran his hands over the leads, mindful not to burn his fingers. Once covered in oil, he rubbed them on his face and shirt. This was the best excuse Millie had come up with. While she didn't want to get involved and live with lying to Marina, she also wanted to give him a chance to repair the damage he'd done. So he'd broken down after the pub and slept in the motor until it was light enough to fix it.

His mind was still torn between thinking about Pete and the last words Tommy Lee had muttered to him.

I'm ashamed to be related to you.

He couldn't argue with that, he felt ashamed of himself. He tugged a couple of leads off and then wiped them on his top. Job done. Now he would return home and blag it—it would either work or he'd face the music.

The drive was only five minutes from where he'd stopped. His heart pounded when he drove onto the ground. It was only six-forty, but he knew Marina would be up waiting, worrying, because of him.

He stopped outside the trailer, Marina appearing at the door immediately, her eyes red from crying, her shoulders slumped. PJ hated himself more in that instant that he had done his entire life. He jumped out of the pickup truck and held his grimy hands up.

It was show time.

+++

Tommy Lee leaned on the metal banister at the top of the stairs overlooking the gym, the slow rhythmic thud of the punchbag the only sound he could hear. His mind was still stuck on PJ. How could one man be so stupid, risking everything, and for what? He couldn't understand it, he'd seen pretty women, but none could ever tempt him to stray. Millie was the only girl for him, even though she was barely talking to him. Millie and his children were his life.

PJ had overstepped the mark. Coming to his home at such an ungodly hour when his wife and kids were sleeping. The fact he'd upset Millie was something he'd not allow.

He turned when the door opened. There, stepping through, was Terrence. He sauntered down the stairs.

"Terrence." He nodded. "Wasn't expecting you so soon."

"I've nothing else to do." Terrence shrugged. "Had enough boredom inside so may as well work… Nice place you've got here."

"I've got a bit of business to take care of, so I'll get Scott to show you around. You won't be here long." He motioned to Scott. "Do the honours."

He'd told Millie he'd have him here so he could keep an eye on him. Once he knew he was to be trusted, he could go and work at the docks.

Tommy Lee ran back up the stairs and grabbed his keys. He needed to put PJ in his place once and for all, and then he'd make things right with Millie.

***

Maeve came rushing out when Tommy Lee drew up, her smile dropping when she obviously saw Millie and the children weren't with him.

He climbed out and pecked her on the check. "Morning."

"Where's the babies?" she said, eyes on the empty seats.

"At home with their mother. Stick the kettle on, I just need a quick word with PJ." He marched off towards his trailer.

A quick knock on the door, and instantly, Marina answered.

"PJ there?" he asked.

"He's in the paddock. I swear he loves those horses more than he does me." She smiled.

"I'm sure he doesn't," he said. "I'll go find him."

Tommy Lee headed to the paddock. He spotted PJ by one of the stable blocks, shovel in hand.

"PJ. A word," he called.

PJ's face coloured up. He held his finger to his mouth and hushed him.

Tommy Lee's temper flared. "Don't you hush me, boy."

"Christ sakes, keep your voice down, Father's in the next block." PJ walked to the edge of the field and motioned for him to follow.

"Look, I got the message this morning when yous wouldn't help," he said, his voice dripping with petulance.

Tommy Lee balled his fists, temper building. "So you think we're in the wrong?"

PJ sighed. "All I know is family are supposed to be there in times of need, and I needed you this morning. My marriage was hanging in the balance."

"You should've thought about that before you messed around with another man's cock," he said.

"You've as much to lose as me. If the family find out you've covered for me, do you think you're going to be a hero or a villain?" PJ glared.

"You should know better than to threaten me. Do you know it's taking all my strength not to knock you on your arse right now... What I've done is protect Mother and Father, so this is the last time I'm going to say it: keep your sordid life away from me and my family." Tommy Lee turned to walk away but stopped when PJ spoke.

"Just remember, your involved in this up—"

Tommy Lee's fist collided with PJ's cheek, knocking him to the ground. "And you just remember, you're the one who prefers men to your own wife."

Paddy stood just behind the stable, out of sight, listening. But what he was hearing didn't make any sense. Men. Cock. PJ. Did he hear right?

CHAPTER 38

Tommy Lee opened the kitchen door and stepped in. He could hear Millie in the front room playing with the twins. He crept to the doorway and watched with a smile on his face. She had built a tower out of blocks, and the boys were waiting to knock them down.

"Okay, it's Duke's turn. Count with me… Ready? One, two, three, go." She giggled when Duke kicked out at the blocks and they scattered across the room.

"Having fun?" he said and flopped onto the sofa.

"How long have you been there?" she asked.

"Long enough." He grabbed little Tommy boy when he lunged towards him. "Have yous boys been good for Mummy?"

"Yes," they replied in unison.

"I'll put the kettle on." Millie stood, checked on Millie Mae, who was fast asleep in her pram, and then left the room.

He followed behind, close, wrapping his arms around her waist when she stood at the sink filling the kettle. "Thought we could go and see your parents later, if you want."

She spun around to face him. "We just gonna forget about this morning?"

"I've spoken to him, told him never to bring that shite to our door again… I'll not have you upset." He let go of her and took a seat at the kitchen table. "I don't know how to deal with this, Mil. It doesn't just concern him, it's my parents I'm trying to protect." He sighed.

She sat next to him. "I know… But I can't help worry about Marina. If that were me, it would kill me to know my husband would rather be with a man. I mean, why the fuck did he get married?"

"It's not our problem anymore, I've made it clear that—" He paused. "Someone's at the door. I'll get it."

He yanked open the front door, and just for a moment, froze. "Father, come in, we're in the kitchen."

He knows.

"Hello, Paddy, where's Maeve?" Millie glanced at Tommy Lee.

He shook his head in warning.

"I need a word with my son, in private," Paddy said, solemn.

"I'll be in the front room." She left and closed the door behind her.

Paddy didn't sit. He never did when something serious was in the air. He stood just inside the kitchen door, arms behind his back, the stiff edge of his coat catching against the frame. His eyes were fixed on Tommy Lee, and he wasn't angry, not yelling, just watching, the way a man does when he's already made up his mind but still needs to hear the lie before he calls it out.

Tommy Lee took a seat at the table. He gave his father a tight nod. "You want tea?"

"I heard something," Paddy began flatly. "Something that wasn't meant for my ears… What were you arguing about this morning?"

He remained quiet. How much had his father heard?

"I was walking back from the stables, heard the two of you. Raised voices. PJ sounded like he was pleading with you. Then you said something about 'keeping it away from the family'."

Tommy Lee swallowed, his throat dry, eyes focused on the table.

Paddy stepped in further. "So I'll ask again. What was it about?"

He sighed and stared at his father. "It's nothing. He's just… PJ's had a few things on his mind. Trouble with Marina. Work pressure. You know how he gets."

"Don't lie to me," Paddy snapped, quick and sharp. "I know what I heard. I know when something's wrong."

Tommy Lee's shoulders stiffened. "You want to know about your son? His not like us, he's different, always has been."

Paddy blinked. "Different how?"

He stared down at the table again. He couldn't say it. He'd said it before, in that argument, in a dozen furious whispers behind closed doors, but not to his father. Saying it now was like carving it in stone.

Paddy sat opposite him, arms resting on the table. "Different how?" His voice was now softer.

"He likes men," Tommy Lee mumbled.

The silence that followed was peaceful, like the volume had been turned down on the world. He exhaled. It almost felt good to release the burden. He glanced across to Paddy. He was still, silent, staring, like he was trying to make sense of his words.

"I told him to stop it," Tommy Lee went on. "Told him to bury it, walk away, forget the whole thing ever happened. I've been covering for him for a while, Father. He tried. He married Marina. Had the baby. Did everything right. But it's still there."

Paddy continued to stare, his face pale.

"You think I haven't wanted to tear it out of him? To fix it? You think I haven't lain awake wondering how the hell I'm supposed to protect him from people like you?"

"It's not people like me, son, we need to worry about. The family, cousins, uncles, they would make his life hell. That's if they let him live… I should've known," he said, barely audible. "The softness. The way he kept close to your mother. It was there the whole time."

Tommy Lee's fists curled. "He's still PJ. Still your son. Still the one who helped you, as a nipper, with the cobs."

"Who else knows?"

"Millie, because he came here for help, John Jo and Sean Paul because I told them. Between us, we watched him… He promised us he was over it. Patrick was more important to him than anything else."

Paddy stood and walked to the door. He paused, one hand on the frame. "This'll kill your mother if she finds out."

"Then we make sure she doesn't," he said firmly. "This goes no further."

Paddy gave a simple, sad nod, then left.

Millie appeared, her face etched with worry.

"How much did you hear?" Tommy Lee sighed.

"All of it… This isn't your fault." She slipped her arms around his shoulders.

He felt the comfort, but the guilt still consumed him.

***

The September sun was shining, although the days were now cooler. The leaves were starting to go golden brown as they clung to the branches. Tommy Lee slowed, ready to veer into John Jo and Sean Paul's ground. He spotted his father's motor; good, he'd come home after the conversation they'd had. He pulled up away from them all and cut the ignition. He was here for damage limitation. Had his father spilled his guts to PJ? He hoped not. After Paddy had left earlier, Tommy Lee had thought of so much more to say. Well, what he'd missed out earlier he was here to put right.

He slid out of the Range Rover and started to walk towards John Jo's. He'd warn him first.

"Afternoon," John Jo called as he opened the door. "Jaysus, you've a face like thunder."

"We need to talk," he said. With a flick of his head, he indicated somewhere private.

He walked back towards his motor, then stood leaning against the door. He wasn't quite sure how to begin, probably from that morning and PJ's five-thirty a.m. visit.

"What's this about?" John Jo walked towards him.

Tommy Lee glanced over to PJ's place. "Is he here?"

"No, he's taken Marina to see her parents… What's going on?"

Sean Paul approached. "What's this? A mother's meeting?" He laughed.

Tommy Lee remained straight-faced. "PJ paid me a visit this morning. I say morning, it was still dark. He'd spent the night with a man and wanted me to cover for him."

"The fecking eejit," John Jo said.

"I thought he'd stopped all that?" Sean Paul added.

"Let me finish, it gets worse… He wanted an alibi, I said no. To cut a long story short, I came over here, told him never to bring that shite to my door again, and Father overheard the conversation."

"Watch out," John Jo warned.

Tommy Lee glanced around. Their father was storming towards them.

"You come here to warn them, boy?" Paddy said, his mouth set in a thin straight line. "Don't you think you've done enough damage?"

"I've done the damage, really?" Tommy Lee stepped away from the men and paced. "You know I've got a good life. It's the life I always wanted. A beautiful wife, three gorgeous children, a home and business." He stopped and faced his father. "I am sick of sorting this family's problems out. You want to know why I never told you? For starters, when I first found out I thought I'd dealt with it. I terminated the problem and warned PJ that his actions would have consequences. Then the fecking little prick tries to take an overdose, which again I dealt with by taking him to Spain with me, and those two," he pointed to John Jo and Sean Paul, "I took them to stop them from doing a bank job and getting locked up." He stepped closer to Paddy. "Everything I've done has always been to protect you and Mother, and this is the thanks I get for it… Total blame. Just look around. The one who's caused all this is away with his wife and son having a day out, oblivious." He shook his head. "Yous lot are on your own. You sort your own fecking problems out, because I'm done."

Tommy Lee pulled open the door to his Range Rover while calling over his shoulder, "You should all be happier now the black sheep's gone."

CHAPTER 39

November

Millie pulled the cardigan around her body. It was fucking freezing today. She couldn't quite remember being this cold in November. Her own fault, she should have put a coat on.

She threw the bags into the back of the motor, then climbed in ready to head home. Tommy Lee was looking after the children while she visited the shop. She'd promised him an Irish stew and had to get the ingredients. Millie Mae was now five and a half months old and easier for him to handle. The twins, well, she didn't think anyone would ever be able to handle them.

It had been a strange couple of months. Tommy Lee had refused all contact with his family. They had been so close that it broke her heart. Paddy had hitched the trailer up and gone to see his brother down in Dorset. They'd been gone seven weeks now. Maeve had asked what had happened before they'd left. Millie had played dumb; this wasn't her story to tell.

She parked on the driveway and carried the bags in. "I'm back," she called, trudging through the front door then placing down the bags.

"Kids are all napping." He grinned.

"Seriously, you want—"

"Of course I want." He grabbed her hand.

He led her upstairs to the bedroom. "You gonna strip, or shall I help?" He winked.

Millie sighed. He'd been like this ever since he'd fallen out with his father and brothers. Not that she was complaining, the sex was out of this world, but it wasn't what he needed. She dropped her cardigan to the floor then lifted her T-shirt off over her head and lay on the bed. He climbed on top of her.

"You want me to do the rest?" He reached for the clip on her bra.

She felt it release.

His mouth immediately found a nipple. She moaned when his hand slipped between her thighs. He pulled her panties down, knelt, and flung them over his shoulder. He was inside her seconds later, thrusting with a slow, gentle rhythm. His right hand massaged her breasts, his left elbow held him up away from her. She glanced at him; his gaze roamed her body. The thrusts grew more urgent, quicker, harder. His moans louder. Millie closed her eyes when her orgasm took over, her body trembling as it subsided.

"I love you," he murmured, before he collapsed on top of her.

"I love you, too," she said, her breathing deep.

They lay there for a few minutes, recovering.

He leaned up on his elbows. "It's nice, just us. Nobody else's problems."

"You still need to sort things with your family, Tommy Lee, they miss you." She nudged him off and then snuggled into his side.

"No, Mil, they miss having someone to clean up all their messes." He kissed the top of her head. "I'll never forget the way Father looked at me, like I was the cause of everything."

"Maybe he was hurting. He'd just found out PJ was one of them gays, and you told him. You know what they say about shooting the messenger."

"Why are you trying to defend him?" He sighed.

"I'm not, I just don't want you regretting this." She heaved herself up. "You know I love you, and you know I think you're right, but your dad's not getting any younger, and he has phoned a few times to speak to you. He clearly wants to make up."

"I don't want to talk about him, can we just cuddle in silence?" he asked.

"Okay, but do one thing for me, just think about making contact." She lay back down and kissed his cheek. "And remember, me and the children love you more than anyone else ever could."

***

The sky had turned the colour of old bruises by mid-afternoon. The wing always felt heavier in the run-up to Christmas, short tempers, longer nights, and the cold creeping in through the cracks of old bricks no matter how hard the screws rattled the radiators.

Carl was due out in two days. Brian had counted them like a man counting breaths underwater. Not because he was desperate to see Carl go, but because it meant one thing: he would be out three weeks later. They sat next to each other in the mess room, backs to the wall, mugs of stewed tea warming their hands. A few lads were playing cards at the far table. Laughter. Tension. Someone shouted down the corridor. But between them, everything was quiet.

"You all right?" Carl asked with a nod at Brian.

Brian smirked. "Three weeks, mate, and I will be."

"I'll be waiting at the gates. No bollocks. No changes. I'll be there."

Brian looked down into his tea. "You don't have to—"

"I want to. We said, didn't we? You and me. No one else," Carl cut in.

Brian nodded slowly. They had said it. Late one afternoon, a couple of months back, when the screws were half-asleep and the lights were low, Brian had told Carl everything, about Tommy Lee,

275

about his father being murdered at his hands. About how he'd sat in his cell night after night, chewing the same thought over and over. "If I don't do something about that pikey bastard, he'll just keep walking," he'd told him.

Carl hadn't flinched. No questions. No judgment. Just an 'okay, let's sort him.' Now the plan was alive, breathing, waiting for action.

"Got a flat sorted in Dagenham." Carl scratched the back of his neck. "Bit rough, but no one'll ask questions. One bed, sofa bed, kettle works. Close enough for the hit, far enough to be out of the way."

Brian raised a brow. "You serious?"

Carl grinned. "Deadly."

A moment passed, and then Brian leaned in slightly, dropping his voice. "He'll never see it coming, you know. Not from you."

"I'm counting on it." Carl nodded.

They both went quiet again. The hum of the wing settled into a low murmur.

"You think you'll miss this place?" Carl asked suddenly, a smirk tugging at his mouth.

"I'll miss the sleep. Nothing else." Brian chuckled. "And especially not that shit they pass off as mash."

"Won't miss that gobby shit giving it large in the canteen either," Carl said. "Apart from watching him slip on his own ego... You know, when you get out...it's different. Not just the air. People stare at you like you're carrying a disease. Even the ones who smile, they're checking if you're gonna go off. You gotta stay sharp. Stay under the radar."

Brian nodded. "I'm ready. Been ready for a long time."

Carl glanced at him, then reached out and tapped his knuckles lightly against Brian's mug. "Three weeks."

"Three weeks," he confirmed.

"Keep out of trouble, and don't let them wind you up, and then, three weeks' time we can finish that pikey prick off once and for all."

***

It was just after three a.m. The street was dead silent, save for the low rustle of leaves scraping along the kerb and the distant hum of a motor somewhere in the night. Terrence stood on the opposite side of the road, half-shrouded in the shadows of a skeletal tree. The house stood quiet. Still. Exactly how he wanted it. His breath curled in front of him like smoke which rose from his lungs. Cold November air bit at his fingers as he loosened the cap of the jerry can he'd been carrying for the last half mile. The time had come to sever the ties to his old life.

He hadn't driven. Too risky. He'd walked it, tucked in the back lanes, hood up, boots silent on the tarmac. No one saw him leave the flat. No one would see him now. The house looked just like it had before prison, maybe cleaner, maybe repainted, but still his in shape and memory. And yet every window, every brick, now belonged to someone else. The one Megan had brought in while Terrence had rotted in a cell. The one who mowed the lawn and probably drank in his old local.

He crossed the street in long, deliberate strides, moving as a spectre. No lights inside. Curtains drawn. Car not on the drive, probably parked in the garage. That was good. Let them sleep.

He stepped around the back gate, still jammed in the same spot, still needing that little lift, and crept into the rear garden. The shed was padlocked now. Smart. But the old metal dustbin would have everything he needed, junk mail, receipts. Paper. Kindling.

He soaked it all. The sharp scent of petrol stung his nose, watered his eyes, cutting through the cold. He poured a steady line from the bin to the back door, trailing it so it acted as a fuse. Then inside the letterbox, just a splash. He didn't want a full explosion. Just a crawling blaze that would chew the place to the bone along with its inhabitants. The last drop emptied onto the doormat. He stepped back, glancing up to the bedroom window, and smiled. He struck the match against the box. For a moment he stared at the flame, trembling in the wind as if it were nervous, too.

Then he dropped it.

The fire caught fast, a soft *whump* and a hiss as it kissed the petrol. It slithered, a serpent, straight up the line towards the house.

Terrence stepped back into the garden, watching the flames lick at the frame of the back door, orange light blooming across the patio. Inside, shadows began to dance. Then, a noise, a bang on the window. A face. Megan. Her hand banging against the glass. Terrified.

He smiled, raised his hand and gave a little wave before turning away. No panic. No rush. Just the slow, satisfied pace of a man cutting a cord.

By the time he reached the corner of the street, he peeked back. The house was now well and truly unsavable. A woman's scream, muffled and high, rang out. He turned and continued on his way. He didn't look back again. The house didn't belong to him anymore, and now it didn't belong to her either.

CHAPTER 40

The cold had settled in for good now. Frost clung to the long grass by the fence line, brittle and silver in the low morning light. Every breath hung in clouds resembling fog, and the horses puffed steam through their nostrils as they shifted restlessly in their stables.

John Jo rubbed his gloved hands together and gave the closest cob a firm pat on the shoulder. "Come on, girl. You've had worse winters than this."

Sean Paul was already soaked to the knees, muck fork in hand, boots caked with slurry. "Them foals need blankets on. It's bitter out here."

"I told PJ to see to it," John Jo muttered. He peered over the stable door. "If he's even gonna bother showing his face."

As if summoned by his name, PJ appeared at the edge of the yard. Hood up, hands jammed in the pockets of his old coat, walking slow like he knew the welcome would be thin. The frost cracked under his boots. He paused at the gate before slipping inside.

"You're late," John Jo barked.

PJ had been a complete prick since Tommy Lee had been off the scene; that's not to say he was much better before.

Sean Paul leaned on the fork. "You forget how time works or just not fussed anymore?"

"Patrick is unwell," PJ said flatly. "I had to go chemist and get some medicine." His eyes flicked to the three foals in the pen. The smallest, a dark bay filly, shivered, its coat still patchy where the winter hair hadn't fully come in. He moved towards the feed bin. "I'll sort the blankets."

John Jo stepped in front of him. "Before you do anything, you and me need a word."

PJ visibly stiffened. Did he know what was coming?

"We know," John Jo said sharply. "You and Tommy Lee. What happened between you. Why he left."

PJ's breath caught in the freezing air. "I'm not doing this here."

"We are doing it here," John Jo said. "This is the yard. You don't get to walk back in like nothing happened… We've kept our mouths shut because Father told us to."

"Father knows?" PJ gasped.

"He overheard you and Tommy Lee arguing, so then Tommy Lee had to come and tell us… We've kept your dirty secret, PJ, but now it's affecting the family. You," he stabbed a finger in PJ's chest, "You need to go and make things right with Tommy Lee. Mother and Father are both heartbroken, and no, Mother doesn't know what's happened."

"This is your fault," Sean Paul added. "And it's down to you to sort it out. "

PJ's jaw tightened. "I didn't ask to be like this."

"No one asks," John Jo growled. "But they *choose* what to bring home. What to shame their family with."

Silence followed.

The foals shifted, their hooves clicking softly on the frozen ground.

PJ looked from one face to the other. "You think I haven't spent every night wishing I could change it? That I could turn it off and be what you want? I've tried. God knows I tried. I fight it every day."

"You should've kept it buried," Sean Paul said, flat and cold. "For your mother's, your wife's, and your son's sake. Hell, for the whole family."

"I did," PJ said. "It was a one-off mistake."

John Jo stepped forward, voice barely above a whisper now. "You bring that mistake back here again, and it won't just be Tommy Lee who walks away. You'll find out how small your life can get."

PJ looked down at his boots. Frost had started to cling to the rubber soles. He nodded once, then moved to the foals, gently laying a blanket over the bay filly's back. She didn't shy from him. She never did. It wound John Jo up; his little brother was so good with the cobs, why wasn't this life enough?

***

Carl jumped off the bunk and made his way down to the mess hall. He spotted Brian hovering by his cell door. "I'll be off shortly, just waiting for that fucking screw."

Brian ushered him into his cell. "I've been thinking." He poked his head out to check for any earwiggers. Once satisfied, he ducked back in. "Tommy Lee's got a wife and kids. How about we grab them first? Rape her, cut her tits off, and then cut the pikey kids into pieces and post them back to him." He grinned.

"Bit late to change the plan now." Carl rubbed the back of his neck. "Plus that would alert him... Look, I'm happy to go along with whatever, but think about it first. At the moment you have the element of surprise." He turned, about to leave, then stopped. "You're one warped fucker." He grinned. "But I like your style."

***

PJ ground the pickup to a halt outside Tommy Lee's house. His and Millie's motors were both on the drive. His heart thudded as he sat

281

chewing at his nails. This was a bad idea. Why had he let John Jo and Sean Paul talk him into it? Begging seemed to have become his thing lately, but that didn't mean he was used to it. He climbed out, the knot in his stomach twisting tighter. He moved towards the front door like a man heading to the gallows. His knock feeble.

The door opened, and Millie appeared. "PJ, you'd better come in."

She walked in front of him towards the kitchen.

"PJ's here. I've got to pop out for a while, please don't kill each other." She smiled at both men, then left.

"You want to kill me, that's reassuring." PJ swallowed.

"No, I don't want to kill you. Why are you here?" Tommy Lee frowned.

"To say sorry for all the shite I've caused… I haven't strayed since." Shame coloured his voice.

Tommy Lee just stared silently.

"I don't like what I've done to the family, splitting it… We used to be close, all of us…"

"No, PJ, you and me used to be close… D'ya know, Father blames me for your—I don't even know what to call it—perversion?" Tommy Lee sat at the table. "He looked me in the eyes and said hadn't I done enough. A man doesn't recover from that, and I certainly don't forgive."

"I'm going to talk to Father, when he gets back, tell him everything… You're my brother, and I miss you. We all do, and that includes Father." PJ turned towards the door and paused. "I hope we can sort this out, because life really isn't the same without you."

***

John Jo knocked on the door and stood back, waiting to face his brother. This feud was getting out of hand. Sean Paul and himself had nothing to do with it, and yet Tommy Lee was avoiding them as if they carried the plague.

The door opened.

"What do you want?" Tommy Lee asked.

"That's a nice greeting," John Jo stepped in.

282

"I've already had PJ here this morning, I don't need any more shite, John Jo. Not today."

"This shite, as you put it, has got out of hand… Since when do you not speak to Father? I mean, he's done and said some stupid things in his time, we all have, but we've always stuck together," John Jo said.

"I'm not talking about this, what's done is done." Tommy Lee turned and marched to the front room. He picked up a glass and poured himself a whisky. "Do you want one?"

John Jo gave a nod. "We have other business to discuss."

"Such as?"

"The prick who's due for release in a couple of weeks… I want to know what's happening." He took the glass offered.

"It's all under control."

"Jaysus, Tommy Lee, we want in on this, it was Sean Paul who ended up in a hospital bed."

"You will be, I'll let you know when the details are finalised." Tommy Lee took a sip of his drink. "Anything else?"

"No, but—" The sound of the door opening stopped him.

"We're home," Millie shouted over the din of the twins.

The boys rushed into the front room and lunged at Tommy Lee's legs. He knelt and kissed them both. "Have yous been good for your mother?"

John Jo stared at their angelic little faces when they both said 'yes' and smiled. "Right, I best get going. I'll drop into the gym in the week, and you can give me an update."

He was met with a nod.

He rolled his eyes. So much for sorting things out.

CHAPTER 41

December

The wind blew bitter off the Hammersmith rooftops, the kind of cold that got into your wrists and knees and stayed there, no matter how fast you walked. December 10th, 1978. The streets were still damp from the night's frost, and the city looked grey in every direction, as if colour had packed it in for the winter.

Carl waited near the prison gates, leaning against the bonnet of an old Ford Granada, his collar turned up, breath curling in front of him. He rubbed his hands together, attempting to spark some warmth, his nerves on edge. Everything had to go like clockwork today.

A bell rang inside the walls, hollow and metallic. A few seconds later, the gate creaked open. Brian stepped out with a canvas holdall slung over one shoulder and no coat, just a thin jumper with the elbows worn through. Carl watched as his gaze darted left, then right, squinting in the late morning glare, then landing on him.

Brian strode across the road, a small smile on his face. "It's good to see ya, mate." He glanced back once at the prison, then turned fully to the car. "Doesn't seem real, does it?"

"What doesn't?"

"Being out. The colour of the road. People without uniforms on, it's all surreal."

Carl opened the passenger door. "It'll settle. Give it a day or two."

Brian slid in, dropping the bag between his feet. The engine rumbled to life, the heater barely working. The radio hissed static before landing on Rod Stewart's 'Da Ya Think I'm Sexy' just starting up.

"This is my song." Carl laughed. "Sing it to all the girls." He glanced at Brian. "So you managed to keep ya nose clean."

"Told you I would," Brian said. "Got plans, ain't we."

They drove in silence for a few minutes. The traffic was light. The world moved differently in December, especially this close to Christmas, like everyone was happy and at peace. People would say a cheery hello instead of the usual grunt. It was Carl's favourite time of the year. He glanced at his watch; it was nearing lunch time.

"You eaten?" he asked.

Brian shook his head.

"Didn't want what they were serving?"

"Last thing I needed was another bowl of cereal, burnt toast, and dishwater."

Carl smirked. "There's a café in Shepherd's Bush. Proper fry-up. We'll stop there, then head out."

"To Dagenham?"

Carl nodded. "Flat's ready. Bit rough, but no neighbours asking questions." He glanced at Brian who was reaching into his bag. "What's that?"

"This…" Brian held up a piece of paper and waved it in front of him. "…is the plan. I'm gonna make that pikey bastard wish he'd never been born… Did you get eyes on the wife?"

Carls jaw tightened as he shifted gear. "Yes, but she's always got people around her, she may be difficult to grab… This needs to be done clean, no loud mess, no police."

"And it will be," Brian confirmed. "I still want her, though, even if it's after we nab him."

"I have got some good news," Carl said with a grin. "I've found an old abandoned warehouse, out the way, perfect for a bit of payback… No one will ever know he is there."

"That's excellent, mate, you're a fucking diamond. " Brian grabbed his shoulder and gave it a squeeze.

Carl pulled into the side of the road. "Right, let's eat, and then I'll take you to see the warehouse."

Brian chuckled. "Let's rename it the slaughterhouse."

***

John Jo piled the last of the logs into the shed with the help of Sean Paul. The weather was expected to get even colder, so they'd stocked up on coal, too. He closed the door and padlocked it just as Paddy and Maeve veered onto the ground.

"They're back." Sean Paul motioned then walked out to meet them.

"We'll put that back for you." John Jo pointed to the Buccaneer. "Yous get in the warm."

Paddy climbed out of his motor. "Tommy Lee been by?"

"No, Father, he's been busy, saw him at the gym a couple of weeks ago."

The age lines on his father's face had doubled. He looked tired and worn out. His temper flared. This was PJ's fault.

"Go in with Shirley Ann, she'll make you a cuppa in the warm. I'll make your fire up," Sean Paul said and helped his mother out.

Maeve remained silent, her eyes sad.

The brothers reversed the trailer into its spot, then opened up the mobile to make the fire up.

"Jaysus, it's colder in here that it is outside," Sean Paul said while he shovelled out the ash.

"Mother always said these were like fridges in the winter, ovens in the summer," John Jo muttered. "Here." He passed the paper and kindling then lifted the bag of coal. "Be toasty in no time."

"John Jo," Gypsy called from the door. "Tommy Lee's on the phone."

"I'll go see what he wants." He followed Gypsy out. "I can let him know Father's back."

***

Carl paid the waitress then grabbed his things. "Right, let's get going. We can stop for a quick one in the pub if you want?"

"I'd rather get settled first, once you've shown me the slaughterhouse," Brian said. "Plenty of time for drinking later."

The two men crossed the street to the car, both sliding in.

"I couldn't wait for a pint when I got out, that first sip was fucking heavenly. Still, I reckon you're gonna like this even more." Carl grinned.

"I reckon I will," Brian agreed. "I'm gonna visualise his tart tied down while I rape her, him tied to a chair watching… Might have to slice of his eyelids off, so he can't close them, and you can hold his head. Then when she's screaming out in pain, I'll slit her throat. It's gonna be fucking bliss."

"What about him?" Carl asked.

"I'm gonna take my time with him, real slow. I'll need a tool kit, pliers, hammer, scalpel, you know the drill. This needs to be done properly."

CHAPTER 42

The sun was already dipping by half past three, throwing long amber streaks through the bare branches that bordered Duke and Connie's ground. The sky had that washed-out colour it always wore in December, pale lilac fading to steel, with clouds the colour of a battleships slowly rolling in from the east.

Millie sat at the kitchen table, hands wrapped tight around a mug that had gone cold twenty minutes ago. Connie moved around the kitchen in her usual rhythm, chopping carrots for the stew, her slippers whispering against the linoleum. The radio muttered quietly from the counter playing Christmas carols. She loved the songs, but they barely registered.

"You all right, love?" Connie asked without looking up.

Millie jumped. "Yeah, fine. Just cold, that's all."

She wasn't. Between the roaring fire in the other room and the cooker behind her throwing off waves of thick heat, she was almost sweating, or was that her nerves? She'd been jumpy all afternoon, like her skin didn't fit right.

Connie shot her a look. "You're worrying about that man of yours again."

Millie forced a smile, sipping her cold tea. "No more than usual."

She stood and sauntered to the door, peeking into the front room. The twins were playing nicely for a change, little Nelson sitting between them showing them his toys. Millie Mae was having a nap.

Duke coughed. He was nodding off in his chair, paper across his lap, a half-drunk beer next to him. The whole house smelled of onions and damp coats and the faint tang of turf smoke from the fire.

She ran her hand over the window. The condensation that had gathered ran down in lines. She glanced outside; the ground was quiet, Jasper in his trailer, Arron in his. A single crow hopped along the fence, black against the white-rimed grass.

Today was the day, Brian was out. That was all she could think of. She'd played her part, helped set things up, done all she could, and yet she worried. She'd come to learn that even with the best-laid plans there was always a what-if?

***

The building sat low against the tree line, tucked behind a disused rail siding and a scrapyard no one bothered guarding anymore. Upminster had grown up around it, but this place hadn't moved in years, just leaned further into itself, walls blistered with age, roof tiles like old teeth missing in patches. Tommy Lee got there early. Always did. Especially when he didn't trust what was waiting on the other side.

He pushed the side door open and stepped into the cold rot of wood and silence. It was just past four p.m. but already felt like evening. Pale light filtered in through broken windows, dust thick in the air. The old floor groaned beneath his boots.

Millie had done well. He hadn't expected anything less from her. He liked it, the emptiness, the stillness. No eyes. No judgements. Just space. He ran a hand along the edge of an old workbench, then took his place by the far wall. From there, he could see the door, the windows, the angles. He could see everything coming.

The door creaked. Two sets of footsteps.

He didn't move. Just listened. Judged the pace. Then turned slowly as John Jo and Sean Paul stepped into the room.

Both men gave a short nod.

"I was glad you called." John Jo pulled his collar up. "Father's home, he don't look well."

"He's aged, Tommy Lee, and Mother has a sadness to her I've never seen the likes of," Sean Paul added.

"Yous are speaking as if I caused this… I'm fed up of fixing the family problems and I'm even more fed up of being blamed for them. Tell me, has Father had it out with PJ yet, or has the baby of the family got away with it yet again?"

Sean Paul shrugged. "This isn't about PJ, it's—"

"It's what, about me? Look, I'm not having this conversation now, I bought yous here for another reason."

"And that is?" John Jo asked.

He grinned. "You're about to find out. Follow me."

***

It was already dark when Carl headed off the main road, the kind of dark that swallowed everything, the kind that made the back of your neck twitch. He continued down a narrow lane. The only sound was the low rumble of Carl's old motor.

Brian sat in the passenger seat, hands tucked under his armpits, the chill creeping in through the metal doors. The windows fogged slightly with each breath.

"What's this place again?" he asked.

"Abandoned warehouse," Carl muttered. "Disused. Quiet. No one around. This place won't be on Tommy Lee's radar."

"Good. After I check this place out we'll head back." Brian smirked, a flicker of bitterness in his voice.

He stared out the window as they pulled into a narrow, unlit road flanked by overgrown bushes and chain-link fencing. The motor rattled over potholes. Ahead, a silhouette of a building loomed, half-collapsed roof, shattered windows. It looked like it had been forgotten by the world.

"Perfect," Brian mumbled. Although he would have preferred to see it in daylight, and he would have done if Carl's motor hadn't conked out. Piece of shit.

Carl pulled up beside the building and cut the engine.

"This it?" Brian narrowed his eyes.

Carl nodded. "The entrance is round the other side."

The cold slapped them both as they stepped out. Brian zipped his coat up higher, breath billowing white. The mud squelched beneath their boots.

Carl led the way, ducking underneath a half-rotting door, and disappeared into the dark.

Brian hesitated, then followed. It smelled like rust and ancient oil. Something dripped steadily in the distance. The kind of place where ghosts settled.

"Carl?" he called out. "Where'd you go?"

And then the sound of footsteps. Three sets. He spun around. Suddenly the place illuminated, a makeshift lamp glowing in the corner. There they were, already waiting.

Tommy Lee, John Jo, and Sean Paul stood together in a line, just past the beams, still shrouded by shadows. But he could see them, he knew who they were.

Brian's stomach dropped.

"What's this?" he asked sharply. "What the fuck is this?"

Carl stepped out from behind him, slow and quiet.

Tommy Lee didn't move. "Hello, Brian."

EPILOGUE

The kettle whistled gently on the stove. Maeve stood at the sink, drying her hands on a dish towel, humming under her breath. Outside, a frost had crept across the windows, feathering the glass with delicate, icy webs. The wind curled around the eaves of the mobile, moaning low and constant. Frost glistened on the lawn, catching the light from the back lamp like scattered shards of glass. The roads were quiet, only the odd pair of headlights passing by on the lane, too distant to matter. Inside, it was warm but heavy with quiet.

Maeve moved to the stove, stirring stew in a cast-iron pot. The smell filled the room, rich and familiar. But she stirred it without focus, her gaze flicking again and again to the window above the sink, where nothing moved. Behind her, Paddy sat at the table, shoulders hunched, cap still on, a cup of tea untouched in front of him.

He hadn't been the same lately. He'd been quiet, even at his brother's, like he carried a secret.

"You've hardly said two words all day," Maeve said, still facing the stove.

She received no answer.

She turned to face him. "Paddy?"

He raised his head, eyes red around the edges, not from drink, but from something heavier. She stepped away from the stove and sat opposite him, wiping her hands on a tea towel.

"What's going on love?" She rested her hand on his. "You've been like this the last couple of months."

"It's nothing for you to worry about, girl, it'll be sorted tomorrow," he assured her. "I'm going to check on the cobs."

She watched him leave. Whatever this was, it was bigger than she'd first thought. Her family was falling apart.

The End

ABOUT THE AUTHOR

Carol Hellier was born in Oldchurch Hospital, Essex, in the mid-sixties. When she was in her mid-twenties, she discovered her parents were in fact her grandparents, and her eldest sister was her mum.

She married a Gypsy and started her married life off living in a caravan/trailer. This has given her a useful insight into the Romany world which shows in her writing.

She has lived in many different counties but now resides back in Essex. She spends her time working for the NHS, writing, and with her large family.

Book One – *The Ward Brothers, Meet the Travellers*
Book Two – *The Ward Brothers, Vengeance*
Book Three – Title to be announced – Coming Winter 2025

Previous books:
Book One - *The Stepney Feud*
Book Two – *The Stepney Alliance*
Book Three – *The Stepney Takeover*

You can follow the author on:

Instagram: author_cahellier

Facebook: https://www.facebook.com/carolhellier

TikTok: carolmc441_author

Printed in Dunstable, United Kingdom